A WISH FOR BETH

AUDREY DAVIS

vinci
BOOKS

Vinci Books

vinci-books.com

Published by Vinci Books Ltd in 2026

1

This work is a work of fiction. Names, characters, places and incidents are the product of the author's imagination or are used fictitiously. Any resemblance to actual persons, living or dead, places and incidents is entirely coincidental.

A CIP catalogue record for this book is available from the British Library.

Paperback ISBN: 9781036733957

The EU GPSR authorised representative is Logos Europe, 9 rue Nicolas Poussion, 17000 La Rochelle, France contact@logoseurope.eu

By Audrey Davis

Cranley Wishes

A Wish for Jinnie

A Wish for Jo

A Wish for Wilma

A Wish for Beth

More by Audrey Davis

Lexicon of Love

The Haunting of Hattie Hastings

A Clean Sweep

A Clean Break

Lost In Translation

Chapter One

Beth Calder watched her life disappear box by box.

The removal men hefted the last crate into the truck, her colour-coded stickers flashing like small flags of surrender. The heavier things – the dining table where laughter had lived – were already waiting at the new place. The sofas that had held her through long nights were gone.

'Anything else to go, love?' asked the foreman.

Beth shook her head. She would set off shortly in her trusty Volkswagen Beetle. Although not hers for much longer, as she'd already sold it. First, she wanted one last wander through her home of the past twenty years.

Now stripped back to the bare minimum, Bilberry Cottage echoed with a quiet sadness. Devoid of the colourful rugs, eclectic artwork and knickknacks accumulated over time, it tore at Beth's aching heart. So many memories to walk away from, but she couldn't stay.

'A fresh start.' That's what her friends had said. 'But we'll visit you all the time!'

She passed through each room. The lounge where they

had once snuggled up together, arguing good-naturedly about what to watch and whether a second bottle of wine was too much. The kitchen, now stripped of Beth's beloved mismatched china, the Le Creuset set she'd always insisted was too heavy, and the solid pine table where they had eaten virtually every night.

Upstairs, Beth paused outside the master bedroom. She touched the door, as if she could pick up good vibrations from its varnished surface. Nothing.

Crossing the small landing to the other two bedrooms, Beth hesitated. The one on the left had been for guests: small, but with an en-suite shower and toilet. The one on the right…

Her instincts screamed *Step away. Do not go in.*

She went in.

It was unchanged since they had decorated it over ten years ago. Filled with excitement, every brushstroke and carefully selected item had felt like a step closer to being a family. Beth had sold or given away the bulk of the things. All that remained were the Disney character stickers, the pale-blue fluffy carpet, and a light fitting she had found online with genies spiralling out of golden oil lamps, wispy and magical.

'That's a bit random,' he had said, raising the eyebrow that bore the scar from a cricket injury in his late teens.

'It's quirky, and I love it. And I love you.'

Beth gasped at the memory. So many times they had said 'I love you' within the close confines of the cottage. Always in the morning, always at night. On the rare occasion they had fought, the tension had evaporated as easily as mist on a hazy day.

'If you'd come along, we'd be together now.'

Still, after all she'd been through, Beth could picture her

child. *Their* child. Sometimes with Beth's dainty nose and Luke's chiselled chin. Sometimes with auburn hair and curls. But always perfect in every way.

'Why didn't you stay?'

Beth knew she was speaking to a ghost. Or rather, a person who had never made it beyond the early stages of life.

'We can't keep doing this,' he had said on so many occasions. Painful but pragmatic. 'Let's accept it's over and focus on being us. Us. Like we were at the start.'

But they hadn't been able to get back to where they were. You couldn't fix what was broken beyond repair.

From a drawer, Beth pulled out the envelope containing the twelve-week scans. Blurry yet miraculous. Each one offering hope of a bright future. Each one doomed to failure.

Screwing up the envelope and its contents, Beth stomped downstairs and tossed it into the bin.

Her phone buzzed. It was a message from Diana, her best friend and absolute legend. The kind of person who knew what rawl plugs were, how to unblock sinks, and how to stop someone sinking into a quagmire of despair.

If you're still in the cottage and in full-on wallow mode, I'll be there in ten minutes. Maybe fifteen, as there are roadworks. You OK?

Beth sniffed. Sniffed again. Headed to the bathroom. The principal one, as the master bedroom didn't have one. Another quirk of the cottage.

I have toilet roll to wipe my face, she texted. *It's not pretty right now.*

She was appalled at how awful she looked. As if someone had melted down her face and rearranged it, Picasso-style.

Sweetie, no one's expecting you to grace the cover of a magazine. Stay put, and we'll sort it when I get there. See ya.

Beth hadn't wanted to stay put. She had wanted to run – drive – gallop away from the place that once was happy and now stuck pins in her soul.

Wait, OK? Diana had never taken no for an answer.

Beth was adrift. She needed to get in her car, drive to Cranley, and draw a line under the life she was leaving.

Instead she wandered into the neglected garden, wishing she had a restorative cup of tea. On a chilly June day, it looked as unloved as she felt.

Beth sat on the weathered wooden bench she'd bought with Luke over a decade ago. She ran a hand over its surface, wincing as a splinter pierced her skin. She welcomed the pain.

At least it meant she was still alive.

The screech of tyres and the slam of a car door signalled Diana's arrival. Beth's friend didn't do quiet. Seconds later she appeared round the corner of the cottage, a wicker basket draped over her arm.

'I knew it. Wallowing. And why are you out here when it's colder than a penguin's arse?'

Beth shrugged. 'I needed to be outside.'

Diana fixed her with the look that said: 'You are borderline nuts, but I am here to take charge.' She shooed Beth into the cottage and emptied the contents of the basket on the kitchen counter. 'Right. We have brie, grapes, a baguette and some cold sausages. Oh, and a bottle of alcohol-free fizz that may or may not be drinkable.'

'I don't have any plates or glasses, or—'

Diana harrumphed and delved into a handbag that could double up as a small tent at Glastonbury. 'Paper plates, plastic glasses, a less-than-sharp knife but we can tear the bread apart. We can chew and chat.'

Spreading brie on a chunk of baguette, Beth couldn't remember when she'd last eaten. Maybe yesterday morning. Her appetite had dwindled to that of a field mouse. Ironic, considering her profession was cooking: serving delicious food to hungry customers. She hoped she'd be up to the new job.

'Eat.' Diana tossed a grape in the air and caught it in her mouth.

'If you ever quit being a physiotherapist, you'd make a great children's entertainer,' quipped Beth.

'Ha, you haven't seen my balloon-bending skills,' retorted Diana. 'Now, tell me more about the job and the delights of Cranley. I know you've told me before but my head's like a sieve.'

Between nibbles of bread, cheese and sausages, Beth explained how a friend of a friend had mentioned the vacancy at The Jekyll and Hyde pub.

'The landlord Ken McCroarty and his wife have taken an extended break on health grounds. Their son Ed and his partner are running the place, and the couple who did the catering moved south to look after an elderly parent.'

'And you needed a complete change of scenery, or an escape from your annoying bestie.' Diana pulled an exaggerated downcast face but her eyes glistened.

'Do not, under any circumstances, cry.' Beth's own eyes filled up. 'I've done enough of that over the years to fill a small Scottish loch.'

Diana nodded. 'And with very good reason. I just wonder if upping sticks now is the right thing to do. What if Luke comes back?'

Beth had thrashed around for countless sleepless nights

wondering the same thing. If he'd appear on the doorstep one day, out of the blue, asking to give things another go.

'He won't come back.' It hurt to say it, but the truth often did. 'The cottage is in my name, it's rented out for six months minimum, and I've enough in the bank to keep me afloat if the job doesn't work out.'

Beth had no idea what faced her. She'd visited Cranley once, for the job interview, and clearly impressed them with her resume. Catering college, a spell in London and several positions in gastropubs. Latterly, she'd taken a break. Partly to spruce up the cottage before renting it out, but mainly because she was running on empty. A tank once filled with love and dreams of a family unit had been drained to fumes and despair.

'Whatever happens, you know I'm here.' Diana squeezed Beth's hand. 'And not just me. You have friends, Beth. We all know what you've been through, and there will always be a comfy bed and ears to bend and shoulders to cry on. Just take it one step at a time.'

'I told you, I'm done with crying.' At which point Beth let rip with a snot-filled howl. Diana gingerly gave her a 'there, there' hug, mindful of her pristine white blouse, as Beth wondered if she'd gone completely mad.

Chapter Two

'Prom. Prom!'

Kieran rattled the food dish. Admittedly, the cat food looked as appetising as his solo dinner last night of microwaved cod in a white-wine sauce, but he'd eaten it.

Prom sashayed into the kitchen, took one derisory sniff, and sashayed out again.

'Fine, starve! See if I care.'

Prom had arrived in Kieran's life at precisely the point he didn't need any more complications. Or people or animals to feed. He was a rangy, smoke-grey tom with the swagger of a street fighter and the attitude of a minor aristocrat. His left ear, torn neatly through at the tip, gave him a jagged, battle-scarred edge that never quite lay flat. He didn't walk so much as saunter, tail high, as though the place belonged to him. He'd strutted in one day, deposited a dead field mouse at Kieran's feet, and never left.

At least Prom now had a garden to roam around in. When he'd first appeared, Kieran had been living in a ground-floor flat on the outskirts of Edinburgh. Nice enough as a bachelor pad, and with an easy commute into the city. But its outside space was a tiny courtyard where Kieran had tried (and failed) to grow plants and herbs. There was barely room to swing a cat. Not that he was into animal cruelty – which Prom would no doubt argue about loudly.

'Home sweet home.' If he said it often enough, he might believe it.

Kieran had bought the cottage in the village of Cranley after a heads-up from his aunt Janette, who ran the local corner shop/post office. Technically she wasn't his aunt – more a distant relative of his mum – but during the handful of times they'd met, she'd insisted on the honorary title.

'It's a wee gem, lad. A bit of a doer-upper, but if you need to get out of the city, it ticks all the boxes.'

Kieran recalled his brief visit to view the property. It sat next to Brae Cottage which, Janette gleefully informed him, used to be rented by the actor Harley Quinn.

'He's a bit of a star these days. Mind you, when he first moved here I thought he was a bad 'un. Turns out I was wrong. Now he's all loved up with Jo, who runs A Bit of Crumpet.'

Janette had listed a cast of Cranley locals: names of people he hadn't yet met, some Kieran doubted he ever would. Bit-part players in a world far removed from the one he'd inhabited since his university days.

'You're burnt out, son. Step back and take time to smell the roses.' Ha! The roses doomed to shrivel and die at Kieran's less than green-fingered touch. Those were the words of his dad, retired early and content to potter, read and take his mum out for drives to country pubs. Married for thirty-five years, he'd made a killing on the stock market and chosen to step away from the cut and thrust of corporate life. Lucky him.

'Miaow.' Prom interrupted Kieran's train of thought, following up with a more strident 'miaow' that meant 'feed me now or I will not be responsible for my actions.'

Kieran had named Prom after the Greek god Prometheus. He wasn't particularly up to speed with Greek gods, but something had stuck in his brain about eternal punishment. Zeus condemning Prometheus to being pecked in the liver by a zealous eagle daily.

'And you do that too, don't you?' Kieran knew he should change the screensaver on his phone. Stop torturing himself with the photo of gorgeous Lisa, who'd been the centre of his world for three years. Until she went on a wellness retreat and came back not only rejuvenated but wrapped around a yoga instructor called Sven. His photo on the retreat website – Kieran couldn't help looking – recalled a younger Yoda, with marginally smaller ears and more hair.

'He completes me,' Lisa told Kieran on her return. Which suggested she'd been less than whole during her time with Kieran.

To cope with the pain, Kieran had thrown himself into work. With a first-class honours degree in computer science, he'd worked his way up the career ladder. Lisa had cheered him on, always urging him onward to bigger and better things. Until she wasn't there anymore.

'Eat this, you greedy wee beggar.' Kieran spooned some tinned tuna into Prom's bowl. Lisa hadn't been a fish fan. More into chickpeas, beetroot and avocados sliced, diced and smashed. Although he'd once caught her tucking into fish fingers and beans when she thought he was working late.

'Delete.' Kieran's finger hovered over the photo. Those

crazy, crinkly auburn curls. Emerald-green eyes that sucked you in. That lopsided smile she'd hated, which only added to the overall charm factor. They'd been good together. But that was in the past. Time to move on.

He tapped the screen.

Done.

The relief was instant yet still painful. Like peeling a plaster off skin that was still tender underneath.

Kieran stared at the blank lock screen, waiting for something to change. For the tightness in his chest to ease. For the past three years to rearrange themselves into something neat and survivable.

Nothing obliged.

What followed wasn't sadness so much as irritation. Sharp and unwelcome, fizzing under his ribs.

He hadn't been *held back*. That was the thing. Lisa hadn't clipped his wings or demanded he settle. She'd done the opposite – pushed, encouraged, praised.

You could do more.

You're wasted here.

Why think small when you could think huge?

He'd believed her. Swallowed the ambition whole. Worked longer hours. Taken bigger risks. Chased the version of himself she seemed so proud of.

And then she'd decided she wanted a quieter life. Less grind, more breathwork.

With Sven.

The irony tasted bitter.

Kieran dragged a hand through his hair. 'So I wasn't enough as I was,' he muttered. 'But I was useful as a launchpad.'

Prom flicked an ear, unimpressed.

Kieran moved to the window and looked out at Cranley's single, winding street. Stone cottages. Hanging baskets. The shop, where Janette would undoubtedly clock his movements and provide commentary.

It was … small.

Comfortably, undeniably small.

There was nothing here that matched the scale of what he'd been building in his head – the investors, the pitch decks, the sleek offices he'd imagined. Cranley didn't care about growth curves or disruption. It cared about bins going out on the right day and whether you waved back at a smiling local.

That scared him more than he liked to admit.

Because small meant stillness. And stillness meant feeling things.

Kieran exhaled slowly.

Maybe this wasn't a retreat from city life. Maybe it was a pause. A recalibration. He hadn't abandoned his ambitions. They were still ticking away quietly in the background, waiting.

He just needed space to remember which parts of them were actually his.

Prom leapt onto the windowsill and headbutted his arm.

'All right,' Kieran said softly. 'You can stay.'

The cat purred like he'd won something.

Kieran wasn't so sure.

Chapter Three

'We're so thrilled you're here!' Angela squashed Beth into a hug. Beth accepted it, reluctantly. She was here to do a job, not become besties with the people who paid her wages.

'Good to see you again.' Angela's partner, Ed, extended a hand instead. Beth noted they both had tattoos. Ed had several, Angela one on her shoulder that said *Be Brave*. Beth wasn't a tattoo fan. Although she'd briefly, madly, imagined one that said *Failed Mother*.

'The removal men have already put your stuff in your quarters, though not in any particular order,' said Angela, with a wry smile. 'But Ed's here to help you arrange things how you like.'

Ed smiled. 'We already sorted the bedroom and lounge, as well as the kitchen area. But it's a bit of a squeeze, sorry.'

'Please don't worry,' said Beth. 'I should have measured before bringing half my life with me.'

'There's a big storage area in the basement which we don't use,' said Ed. 'Anything you don't need can go in there.'

Angela and Ed insisted Beth eat before unpacking.

'Ray and Liz left a well-stocked freezer. But the locals will be excited to sample what you conjure up.' Angela clapped her hands together in glee.

'I hope I don't disappoint them,' Beth said. Her hands twisted in her lap. She *was* a good cook, she knew that, but lately her confidence had shrunk to the size of a walnut.

'Don't be daft. The sample menus you showed us at the interview were amazing.' Ed looked at Angela, who nodded in agreement. 'Right, I've defrosted some of Ray and Liz's epic lasagne with a side of garlic bread, if that's OK with you.'

'Perfect,' Beth said, though her appetite had gone the way of her sleep. Still, she'd need fuel to tackle the mountain of boxes upstairs.

They'd just finished eating when a young woman wheeled in a double buggy.

Beth froze. Her stomach lurched, the lasagne turning to lead. *Don't react.* She forced herself to breathe, to smile. Seeing babies shouldn't hurt anymore. But it did.

'Jinnie!' Angela shot to her feet, hugging the newcomer. Ed followed at a slower pace. 'How's the dynamic duo?'

Beth stayed seated, feigning fascination with her napkin as Angela reached into the buggy and extracted a wriggling child. From here, she couldn't tell if it was a boy or a girl. The woman called Jinnie unstrapped a second baby. Dressed head to toe in pink, she'd put money on it being a girl.

'Beth, say hello to the newest arrivals in Cranley. Oh, apart from yourself, of course.' Angela cradled the baby close to her chest, her face glowing with unfiltered love.

'The other new arrival is here, too,' Jinnie said cheerfully. 'Kieran, the one connected to Janette from the shop.'

Beth rose, praying her expression stayed neutral. She crossed the short distance to the doting mums, although Jinnie might be a childminder.

'Beth, this is Jinnie and her gorgeous girl, Dahlia. Jinnie takes care of our wee boy Ruairi four days a week. They were born close together last Christmas, and we're hoping they fall in love and get married one day.' Angela giggled and Ed rolled his eyes.

'We're *actually* hoping they both sleep through the night before they turn eighteen,' he said, taking Ruairi from Angela's arms and pressing a kiss to his head.

Beth wanted to run. Take off through the pub door and scream into the abyss. Her new life was meant to start today. Screwing it up by acting like a madwoman wasn't an option.

'You're so lucky.' The words came out before Beth could stop them.

Three pairs of eyes turned to her. For a moment, she thought they could see straight through her. Into the hollow space she carried everywhere.

'Yes, we are,' Angela said softly. 'You look tired, Beth.'

Beth forced a smile. 'Just the move catching up with me. I'll be fine once I get some sleep.'

Angela took her arm and steered her gently towards the stairs. 'Take your time settling in. Supplies will be here first thing, all locally sourced just like you wanted.'

'Perfect,' Beth said.

'And remember,' Angela added at the doorway, 'Cranley's special. Everyone's kind here. When I hit rock bottom, Jinnie was there for me. Just … take your time, yeah?'

Beth nodded. Her throat was too tight for words.

Beth wearily climbed the stairs to her new home. Every step emphasised her exhaustion. She wondered how she'd cope in the morning, faced with the reality of providing quality pub grub. They'd agreed to start small: a handful of new dishes to tempt the palates of the regulars.

'But we want to put the pub on the culinary map.' Beth recalled Angela's enthusiasm at the interview. Ed had been more low-key.

'What Angela's saying is that dining choices are limited in the area. Ray and Liz did an ace job, but your vision will draw in punters from a wider area – fingers crossed – and we can look at expanding.'

Beth admired their energy, but right now hers was hitting an all-time low. She pushed open the door to her living space and sighed heavily at the chaos before her.

Yes, she had a bed, but she needed to find the bedding. Ditto her toiletries and the spreadsheet she'd created for the first few days of catering at The Jekyll and Hyde.

After making the bed and arranging her products in the bathroom, Beth opened her laptop. She'd gone for a themed menu, playing on the Jekyll and Hyde connection and adding a general gothic vibe.

Dr Jekyll's Venison Remedy: a venison and wild mushroom stew cooked in red wine.

Mr Hyde's Haggis Bomb: haggis (both regular and vegetarian) croquettes on a neeps and tatties purée, with a whisky peppercorn sauce.

Cauldron Mac: Skillet macaroni cheese tossed with bacon jam and crispy shallots.

Angela and Ed had loved the gothic theme. They'd also insisted on the classics – fish and chips and steak pie – to cater for those with simpler tastes.

Rose, the newly trained kitchen assistant, would help with prep and plating. Beth was grateful. She hadn't found her rhythm again; maybe shared laughter over peeling potatoes could coax it back.

When the room finally resembled something like home, she cleaned her teeth, tied back her hair and crawled under the duvet. She set her alarm for six thirty.

Sleep, however, refused to come.

Beth popped in her earbuds and opened her meditation app. A calm voice guided her breathing, repeating affirmations she was trying to believe: *I am stronger than I realise. I have the power to build a new life. I will allow myself to heal.*

The words washed over her.

As her breathing slowed, the ache in her chest eased to something bearable.

Tomorrow is a new day, she told herself. *Let the adventure begin.*

Chapter Four

By half past twelve, Beth wondered if she'd made a mistake.

Not a catastrophic one – no kitchen fires, food poisoning or customers storming out threatening legal action. Just a creeping, insidious feeling that lodged in her chest and whispered: *You're not ready for this*.

She stared at the tray of pies cooling on the stainless-steel counter. Venison and mushroom. Exactly what Beth had come up with when she pitched her menu ideas.

They were cooked to perfection, with golden pastry and rich filling. She'd tasted one herself, forking up a delicious mouthful.

And yet…

Something felt off.

'They look amazing,' Rose said, popping her head round the door. Her cheeks were already flushed from carrying plates out and chatting to customers. 'Angela's chuffed.'

Beth smiled automatically. 'Good.'

Rose lingered. 'Are you OK?'

There it was. The question she'd been dodging from the moment she arrived in Cranley.

'I'm fine,' Beth said, a little too brightly. 'Just … first-week nerves.'

Rose nodded, unconvinced but kind enough not to push. 'Shout if you need anything.'

Beth waited until she'd gone, then placed her hands flat on the counter and let her shoulders sag.

The kitchen was quiet in that rare, in-between way. Not rush, not rest. The extractor fan hummed. A pan ticked softly as it cooled. Outside, she could hear voices from the bar – laughter, the clink of glasses, the low, comforting murmur of people who knew where they belonged.

Then a child laughed.

The sound sliced through her without warning. Her nerves jangled and she felt the room tilt around her.

Beth stilled, her breath catching. It wasn't particularly loud. It wasn't even near. Just a high, unselfconscious giggle, followed by an adult voice saying, 'Careful, sweetheart.'

She closed her eyes and pushed down the wave of internal panic. *Get a grip.*

Children existed: they always would. She knew pretending otherwise was beyond ridiculous. Most days she carried the knowledge like a smooth stone in her pocket – always there, but manageable.

Today, it felt jagged round the edges.

It shouldn't still hurt this much.

She forced herself to breathe, counting silently. *One. Two. Three.*

When she opened her eyes, she caught sight of one of the small chalkboards Angela had prepared to showcase the new menu. It listed the options, with *Made by Beth, With Love* written underneath.

Beth snorted softly. Love. If only it were as simple as dishing up food to starving punters.

She busied herself with washing things that didn't need washing, wiping surfaces already clean. Keeping busy helped. Thinking was dangerous.

'Beth?' Angela appeared in the doorway, baby Ruairi balanced expertly on one hip. He stared at Beth with solemn intensity, as if judging her worth.

Beth's stomach clenched.

'Everything OK?' Angela asked gently.

'Yes,' Beth said quickly. 'All good. Just finishing up.'

Angela smiled. 'I've had three people ask if you're staying.'

Beth blinked. 'Staying?'

'Long term.' Angela shifted Ruairi, who immediately grabbed a fistful of her hair. 'I told them we're hoping so, but I didn't want to speak for you.'

A thousand answers crowded Beth's brain.

I don't know.

I'm scared.

I can't promise anything.

Please don't make this mean something yet.

Instead, she said, 'I like it here.'

Angela's smile widened. 'Good. We like having you.' She turned to go, then paused. 'And Beth? You don't have to be brilliant all the time. Just … be here.'

After she'd gone, Beth sank onto the metal stool by the prep table.

Be here.

She stared at her hands. They were steady. Capable. These hands had cooked for hundreds, maybe thousands of people. They knew what they were doing.

It was the rest of her that felt unmoored, like a small

boat on a rocky sea.

Later, when the pub had quietened and Rose had gone home, Beth slipped back to her quarters. An hour or so of unpacking and sorting might help clear her mind of negative thoughts.

With a pair of scissors, she slashed at tape and unearthed items she'd already forgotten about. Ceramic dishes for storing jewellery – not that she owned much – candle holders and photo frames. All empty, bar one. A snap of her and Luke, grinning at the camera, eyes sparkling with joy. Taken several years ago, before the joy shrivelled up and died.

Beth stared at the photo. Tried to bolster her current mood with a smidgeon of how she'd felt back then.

'You're wallowing again,' she muttered to herself, shoving the photo back in the box. 'If Diana were here, she'd give you a bollocking.'

Half an hour later, Beth surveyed the living room with a satisfied eye. She'd found a few plaid throws, a jade-green tufted rug and a print of Edinburgh's rainbow-coloured Victoria Street that brightened the otherwise dull white wall.

A sense of calm washed over her. It was still early days, but Beth prided herself on not being a quitter. And it was normal to feel jittery starting a new job in an unfamiliar place.

Turning off the table lamps, Beth returned to the warmth of the pub. She inhaled the smell of beer and pie, smiled at the animated customers chatting together and felt the shard of tension in her chest subside.

She spotted the child: a little boy, engrossed in colouring in a picture with chunky crayons. A knot of tears threatened to overwhelm her, but she swallowed them down.

For the first time since arriving in Cranley, Beth allowed herself to think a dangerous thought. *Maybe this could work.*

She didn't push it any further than that.

One step at a time, Diana had said. And Beth valued her friend's wisdom more than anyone else's on the planet.

You can do this, she said quietly. *One step at a time.*

Chapter Five

The cottage still resembled a bombsite. Kieran had unpacked the essentials, but he feared a trip to the dreaded Swedish store might be on the cards. His meagre jacket and coat collection dangled from a cheap and not-so-cheerful clothes rack, while T-shirts and shirts remained higgledy-piggledy in a box. As for underwear…

The irony of Kieran being clueless on the fashion front didn't escape him. His brainchild – an app provisionally called ClosetAura – aimed to help men and women organise their wardrobes. Purge them of unused and unloved items, help them streamline their outfits and curb impulse buying.

'Steve Jobs did OK,' Kieran mused. 'Black turtleneck, jeans, trainers. Sorted.' Except Jobs had helmed a global empire. Kieran's fledgling business depended on customers caring about their appearances and making smart choices. Kieran looked at *his* uniform of whatever passed muster on the cleanliness front and laughed.

'No one in Cranley gives a rat's arse what you look like. They'll think you're some eccentric tech person who needs to be left alone. Which suits me right now—'

Ding-dong.

Oh, joy. The doorbell. As welcome as a verruca.

He considered pretending he wasn't home. Except the person now hammering loudly and shouting his name made that impossible.

'I know you're in there, so open up!'

Janette. Of course.

Kieran forced himself to the door. Good manners and a Scottish upbringing overrode the very real desire to hide in a cupboard.

'Hi, Janette.'

'Hi yoursel', laddie. You're looking a bit peely-wally. Isn't he, Alison?'

'Hi, Alison.' Kieran blinked at the woman beside Janette. She was elegance personified in wide-legged cream trousers with matching cardigan – cashmere, he thought – and a chocolate-brown silk top. Janette, in contrast, wore a floaty kaftan covered in tropical birds. On anyone else it would look ridiculous. On her? Weirdly magnificent.

'Thanks for the supplies,' he said. 'Sorry, I should have dropped by, but I've been busy getting the place in order.' He tried to keep the door ajar, in case they saw the stacks of boxes in the hallway.

Janette harrumphed. 'Your mum said you're a bit of a Harry Hermit. And that you live on toast, beans and enough caffeine to give you the skitters. So we're taking you to A Bit of Crumpet for the finest pastries and coffee Cranley has to offer. Oh, and this is my partner, Alison.'

Kieran's brain did a tiny double take at *partner*, then

settled. Life was complicated, relationships even more so. He wasn't about to make assumptions.

'Nice to meet you,' he said to Alison. She gave him a warm smile in return.

He grabbed his keys, resigned to his fate. At least pastries were preferable to another microwave meal.

They walked into the village, Janette delivering the local gossip with the enthusiasm of a veteran commentator.

'Ken and Mags who ran The Jekyll and Hyde have taken a wee sabbatical. Mags, bless her, has dementia, and it got too much for Ken. Their son Ed and his girlfriend Angela are running the show now, and a little bird tells me they've hired someone new for the food.'

'Her name's Beth,' Alison said quietly.

Janette stopped mid-stride. 'And how do *you* know that? Have you been keeping secrets from me?'

Kieran's mind struggled to keep up with the deluge of names. His brain felt like a badly indexed database. But one person he *had* met sprang to mind.

'I think I bumped into Jinnie,' he said.

Janette halted, her arm shooting out like a traffic warden. 'You think? You either did or you didn't. How, pray tell, did that happen?'

They'd reached the café. Through the window he saw customers chatting, laughing, consuming obscene amounts of pastry. His stomach grumbled. Escape was futile.

'How did you meet Jinnie?' Janette demanded again, blocking the entrance like a human barricade.

Kieran resisted the urge to sigh. 'It wasn't a meeting. She walked past while I was taking rubbish out. We exchanged about three sentences. Hardly a summit.'

'Janette, honestly,' Alison said, nudging her. 'Leave him alone.'

Inside, the warmth and the smell of buttered pastry hit him like a nostalgic punch to the gut. It reminded him of a café he used to visit with Lisa—

Stop.

Do not go there.

'Hey, ladies. Good to see you.' The woman behind the counter beamed at them – Jo, if he remembered correctly. Her display of baked goods was nothing short of seductive.

'Hi, Jo.' Janette cackled. 'We've brought fresh meat, but no' tae fill one of your legendary Scotch pies.'

Kieran lifted a hand. 'Hi. I'm Kieran. Moved into the cottage next to Brae.'

Jo's smile widened.

'Jo's husband is a famous actor,' Janette announced, pointing at an iced bun. 'Star of that dark show *Chasing Shadows* – not my cup of tea – and that other one … what's it called again, Jo?'

'*Dad To Me*,' Jo said proudly. 'He's away filming the next series.'

They placed their orders. Kieran chose a Gruyère and leek quiche and a decaf latte, because regular coffee might nuke his nervous system at this point.

He settled at a corner table. Janette scanned the room as if conducting surveillance.

'Shame Wilma's not here,' she said. 'Not technically a local, but she's Jinnie's gran and an absolute hoot. Late eighties and shacked up with a younger man.'

'Not *that* much younger,' Alison said drily. 'Before Kieran thinks she's robbing the cradle.'

Kieran sampled his quiche. Good. Too good, in fact. If he wasn't careful, he'd get used to this level of civilisation.

The bell jingled.

'Speak of the devil. Here's Wilma hersel', and Jinnie.'

Kieran looked up.

Jinnie beamed. 'We meet again!' Beside her stood a tiny woman with sharp blue eyes and a mischievous smile. 'Kieran, this is my gran, Wilma.'

Wilma inspected him as if she was reading his soul. 'There's an aura of sadness about you, laddie. Dark purple, with a hint of magenta.'

Kieran blinked. Twice.

Jinnie groaned. 'Gran, please. Not the colour stuff again. I preferred you with the tea leaves.'

A full-body shudder rippled through him. He had no time for crystals, colours, or psychic grannies. But *aura of sadness* hit too near the mark.

'Ignore her,' Jinnie said brightly. 'She's going through a phase.'

'Less of the phase.' Wilma sniffed. 'There are things in this world that defy explanation. Right, Jo?'

Jo, who was wiping down a table, launched into a spectacular coughing fit.

Jinnie buried her face in her hands. Alison continued eating her almond slice without comment.

Kieran decided he'd had enough village initiation for one day. 'Well, this has been … lovely, but I've work to do.'

He stood, headed for the till, slapped down enough cash to cover the lot and made for the door faster than was polite.

'See you soon, Kieran!' Janette hollered.

'Let me know if you need your aura analysed!' Wilma called after him.

When hell freezes over, Kieran thought.

Outside, the fresh June air hit his face. He took a deep breath and stared down the quiet street. Time to head home.

The cottage lights were off. Prom would be asleep somewhere inconvenient.

Kieran lingered by his gate, hands shoved into his pockets, telling himself that he needed to make more of an effort. To try and fit in, even if it pained him to do so.

Across the road, a couple of neighbours were chatting beside a parked car, laughter bubbling easily between them. They noticed him and smiled.

Right. This is it.

'Hi,' Kieran said, moving closer. 'Evening.'

'Evening,' one of them replied, friendly and open.

'I'm Kieran. Just moved into the cottage there.' He nodded vaguely behind him, instantly annoyed at how defensive that sounded.

'Oh yes,' the woman said. 'Janette mentioned you. From Edinburgh, aren't you?'

Again with that.

'Guilty,' Kieran said. 'Trying village life.'

They smiled and nodded. Pleasant. Waiting.

He searched for something to add. 'Nice place,' he offered, gesturing at the street as if they might have missed it.

'It is,' the man agreed. 'Quiet.'

'Very,' Kieran said, too quickly.

A pause settled. Not awkward for them. For him, it stretched.

'Well,' the woman said kindly, 'good luck getting settled.'

'Thanks. Yes. Lots of boxes.'

They returned to their conversation.

Kieran stood there for a beat longer, waiting for … something. An invitation. A follow-up question. Proof he hadn't already overstayed his welcome.

Nothing came.

He nodded, retreated through his gate and let himself into the cottage, closing the door softly behind him.

Prom opened one eye.

'I tried,' Kieran told the cat.

Prom yawned, turned his back and went back to sleep.

What exactly have you got yourself into?

Chapter Six

If Kieran had been the sort of man who enjoyed euphemisms, he'd have described recent hours as 'a learning curve'.

As he wasn't, he called it what it was: a barrage.

Cranley didn't do gentle introductions. It did full-frontal friendliness, served with pastry and unsolicited personality analysis.

He stared at his laptop screen as if it might provide comfort.

It didn't.

The cottage was silent apart from Prom's vigorous scratching in the corner, which sounded less like grooming and more like judgement.

'Don't start,' Kieran muttered, rubbing his eyes. 'I'm aware I'm failing at life.'

Prom didn't respond. He never did when Kieran talked to him. The cat saved his reactions for important matters, like the opening of a tin, or the appearance of a bird he wished to murder for sport.

Kieran flexed his fingers and tried again. Code. Logic. Systems. The things that always followed the rules, even when people didn't.

Except today the code wouldn't hold still. Every time he focused, his mind ricocheted back to the café: Janette's booming voice, Alison's quiet warmth, Wilma's unnervingly accurate 'aura' assessment.

Dark purple, with a hint of magenta.

He didn't believe in auras. He believed in caffeine, capitalism and the certainty of a well-written algorithm.

And yet Wilma had looked straight at him as if she could peer into his soul.

He pushed the thought away and opened the ClosetAura prototype, the home screen still showing the placeholder logo he'd thrown together at three in the morning. An outline of a wardrobe with a smug little sparkle in the corner.

The sparkle annoyed him.

He clicked into the onboarding flow. The copy felt too earnest. Too glossy. He needed it sharp, clean, useful.

Welcome to ClosetAura.

Let's build a wardrobe that fits your life.

It read like something Sven would say on a yoga mat, smiling with his younger-Yoda face.

Kieran grimaced and reworded a whole paragraph with savage satisfaction. A little better.

Then his email pinged.

He ignored it.

It pinged again and, with a reluctant sigh, he opened it.

Re: Seed Funding Enquiry

Hi Kieran, thanks for reaching out. We've reviewed your deck and—

He didn't need to read the rest. He knew the rhythm of

rejection too well. Polite. Efficient. Disappointingly civil. He skimmed anyway, just to confirm the universe hadn't decided to change tone.

…not the right fit at this stage … wish you the best … keep us updated.

Keep us updated. As if he was sending them postcards from the land of Crushing Defeat.

He shut the laptop.

Prom strutted towards him, tail upright like a flag of judgement. He paused, looked at Kieran, then sat down and began licking his paw with exaggerated calm.

'Oh, I see,' Kieran said. 'You're having a spa day while I sink into a quagmire of despair.'

Prom yawned.

Kieran got up, paced the room, then collapsed into the sofa.

He'd moved here to breathe. To step back. To recalibrate. Instead, he was the same person in a different postcode. Still grinding away. Still lonely. Still convinced that if he stopped moving, the feelings would catch up and tackle him to the floor.

He grabbed his jacket.

Prom's ears flicked.

'Don't get excited. I'm not taking you on a walk. You're a cat, not an Alsatian.'

Prom watched with bored interest as Kieran shoved his feet into trainers and stepped outside.

The air was crisp, the June sunlight welcomingly cheerful. Cranley looked like one of those villages designed to lure people into complacency: stone cottages, hanging baskets, the smell of something baking that made his stomach clench with hunger.

It should have soothed him.

Instead, it made him feel like an intruder.

He walked towards the centre, passing Janette's shop with its cheerful sign and the little bell that would no doubt summon her like a foghorn if he dared go in.

'Not today,' he muttered.

A Bit of Crumpet was open, but he couldn't face Jo's sparkle either. It was too … human. Too warm.

Without meaning to, he found himself drifting towards the pub.

The Jekyll and Hyde sat solid and familiar, as if it had been there forever, holding secrets in its walls. Kieran hesitated outside the door, unsure if socialising was the answer right now.

A cluster of people edged past him, chatting excitedly about something or other. A middle-aged man held the door open for him, but he shook his head and hurried away.

Standing on the street corner, he took a deep breath. 'Wimp,' he muttered. 'Beans on toast it is.'

Back at the cottage, Kieran heated the beans and rammed two slices of slightly mouldy bread into the toaster. Prom, optimistic at the can opening, skulked off when no food came his way.

Returning to his laptop, Kieran vowed to pull on his big-boy pants. He'd venture into the pub soon and try not to behave like a socially inept idiot in future.

As he typed, a flicker of movement caught his eye. Something pale, fluttering in a patch of sunlight filtering through the threadbare curtains.

A butterfly.

Gold-tinged, almost sparkling. Unlike any butterfly he'd seen before – not that he was an expert in lepidopterology.

As Kieran mentally congratulated himself on knowing

the word, the butterfly fluttered above his head. It hovered, as if deciding whether to land.

Kieran held his breath. Even Prom, who'd strutted into the room, gazed upwards.

Then, as suddenly as it had appeared, the butterfly vanished.

Just … gone.

Kieran looked around, expecting to see it flit elsewhere. Nothing. No movement. No shimmer. Just a light breeze that ruffled the curtains and reminded him how crap the window seals were.

'All right,' he muttered, half to himself and half to the universe. 'Either I'm hallucinating, or Cranley's got a weird pest problem.'

Prom miaowed, his gaze still fixed on the spot where the butterfly had been. Seconds later, he yawned and curled up in a ball.

Somehow, Kieran managed to dig deep and polish the ClosetAura pitch. It needed more work, but it flowed better.

Stretching his arms above his head, he outdid Prom on the yawn-ometer. A nap might be in order, although Kieran associated daytime naps with older people. *Much* older people.

'Sod it.' Kieran mirrored Prom's curled-up position, but on the sofa rather than the floor. He tugged a fleecy blanket over his body, for comfort rather than warmth.

His problems hadn't magically vanished. ClosetAura still needed funding. His cottage still looked like a building site. His loneliness still sat in his chest like a stone.

But something had shifted.

Not been fixed. Shifted.

A satisfying nap later, he opened the laptop again.

The rejection email still sat there, smug and dismissive in his inbox.

He didn't delete it.

He also didn't let it stop him.

He clicked into the onboarding flow and began rewriting, fingers moving with renewed purpose.

On the screen, the wardrobe icon still had that ridiculous little sparkle.

Kieran hovered the cursor over it.

Then, despite himself, he left it there.

For now.

Because a little sparkle never hurt anyone.

Chapter Seven

The alarm roused Beth from a sleep so deep she almost forgot where she was. Her earbuds were still in; the relaxation app had clearly done its job.

She swung her legs from the bed and went through her stretching routine – slow, deliberate movements that shook sleep from her limbs and warded off the early rumblings of anxiety. Breathe in … breathe out. A hot shower, a mug of camomile tea and a round of buttered toast later, she felt almost human.

'Morning!' Angela greeted her with a smile. Only a bluish tinge under her eyes suggested she hadn't slept as well as Beth.

'Morning,' Beth replied, then turned at a whimpering sound.

Ed appeared behind her, baby Ruairi strapped to his chest in a soft pouch, his hands automatically stroking his son's downy head. The whimpering subsided instantly.

'Did you sleep OK?' Ed asked, eyes soft with fatherly exhaustion.

'Hopefully not like a baby,' grumbled Angela. 'Which must be one of the dumbest expressions ever. Because who wants to wake up on the hour every hour, either soaked in wee or covered in poop.'

'Yes, I slept fine,' Beth said. *And I'd give anything to spend endless sleepless nights with a baby in my arms.*

She swallowed the thought before it could take root.

By mid-morning, the kitchen buzzed with purposeful noise. Mushrooms sliced into neat crescents, potatoes peeled and piled, raw meat waiting obediently on trays. Rose moved with the unselfconscious energy of someone who hadn't yet been properly walloped by life.

Beth envied her that.

Lunch came and went in a blur of plates and praise. At one point, Ed insisted Beth step out from the kitchen and the applause caught her off guard – warm, genuine, and dangerously close to hope.

By mid-afternoon, with the pub quiet again and Rose heading home, Beth should have rested. Instead, she found herself standing at the top of the basement stairs.

The door groaned as if resentful of being disturbed.

Beth tugged the light chain. The single bulb flickered, steadied, then cast a weak yellow pool over the first few steps. Cold air crept up to meet her.

'You're being ridiculous,' she muttered, but descended anyway.

Each step creaked, the sound echoing too loudly in the confined space. The air smelt of dust and damp, old stone and neglect. This place had been forgotten on purpose.

Halfway down, something brushed her shoulder.

Beth yelped, flailing, then laughed shakily when nothing attacked her.

A cobweb. Of course.

At the bottom, crates and boxes loomed in untidy stacks, their contents surrendered to time. Broken stools. Old signage. Bottles whose labels had long since peeled away.

Then she saw it.

The shape beneath the tarpaulin didn't belong to the rest of the clutter. It had presence. Bulk. Intention.

Beth's pulse quickened. She hesitated, then reached out and tugged the tarp free.

Dust erupted. She sneezed violently, eyes watering, heart racing, then froze.

A pinball machine.

Not plastic. Not garish. Ornate and heavy, with brass trim dulled by age. Sapphire and gold paint curled across the cabinet, the artwork rich and elaborate. On the back glass, a genie reclined on a flying carpet, arms folded, lips curved in a knowing smile.

The Wish Master.

Beth stepped closer. 'I haven't played one of these in years,' she whispered.

A memory slammed into her. She and Luke in a friend's basement, laughing as they battled it out on vintage machines. Her unexpected talent. His mock outrage when she beat him again.

'I won every time,' she murmured, smiling despite herself.

She crouched, tracing the edge of the cabinet. The wood felt cool. Solid. Real.

'You probably don't even work,' she said, oddly disappointed.

Still, she searched for a cable. Found one, old but intact, trailing uselessly along the floor. No socket nearby.

Beth straightened, brushing dust from her hands. 'Just a stupid machine,' she told herself.

Then, because she was tired and human and apparently incapable of leaving things alone, she pressed the start button.

Nothing.

She exhaled, half relieved.

'See?' she said to the empty room. 'Dead as a doornail.'

She turned away.

Then she turned back and pressed the start button again, harder this time.

Still nothing.

Beth huffed. 'Figures. Even imaginary magic needs the right conditions.'

Suddenly she was aware of how quiet the room had become – the sort of silence that felt expectant rather than empty.

Not yet, something in her seemed to say. *Soon. But not yet.*

The thought unsettled her more than the darkness. She headed for the steps.

Behind her, a light flickered.

Beth spun round.

The machine glowed – not brightly, not dramatically. Just … alive.

Beth's heart thudded. 'No,' she breathed. 'No bloody way.'

She crouched again, staring.

No plug. No power. No explanation.

Beth staggered back, her mind scrambling for logic.

'This isn't happening,' she whispered. 'I'm tired. I've inhaled too much dust.'

She reached out and smacked the side of the machine, hard.

The lights blinked out.

Silence crashed down.

Beth stood shaking, breath rasping in her ears. Then her gaze snagged on the lettering etched into the cabinet: *Three Wishes. No Refunds.*

Beth frowned at the words.

No Refunds.

'That's cheerful,' she muttered. 'Who hurt you?'

She ran a finger along the etched letters. The metal felt faintly warmer here – not hot, just … aware. As if it had been touched too often by hopeful hands.

A strange, unbidden thought slid into her mind. *What if it doesn't give you what you ask for?*

What if it gives you what you need – and lets the wanting do the damage?

Beth shook her head sharply. 'Listen to yourself,' she said. 'You've spent too long around menu boards with theatrical names.'

Her throat tightened and a cold realisation settled in her chest.

Three wishes sounded generous. Luxurious, even.

But the truth was that she had been living with dozens of half-wishes for years. Quiet ones she'd never said aloud, because naming them made them sharper.

Wanting a baby.

Wanting Luke back.

Wanting not to feel broken every time someone said *congratulations*.

Three wishes suddenly felt … *inadequate*.

How were you meant to choose which part of your heart mattered most?

'I wish I had a baby,' she whispered, the words spilling out before she could stop them. 'A child.' Her voice cracked. 'That I hadn't failed at something so many women do every day.'

'I wish Luke was still with me. That he'd believed in us.'

A sob tore free.

'And the third?' she whispered. 'I don't even know what to wish.'

Anger surged, hot and sudden. 'Damn it!'

Beth stood, heart hammering, as a peculiar certainty crept over her.

Whatever had just happened hadn't responded to the button. Or the wiring.

It had responded to *her*.

To the tightness in her chest. To the ache she carried everywhere like an invisible scar.

The realisation was enough to send her stumbling for the stairs.

Beth didn't hear the soft *whirr-whirr* behind her.

Didn't hear the faint, shimmering jingle rising from the shadows.

And didn't see the Wish Spinner complete its first, quiet turn.

Chapter Eight

Kieran slurped what was either his fifth or sixth coffee of the day. Considering he'd been awake since five, that didn't seem too bad. Until he realised only two hours had passed and his stomach felt as if he'd ingested battery acid.

'Focus,' he muttered.

But the lines of code on his laptop swam and twisted, refusing to settle into anything intelligible. On a good day, coding flowed through him – logic, structure, clarity. Today it looked exactly like the gobbledygook most people assumed it was.

His stomach rumbled in protest, loud and insistent. A quick inventory of his kitchen revealed a packet of digestives, one lonely teabag and a fridge emptier than his social diary.

'Miaow.' Prom sat at his feet, tail flicking like a metronome set to disdainful.

'Don't worry. There's always food for you.' Kieran had packed cat kibble. He dished out a helping, only slightly tempted to eat some himself.

It became painfully clear he wasn't going to get any productive work done while surrounded by chaos. He shut the laptop and surveyed the cottage with a critical eye. Spartan didn't cover it. The place looked like a cross between a student bedsit and a warehouse clearance.

Right. Step one: make it habitable.

He ordered a few essentials online – a wardrobe, a chest of drawers, a couple of bookcases – because the idea of trekking through a migraine-inducing Swedish furniture labyrinth made him want to weep. Delivery in two days. Better than nothing.

Next, food. He could drag himself to Janette's corner shop, but that risked conversation. Questions. Stories. Enthusiasm. Kieran was in no condition for enthusiasm. He googled supermarkets instead and snagged a delivery slot for that evening. Half an hour later he'd completed an uninspired but functional shop: bread, milk, pasta, veg, coffee, cat supplies. Enough to survive a week, maybe more.

What next? The cottage still looked bare and unloved. Lisa knew how to add homely touches: an artfully draped throw or a scatter of multi-hued cushions. Strategically placed lamps which added warmth, and always the aroma of freshly brewed coffee or baking bread filling the air.

'And bloody yoga mats I kept tripping over, and incense sticks that stank to high heaven.' Kieran tried to balance the good with the bad – the yin and the yang, if that made sense – but still his heart faltered whenever he thought of Lisa.

'The pub,' he said aloud. Food, noise, warmth – all preferable to wallowing in his own misery. Not conversation: he had no intention of 'peopling'. But he could sit in a corner and rejoin the world from a safe distance. Not run away from it as he had before.

The Jekyll and Hyde. He remembered the sign – the reference to Stevenson's story, all about the split in human nature. Light and dark. Good and not-so-good. *Do I have a dark side?* he wondered.

Talking to yourself is the first sign of madness, lad. His grandad's voice echoed in his head. Five years gone yet still popping up whenever Kieran veered off course.

The walk to the pub was short and pleasant. June sunlight filtered through the trees, dappling the pavement. When he stepped inside, warmth enveloped him instantly. The place had a comforting, lived-in charm, with its polished wood, soft lighting, the faint scent of old fires and good food. Customers chatted in low voices, glasses clinked, and the atmosphere murmured with an ease he envied.

'Hi there!' A smiling woman approached, as bright and welcoming as the sun outside. 'Welcome to The Jekyll and Hyde. I don't think I've seen you here before. I rarely forget a face.'

Kieran tried to mirror her smile, but his mouth refused to cooperate. 'I just moved here. I bought—'

'The cottage! Next to Brae Cottage. I always wonder why yours doesn't have a name, although I guess it doesn't matter. Maybe you should come up with one.' She laughed lightly. 'I'm Angela, by the way.'

'Nice to meet you. I'm Kieran.' He recalled Janette mentioning an Angela who'd taken over the pub, along with Tom. Or was it Ted?

'I hope you're settling in OK,' Angela said. 'Janette said you lived in Edinburgh before and you're a tech genius.'

'Did she also reveal my blood type, inside-leg measurement and social ineptitude?'

Angela's smile dimmed. 'Janette means well. She's got a heart of gold.'

Kieran considered reversing out of the door. He could wait for his supermarket delivery and order it on repeat for maybe the next six months. Or…

'Sorry. I have a pathetic sense of humour and no filter. I didn't mean to be rude. But I'm starving, so…'

Her smile returned, softer this time. 'Then you've come to the right place.' Angela gestured to an empty table and Kieran sat down. 'The menu's on the blackboard and everything's freshly made by our new chef. We're keeping it small for now, but early feedback's brilliant.'

Kieran ordered a pint, scanned the menu, and settled on Hyde's haddock with triple-cooked potato fingers and a side of terrifying tartare and graveyard purée. Right. Fish, chips and mushy peas.

When the meal arrived, he dug in with embarrassing enthusiasm. The fish was crisp and perfectly cooked, the chips glorious, the peas rich and buttery. He wiped his plate clean and sat back, sated for the first time in days.

'Did you enjoy that?' Angela reappeared, this time juggling a squirming baby.

'I did.' The fact that the plate looked dishwasher-clean might be a massive giveaway.

'This is our pride and joy, Ruairi,' Angela said. Ruairi kicked his chubby little legs like a tiny chorus-line dancer.

'He's, erm, cute.' Kieran cringed internally at how awkward it sounded. *How do normal people talk to babies?*

'Our friend Jinnie just dropped him off. She's got one too, a darling girl called Dahlia.'

'I've met Jinnie,' he said, then blinked as another woman joined Angela. An apron-clad woman with flushed cheeks and an 'I'd rather be anywhere else' expression.

'Kieran, this is Beth,' Angela said. 'Our culinary wizard, shaking things up at The Jekyll and Hyde.'

Beth nodded a tight hello. Kieran reciprocated. Angela nodded too. No one spoke.

Then a disturbance interrupted their brief exchange.

'Ed, give me a blinking second,' Angela snapped at someone behind her, trying to decipher frantic waving from across the room. 'What? I can't hear you!' Flustered, Angela turned to Beth, holding out Ruairi. 'Can you hold him for a minute, please?'

Kieran saw Beth stiffen, eyes widening as she took a step back. Panic flickered in her face, shockingly raw. 'Sorry, I… There's something I need to do in the kitchen. Urgently. Sorry.'

They watched as Beth took off at a gallop, nearly colliding with a woman carrying a tray of drinks.

Angela sighed.

'I can help.' Kieran reached for Ruairi before his brain could veto the decision.

The baby was heavier than he looked and more fragrant than he expected. Prom never smelt that pleasant.

Angela frowned slightly. 'Are you sure you're OK with this?'

'I think I'm holding him the right way up, but if he fills his nappy I'll dump him in a wheelie bin. Joke. Deal with whatever needs doing.'

Ruairi blinked at him, solemn as a judge. Kieran gently stroked his head, unexpectedly moved. What went on inside this tiny mind? Probably not existential dread. More likely: *food soon?*

Beth's reaction replayed in his head. The way her face had changed at the sight of the baby. Fear, yes, but something deeper too. Pain.

'You're a star,' Angela said, and hurried to Ed. When she returned minutes later, she reclaimed Ruairi with coos and kisses. The baby giggled, as if nothing in the world could ever go wrong.

Across the room, a young woman staggered towards the door shrieking profanities.

'Who's that?' Kieran asked.

'That's Kylie.' Angela sighed. 'Who has nothing in common with the Aussie singer apart from a fondness for tight hot pants. Poor old Jimmy over there' – she gestured at an elderly gentleman nursing a whisky – 'nearly had a heart attack when she bent down in front of him one day and he saw more than he bargained for.'

'The toilet's fixed.' Ed appeared, looking dishevelled. 'And Kylie's barred for a month.'

Kieran smiled. 'Well, now that calm has returned, I'd better head home and do some work.' He said his goodbyes and felt a pang when Ruairi, with a little parental help, waved a chubby-fingered farewell.

Back at the cottage, he reopened his laptop and stared blankly at the screen. Code stared back, uncooperative. His thoughts weren't on ClosetAura, algorithms or anything logical. They were on Beth. On the way she'd recoiled from the baby. The flash of anguish she'd tried to hide.

'It doesn't bloody matter,' he muttered under his breath. 'ClosetAura needs your brain, not a stranger with … whatever that was.'

But the image lingered anyway.

And for the first time in a long time, something tugged Kieran out of his self-absorption. Something that wasn't coding, coffee, or a cat named after a mythical troublemaker.

Chapter Nine

'Hon, don't beat yourself up about it.'

Diana's face filled Beth's screen – freckled, fierce, and unflinchingly kind – as she balanced her mug beneath her chin. The familiar sight released something tight in Beth's chest.

'I recoiled from holding their baby!' Beth whispered, horrified all over again. 'As if they'd asked me to mind the spawn of Satan instead of … instead of…'

She pressed her palms to her eyelids, forcing the tears back. The baby had been adorable. Exactly how Beth had pictured her and Luke's firstborn.

'Let it out,' Diana urged. 'Cry. Don't stop yourself because you think someone will judge you. I don't judge anyone. Apart from the dickhead who got hacked off yesterday when I said I didn't offer "extras" with his lower back massage.'

Beth snorted, the sound half laugh and half sob. Diana always found a way to anchor her when she felt one breath away from falling apart.

'Changing the subject, what's the deal with the pinball machine? Are you planning to get your game on?' Diana sipped from her *Knead You to Relax* mug.

Beth had told Diana about the unexpected discovery. Not a big deal, but it had piqued her interest.

'It's nothing. It probably doesn't work, anyway. But if I changed the plug and got it near a socket…'

'So when you're not being a gastronomic goddess, you want to hide in a fusty basement and get all flippery, or whatever the terminology is for playing pinball.'

'No.' Beth laughed weakly. 'I just think it might be fun.'

'Have you mentioned it to Angela and Ed?'

'Not yet. I probably should, but I don't think they'll want it in the pub. Ed said they ditched the fruit machine a while ago.'

Their conversation drifted. Beth talked about the menu launch and Diana grumbled about not having had a holiday in over a year.

'That's because you're a workaholic,' Beth teased. 'You'd rather massage perverts than lie on a beach. And you haven't mentioned the date you had the other night.'

Diana pulled a 'kill me now' face. 'Horrendous, as usual. He had more hair growing out of his nostrils than on his head, and he bit his nails at every opportunity.'

'Maybe he was nervous.' Beth adored Diana but she could be intimidating, especially to someone with chewed nails and fragile confidence.

'Ha! Confidence oozed from every pore, including the blackhead-blocked ones on his bulbous nose.' Diana shuddered theatrically. 'I'm done with dating. Finished.'

'That makes two of us.' The thought of seeing someone else after Luke filled Beth with terror. No matter how nice they might be, her history would act as a massive stumbling block. *Yes, I was married. Still am, technically. But my husband left me. Why? Settle down, and I'll drown you in an ocean of grief.*

'Beth,' Diana said softly, 'you've got that sad face again. Come on, there must be some talent in Cranley. Someone you can discreetly ogle when you're not slaving over a hot stove.'

Beth rolled her eyes. 'Most men I've seen or heard about are collecting their pensions or taken. Like Ed and Angela. Like Jinnie and Sam. With babies. The only single person around my age is Kieran. He's the one who held Ruairi when I—'

'When you didn't want to,' Diana cut in firmly. 'And that's OK. Non-event. Tell me more. Is he gorgeous, with hair on his head and cuticles intact?'

Beth tried to conjure Kieran's face. He'd seemed pleasant enough. Kind, even. But it didn't matter. She wasn't looking. She wasn't capable.

After a flurry of blown kisses, they ended the call. The silence that followed felt heavy. Thick with memories and loss.

Beth glanced at the bags by her door. Two blue IKEA sacks bulging with baby things: bootees, sleepsuits, cot blankets, toys. And the genie-themed lampshade she'd once adored. It had seemed so magical once upon a time.

Magic didn't exist.

She carried the sacks down to the basement.

The air felt different tonight. Colder, yes, but not in temperature alone. The kind of cold that pressed against your skin as if waiting for you to acknowledge it.

'Don't start,' she muttered to herself.

She shoved the sacks into the metal cupboard and slammed the door. It rebounded slightly. She kicked it closed, harder than necessary.

The clang reverberated through the stone walls.

Silence followed.

Not empty silence.

Listening silence.

Beth's shoulders tightened.

Slowly – unwillingly – her gaze slid across the room.

The pinball machine was already lit.

Not in a dramatic flare. No sudden burst. Just a steady, low glow beneath the jewel-toned lenses, as though it had been patiently waiting for her to arrive.

Her breath shortened.

'I didn't touch you,' she said.

The genie on the backboard looked less decorative in the dim light. The painted smirk held a new sharpness.

The Wish Spinner at the centre of the playfield rotated once.

Whirr.

A clean, deliberate click.

Beth froze.

'No.'

The score display flickered. Numbers trembled into life.

000002

Her stomach dropped.

Two.

Not zero.

Not waiting.

Two.

'I didn't—' Her voice faltered. Because she had. She'd stood here before and poured her grief into the air like it was something the universe might collect and return improved.

The lights pulsed faintly, almost like breathing.

'I was upset,' she whispered. 'That doesn't count.'

The machine responded with a soft, crystalline chime.

Not cheerful. Confirming.

The spinner twitched but did not complete another turn.

Two.

The etched lettering gleamed faintly:

Three Wishes. No Refunds.

The words felt heavier now. Less theatrical. Less like an old pub novelty dragged from storage.

More like terms and conditions.

Beth took a step back.

'You don't get to decide what I meant,' she said, anger pushing through fear. 'You don't get to interpret grief.'

The bulbs dimmed slightly, then brightened again.

The genie's painted eyes seemed almost reflective, catching light that wasn't there.

Behind her, the cupboard door creaked open an inch.

Beth spun.

The bags sat exactly where she'd thrown them. No movement. No sound.

When she turned back, the display still read:

000002

Unchanged.

Waiting.

A shudder of cold slid down her spine.

'I don't want this,' she said hoarsely.

The machine did not dim.

Did not flicker.

Did not retreat.

It simply remained.

Alive.

The realisation settled in her bones: whatever had

happened in this room had not required wiring, plugs or logic.

It had required her.

Beth backed toward the stairs, never taking her eyes off the machine.

Halfway up, the lights faded.

Not snapped off.

Faded.

Until the basement returned to dull, ordinary darkness.

Just before she reached the top step, a final, almost playful chime echoed behind her.

And somewhere deep within the machine, metal shifted against metal.

Patiently.

Chapter Ten

'Don't you miss the buzz of city life?' Charlie asked, making a grand sweep of his arm towards Edinburgh Castle and almost decapitating a group of startled tourists.

'No,' Kieran said, dropping a few coins into the battered hat of a man curled against a shopfront. 'I don't miss elbowing my way along Princes Street, that's for sure.'

They reached The Devil's Dram, their old haunt from uni days. The type of pub where the windows wept condensation and the doorway was permanently blocked by diehard smokers. They squeezed inside, jostling through the weekend crush, and lucked into a table just vacated by a pair of students who looked barely conscious.

'Right,' Charlie said, shrugging off his jacket. 'What are you having? Pint of heavy? Wee dram?'

Kieran smirked. He could already see where this was going. 'Just a pint's fine.'

'Or,' Charlie continued, eyes bright, 'I could get you a Flirtini. Maybe a Unicorn Whisper with extra sparkles on top?'

'You're an eejit.'

'Nah, seriously. I'll ask for a tiny umbrella and a pink straw. Something to make you feel special.'

'Just get me the pint, you dafty.' Kieran laughed, a genuine one, grateful he'd escaped Cranley for a few hours. Charlie's ridiculous banter was nostalgic in the best way; it reminded him of a younger version of himself, before life had got messy.

Charlie pulled a theatrical sigh. 'Fine. Pint of lager for you, one Princess Potion with fairy dust for me. Sorted.'

He returned with two pints of Innis & Gunn and a laminated menu tucked under his arm. 'My stomach thinks my throat's cut,' he announced, rubbing his belly.

They ordered macaroni cheese with garlic bread. Comfort food, pub grub. No flamboyant names or themed nonsense. Straightforward and safe.

'So, you don't miss Edinburgh. Is that because Cranley's crammed with gorgeous women desperate to hook up with a soon-to-be billionaire tech giant?'

Kieran spluttered mid-sip. 'Hardly. The handful of women I've met are either happily partnered or old enough to have lived through three recessions.'

The server plonked cutlery, napkins and condiments on the table. 'Thanks,' said Charlie. 'Come on, Kieran, there must be someone close to your age! Ah, don't tell me: you're still pining for Lisa.'

Denying it would be a lie. Admitting it… Heather, Charlie's wife, had been good friends with Lisa. Not so much after the split, since Heather had aligned herself with Team Kieran, but he didn't want to seem like a lovelorn loser. 'It still hurts, OK. Let's leave it there.'

'Fair.' Charlie nodded, which meant absolutely nothing, because he never let a topic go if it intrigued him. He picked at the beer mat. 'But you've got to give me something. Two or three youngish, attractive women in Cranley willing to fall for a saddo like you… Then I'll bore you with tales of fatherhood and the joys of a pregnant wife who now requires assistance clipping her toenails.'

Their food arrived. Charlie tore into his with the enthusiasm of a man facing his last meal. Kieran chased a forkful of macaroni round his plate. Who *had* he met in the younger age bracket? Jinnie, happily married and with a baby. Angela, possibly married, also with a baby. Then there was Beth. He knew next to nothing about her. Except that she cooked very well and appeared to have an allergy to babies.

'Mate, are you not eating?' Charlie asked.

Kieran took a token bite then shoved his plate towards him. Charlie pounced on it like a starved wolf. Fortunately, his friend worked out three times a week at the gym, otherwise he'd be the size of a well-fed bungalow.

'There is someone,' Kieran said. The words escaped before he could apply the brakes. He grabbed a slice of garlic bread and shoved it into his mouth to stop elaborating.

Charlie's head snapped up. 'Now we're talking. Is she another yoga nutter like Lisa, or does she have actual substance? Not that Lisa doesn't have substance. She just needs to stop banging on about chakras and tantric sex.'

Sex. Kieran pretended not to remember what that was. Couldn't care less if he never again writhed around under tangled sheets, making a woman moan with pleasure. Nope, not interested.

'Kieran,' Charlie said slowly, 'you're making a weird face. And kind of a weird noise.'

'No I'm not.'

'People are staring.'

Shit. Kieran scanned the room. No one was looking at him.

'You are so full of shit, Charlie.'

Charlie shrugged, dragging a hunk of bread through the dregs of the cheese sauce. 'Mate, I'll be knee-deep in nappies again come July. Or August. Heather complains I don't listen. I'm more worried about Jacob.'

Jacob, in Kieran's fairly inexperienced opinion, was a sweet boy with a gentle disposition and a fondness for complex Lego constructions. 'Because he'll feel temporarily displaced as the focus of the family?'

'No. Because he said he wanted to chop up the baby and cook it in the oven.'

Kieran blinked. 'Wow. That escalated.'

'He's just being dramatic,' Charlie said breezily. 'Probably.'

Slightly worrying. Possible serial-killer alert. Kieran decided not to pursue that. There were only so many potential serial-killer conversations a man could manage on a Saturday afternoon.

'Send my love to Heather,' Kieran said. 'She's a diamond.'

Charlie softened. 'Aye. She is. And I don't mind the toenail clipping. Or the flatulence. Or the screaming. Or the threats that she'll never pee normally again.' He shook his head helplessly. 'What *is* that about?'

Kieran had no answers. Only a growing ache in his chest.

'Sorry. Got sidetracked there,' added Charlie. 'Tell me about the someone you've met.'

'There's nothing to tell. Her name's Beth. She's the chef at The Jekyll and Hyde pub and we're both newcomers.'

Charlie grinned. 'And the locals aren't likely to drive you out with pitchforks or perform some weird ritual involving wicker and flames?'

Charlie was obsessed with creepy movies. Evil dolls that came to life, or ancient entities hell-bent on wreaking havoc. Kieran had no time for the supernatural. A man of science and logic, he observed the world with a pragmatic eye.

'Not yet. Cranley is more likely to lull me into a coma than a horror film.'

'How's the app coming along?' Charlie owned an upmarket garage selling vintage cars. He knew next to nothing about Kieran's IT abilities, just as Kieran had zero interest in carburettors, gearboxes and the expensive nap of a leather seat.

'It's coming along at a snail's pace. The problem is, I'm a one-man band. Designer, coder, future advertiser and marketer. I need investment to progress. But without something polished, it's hard to get investment. It's a chicken-and-egg situation.'

Charlie glanced down at his immaculate ensemble of suit trousers, pristine white shirt and shoes that gleamed. 'Heather buys most of my clothes. I haven't a clue about what goes with what. So, pitch your product to me. As someone who dresses like a funeral director, what exactly does your app do?'

Kieran rubbed a hand over his face. Ideas usually came effortlessly. Today they flickered weakly at the edges of his mind.

'It helps people find their comfort zone,' he said. 'Streamline their wardrobes. Curb impulse buying. Build a capsule collection that fits their lifestyle. Less clutter, more confidence.'

'Right.' Charlie's expression suggested he'd reached his boredom threshold.

'I'm thinking of a two-tier plan. Freemium – free, duh – and Premium. Where you'll get discounts at certain stores and other extras. I want to offer customers empowering, smart, stylish and sustainable choices, one outfit at a time.'

'Nice,' Charlie said, wiping his mouth. 'No clue what that means. Heather tells me if I look like a sack of shit or gives me a thumbs up if I pass muster. Currently, I daren't say a word about her appearance. She's allowed to use the word "whale". I value my life too much to comment.'

The afternoon drifted towards its end. They finished eating, exchanged the ritual man-hug and promised to meet again soon.

'By which time,' Kieran said, 'you'll have two kids and I'll still be a single, nerdy bastard.'

Charlie checked his phone as his Uber arrived. 'Or you'll be loved up with Beth, eating gourmet meals every night.'

Kieran snorted as he waved him off. Loved up. As if.

On the train back to Cranley, he let his head rest against the cool glass. Outside, the countryside blurred into green and gold streaks.

The only creature that loved him was Prom.

And he wasn't entirely certain the cat was totally on his side.

Chapter Eleven

By day seven at The Jekyll and Hyde, the early buzz had dulled into the usual village rhythm. Steady and predictable, punctured by the odd complaint.

'We've had a few grumbles from the regulars,' said Ed. 'Moaning that sausages, beans and chips aren't on the menu, and what's wrong with a nice gammon steak and pineapple.'

Beth bit her tongue. Pineapple belonged nowhere near savoury food; the very thought made her skin crawl. But the customer came first. Always.

'I can dial the menu down a notch,' she said. 'Keep some quirkiness but add more classics.'

'We've already got pie and fish and chips.' Ed smiled reassuringly. 'It's early days, Beth. Give them time and they'll come round.'

Time. Beth wondered how much of it she'd need before she stopped feeling like an imposter. She'd swept in wanting to prove herself, hoping passion and creativity would somehow magic away the grief that clung to her like smoke. Ed and Angela believed in her. That should be enough.

But she didn't really believe in herself.

'Are you all sorted in the basement?' Angela's voice cut in, bright and warm. She appeared with Jinnie in tow, babies Ruairi and Dahlia nestled against them, and a tall man behind. He was handsome, steady and oozed easy confidence. Judging by the way he gazed adoringly at Jinnie and Dahlia, he had to be Jinnie's husband, Sam. Jinnie headed off to the rest room, cradling Dahlia who'd started to grizzle.

'I'm getting there,' Beth said.

'Have you two met?' Angela nodded at Sam. 'No, I don't think you have. Sam, this is Beth.'

Beth shook Sam's hand. A sudden chill snaked down her spine, and she jerked her hand back too quickly. Brilliant. Now she was the woman who hated babies *and* handshakes.

'Nice to meet you, Beth.' Sam's face remained neutral apart from a tiny twitch of his left eyebrow. That meant nothing, but… His face seemed familiar. Something to do with Luke. Luke, who loved to read thrillers, the darker and gorier the better—

'You're Alistair Scott! My husband loved your books.' Her voice wobbled. 'I recognise your face from one of them. Not my thing: I read fluffy stuff. I mean…'

She stopped. Too late.

Silence swelled between them. Even Ruairi stopped chewing his knuckles and gawped at her.

'Oh, Beth,' Angela breathed, eyes filling. 'We didn't know. We didn't even ask. How long since he … he passed?'

Passed?

'He's not dead,' Beth blurted. 'Luke's alive. We're just … not together anymore.'

Relief flashed across Angela's face. 'Oh, that's great! I mean, that he's not dead. It's great he's still alive, isn't it, Sam?'

Sam made an awkward sound. 'I think we can all agree that's a good thing. Beth, we'll give you some space now.'

Jinnie reappeared, looking flustered.

'Aren't Wilma and Gus expecting us?' said Sam, looking at his watch.

'Are they? Oh, yes.' Jinnie clutched Dahlia possessively. 'Let's get going. Bye!'

The trio beat a hasty retreat, leaving Beth, Ed and Angela in an awkward silence that extended into a vacuum of wordlessness.

Beth spoke first. 'There's a pinball machine in the basement.'

Angela blinked. 'Is there?'

Ed frowned, then recognition dawned. 'I'd forgotten all about that. Dad mentioned it when they took over the pub. Apparently it glitched all the time, so they put it into storage. It should really go to the dump, but we never got round to it.'

'Glitched how?' Beth realised her question might seem odd. Scratch that; borderline barking mad.

'Erm, I was in my teens when they pulled the plug – excuse the pun – so I don't really remember. I think it gave out wonky scores. Oh, and someone claimed it spoke to them.'

Angela snorted. 'It's amazing what a drink or six can do to someone's faculties. I'm so glad I quit. Not that doing so has given me genius status.'

Ed chuckled and kissed her cheek. 'Who needs brains when you've got beauty?'

'What's your excuse for having neither?' she shot back, elbowing him.

Their easy affection pierced Beth like a blade slipped between her ribs. Familiar ache, familiar burn. She swallowed it down.

'Beth?' Angela's voice was gentle. 'Are you OK?'

Beth forced a brittle smile. In another life, she'd have leaned into that kindness. But in this one… Her heart had room for exactly one confidante: Diana. No more.

'Sorry,' she said softly. 'I've got a thing about pinball machines. Luke and I… It doesn't matter. I'll be downstairs if you need me.'

She fled to the basement, half-expecting Ed and Angela to follow. They didn't.

'Hello, Wish Master.'

Nothing. Zip. Nada. The pinball machine remained inanimate.

Of course it did. Some 1970s piece of junk that had entertained in its time, but now?

She approached. The machine loomed in the dim light, silent and harmless.

'I imagined it,' she said firmly. 'Sadness can make you see things. Hear things. Like—' Her throat caught. 'Like a baby you'll never hold.'

'Hey, foxy mama.'

Beth reeled back so violently she slipped and hit the floor.

The bulbs flared to life – red, green, gold – washing the walls in shimmering light. Music chimed, strangely exotic, threads of melody winding through the air.

She froze.

'Welcome, welcome,' a voice boomed. 'Long time since

someone played me. But first, let's put some zing into the ka-ching!'

A figure shimmered into view above the machine. Misty, but human-shaped. Portly, wearing a sequinned waistcoat, absurd harem trousers and a gold medallion, swinging over a rounded belly.

'You've got to be kidding,' Beth whispered.

'Not at all, sweetheart,' the figure crooned. 'The name's Gigi. You got any coins?'

Beth scrambled backwards, reaching for anything solid. The world spun sideways.

Her hand skidded across the floor: her head cracked against a crate.

Stars burst. Then everything went black.

When she came round, the basement was filled with silence. No lights. No music. No Gigi. Just dust motes drifting through weak light and the relentless ticking of an ancient clock.

Beth groaned, rubbing the back of her skull. 'Brilliant. Knocked myself out. Seeing things now, am I?'

Her laugh was half-tremble, half-hysteria.

The pinball machine stood inert. Dead. Nothing more than wood, glass, and peeling paint. A relic from a bygone era.

'All in my imagination,' she muttered, forcing her voice steady.

She rose slowly, dizzy but determined, and walked towards the stairs. Because whatever had happened here…

Beth wasn't ready to let anyone know she'd seen an apparition in harem trousers who'd called himself Gigi.

Not yet.

Probably never.

Chapter Twelve

Kieran eyed the peeling wallpaper in his living room with the same despair he reserved for broken bits of code. The estate agent had optimistically described it as 'charming, with potential.' At present, it was damp, draughty and as appealing as a 1990s office cubicle.

Armed with a stepladder, a bucket of soapy water and an enthusiasm fuelled by three mugs of coffee, he set about stripping the paper. Ten minutes later, he was standing in the middle of a sodden mess, with half a wall bare, and a chunk of plaster at his feet which had come away like an uncooperative scab.

'Looks like yer murdering the place,' came a voice from the open window.

Kieran turned to see Janette leaning on the garden gate. Behind her stood a cute spaniel, tail wagging enthusiastically.

'I'm … renovating,' Kieran said, hoping the word lent him some credibility.

'Renovatin', eh? Last fella I knew who tried that ended

up wi' a hole in his roof and pneumonia by Christmas.' Janette gave a sage nod. 'Best leave it to the professionals. Or at least to my cousin Rab. He's cheap, if ye don't mind him turnin' up three weeks late.'

Before Kieran could reply, Beth strolled past carrying two shopping bags. She slowed, took in the sight of him clutching a scraper like a weapon, and raised an eyebrow.

'DIY disaster?' she asked.

'DIY character-building exercise,' he countered.

'Mm. Character. Right. Let me guess … you've managed to glue yourself to the wall?'

'Not yet,' Kieran muttered.

Beth set her bags down and peered through the window. 'You know, a rug and a couple of lamps would do wonders. You don't have to strip the whole place like you're auditioning for *Homes Under the Hammer*.'

Janette let out a bark of laughter. Her canine companion followed suit. 'Aye, lass, but then he wouldnae have given us such a fine show. You should've seen the plaster flyin' earlier. Thought he was wrestlin' wi' the hoose.'

'Thanks for the support,' Kieran said drily.

Beth picked up her bags and continued on her way. Kieran watched her retreating figure longer than he should, noting belatedly that she looked paler than usual. Which probably meant nothing. Janette gave him a knowing look.

'Och, aye,' she said. 'The chef woman. A bit sharp around the edges, but folk like her. Well, as much as you can like someone you've known for five minutes. Careful, though. She strikes me as a no-nonsense sort.'

'I wasn't—' Kieran began, but Janette had already ambled off, leaving Kieran alone with his wrecked wall and a sense that his private thoughts were less private than he'd hoped.

By evening, the cottage resembled a war zone. Dust coated his laptop, rendering the touchpad temperamental, and his attempt to test a new feature on the app had ended in a frozen screen and a string of expletives that made even Prom look offended.

'Right,' Kieran muttered, brushing plaster crumbs off the keyboard. 'Minimalist wardrobes are hard enough without you crashing every five minutes, you useless lump of crap code.'

The app refused to respond, smug in its silence.

With no energy left for renovations or recalcitrant software, Kieran grabbed his coat and wallet and headed for the pub. A peaceful pint and a bite to eat would make things better.

'Hear you've knocked half the cottage down.' Ed grinned as he pulled a pint.

'Didn't realise you were into demolition,' someone else chimed in.

Kieran held up his hands. 'All lies. I'm simply modernising.'

'Aye, modernisin',' Janette echoed from her stool in the corner. 'By next week, he'll have invented indoor rain.'

The room erupted in laughter, and though Kieran rolled his eyes, he couldn't help the twitch of a smile. Somehow, being teased meant he was accepted – plaster dust, broken code and all.

He drained his pint, already imagining tomorrow's double headache: rebuilding his wall and figuring out why his 'streamlined user experience' now resembled the menu screen of a 1998 video game.

'Penny for them.' Beth had appeared, holding a plate of

Killer Kedgeree. It looked like regular kedgeree to Kieran, but he'd noted the quirky menu names before.

'Sorry, my head's mince, to use a favourite phrase of my dad's.' Kieran patted the chair next to him, and to his surprise, Beth sat.

Her hands trembled as she put down the food. Kieran noted the still-present pallor and the red-rimmed eyes that suggested sleeplessness or tears. Or both. 'Are you OK?'

'Yes. I mean, no. I don't know what I mean. It's just…'

Beth's voice faded away. Kieran forked up a mouthful of rice and fish, chewing as he figured out what to say next.

'Do you believe in otherworldly things?' she asked.

Didn't see that coming. 'Erm, if you mean ghosts, malevolent spirits and things that go bump in the night, the answer is no. Although my mum swore she saw a shadowy figure dressed in Victorian garb. My dad reckoned she'd mainlined too many gins and mistaken a dress on a hanger for some 1800s dame.'

Beth tapped her fingernails on the table: a rhythmic, staccato sound that jarred Kieran's nerves. 'I saw something last night. Here, in the pub. It made no sense, and when I woke up this morning, it didn't feel real. I checked where it happened, and it's simply impossible.'

'A bad dream?' Kieran wanted to find a rational answer to whatever was troubling Beth. 'I dreamt the other night that Kate Bush smashed my sunglasses, we were on the *Titanic*, and everyone was singing "Wuthering Heights" in the style of Black Sabbath.'

Beth laughed. A strained laugh siphoned through whatever was troubling her. 'Ozzy Osbourne channelling Kate Bush? I'd pay money to see that. But I'm babbling on when I should be cooking. Enjoy, Kieran, and pay no heed to my nonsense. See you around.'

Then she was gone. What had that all been about?

'Hi, Kieran.' Jo from the café appeared, with a man beside her. Kieran recalled that her husband was an actor, and he vaguely recognised his craggy but kindly face.

'Nice to meet you, Kieran. I'm Harvey, lucky enough to be married to this gorgeous woman, and not only because her baked goods are legendary.'

Jo rolled her eyes. 'I've hardly got the Greggs bakery chain quaking in their boots, Harvey. Anyway, you're the famous one in these parts. Well, apart from Sam.'

'Who you know very well doesn't like to flaunt it.' Harvey gave Jo a gently reproving look.

Kieran recalled Jinnie saying that her husband was an author. For a sleepy Scottish village, Cranley seemed to have its fair share of celebrities. He'd never be one of them. A quiet life. That's all he wanted.

Chapter Thirteen

'Nice gaff.' Diana prowled around Beth's small living quarters, straightening a cushion here, a coaster there – her natural habitat was any place she could impose order.

'Thank you, my neat-freak friend.' Beth forced a smile. She'd shoved her drying underwear into a drawer minutes before Diana arrived; small victories. 'It's not Bilberry Cottage, but I'm trying to make it feel like home.'

Diana nodded, her dark curls swishing. 'So, how are you really settling in? We've talked on the phone but seeing you in person … something's off. Am I right?'

Beth twisted the stem of her wine glass until her knuckles whitened. She'd opened Diana's favourite rosé; Diana had taken only a tiny measure, pleading driving. The rest of the bottle – well, Beth was on dangerous terms with temptation.

'It's hard to explain. Something happened. And you're the only person I can talk to.'

Diana gave Beth that look. The one usually reserved for obscenely rude shop assistants and patients who thought 'deep tissue massage' meant 'inappropriate touching'. It said: *Don't you dare fob me off.*

'I'm assuming you haven't been fired,' she said. 'Your bosses greeted me like I was a celebrity. Is it Luke? Has he been in touch?'

For the briefest moment, Beth wanted to lie. To fabricate a text, a phone call, a miraculous reconciliation. To pretend Luke missed her, regretted everything, wanted her back. Instead—

'No, it's not Luke. I … saw something. In the basement where I store some of my stuff. And it's seriously freaking me out.'

Diana froze mid-stride.

As if reciting a recipe in a language she barely remembered, Beth explained the pinball machine, the flickering bulbs, the sequinned apparition calling himself Gigi. 'It's called The Wish Master. It's ancient, maybe seventies or eighties at a push. No modern tech. But I hit my head when I tried to get away. I must've blacked out. Because when I came round … there was nothing and the machine was off.'

'OK.' Diana stretched the word like elastic, lacing it with equal parts caution and disbelief.

'OK what?' Beth snapped, exasperation spilling over. She poured herself more wine and slopped some on the floor.

'Steady, hon.' Diana leapt up, grabbed a cloth, and mopped up the spill with military efficiency.

'You think I'm nuts.' Beth felt the tight coil in her chest twist tighter. 'Of course you do. If you were telling me the same thing, I'd think you were nuts.'

Diana's gaze softened. 'Hon, absolutely not. Look, you've been under major stress. The whole Luke thing. And not being able to … you know.'

Anger flared, bright and immediate. 'We don't need euphemisms, Diana. Not being able to carry a baby to full term. There, I've said it. None of which explains what I saw.'

The tears shining in Diana's eyes mirrored Beth's own, and for a moment the room blurred.

'I'm so sorry, sweetheart.' Diana grasped her hands, warm and steady. 'I'm just worried about you. Are you sleeping? Are you drinking too much?'

Beth eyed her glass. 'You know I quit for ages. No alcohol, no raw fish, yoga until my limbs screamed, all the healthy stuff. It got me pregnant several times but didn't give me the one thing I wanted.' Her voice thinned. 'So I have the odd glass now. But I'm not drunk. And I'm not losing my mind.'

Silence settled. Not their easy, companionable kind, but one that crackled with unspoken pain.

Diana broke it first. 'You said you hit your head. Maybe see a doctor? Just to be safe. Concussion can be sneaky.'

Beth touched the tender spot at her scalp. 'I'm fine. Honestly. Let's just forget it.'

Diana didn't look convinced, but she let it go. She gathered her things, pausing at the door. 'Call me, day or night. Even if I'm mid-massage with some hunky footballer, I'll drop my oils for you.'

'Since when have you massaged a hunky footballer?'

'Never.' Diana pulled her into a hug. 'But a girl can dream.'

Beth worked the rest of the afternoon with Rose: chopping, stirring, planning, pretending normality came naturally. *Rome wasn't built in a day*, Ed had said. Beth suspected her confidence would take at least a century.

Later, after a bout of menu research on her laptop, she

found herself restless. Buzzing, and not in a good way. She needed fresh air – or closure.

Instead, she went to the basement.

The cold air hit her like an open fridge. The pinball machine sat in the gloom, silent as a tomb. Dust. Cobwebs. A forgotten relic.

It's fine. Nothing to see here.

Beth took a step forward.

One of the flippers twitched.

Beth's pulse spiked.

A single bulb flickered to life – weak, amber, unsteady.

She heard a faint strain of the tune she'd heard before. That haunting, vaguely Middle Eastern melody that wormed its way under her skin.

Beth pressed a hand to her chest.

'No,' she whispered. 'No, no, no.'

A metallic clatter sounded in the coin return tray. A coin rolled out, circling, clinking against the metal.

Then the laugh. Low, gurgling. Teasing. *Knowing.* 'Back again? Let's play.'

Beth's blood froze.

The room spun. She bolted. Feet pounding, breath torn from her throat. Up the stairs, heart in freefall.

She burst through the door into the hum and chatter of the pub – warm air, human noise, life – slamming the door behind her and pressing her back against it as if she could hold the world in place.

Her pulse thundered.

Her hands trembled.

'This isn't real,' she whispered to herself. 'I imagined it.'

But her brain told her otherwise.

And somewhere, deep in the darkness below, a single bulb flickered again.

Chapter Fourteen

Kieran wrestled with the largest of the cottage's windows. He guessed several hadn't been opened in years, welded shut with layers of badly applied paint. And as the temperature had soared from the low teens to the mid-twenties, he desperately needed to air the place.

'Damn it!' muttered Kieran as he nicked his thumb on the scraper he was using to force the window open. Blood pooled in the cut and dripped on the floor.

'Prom, fetch the first-aid kit,' he ordered jokingly.

Prom remained sprawled on the sofa, giving his rear end a thorough licking.

'On second thoughts, I don't think your hygiene practices lend themselves to first aid.'

In the bathroom he found a packet of plasters he'd bought on a panicked pre-move dash to the chemist. He wrapped one around his thumb, admired the world's saddest DIY injury, and trudged to the bedroom. It remained hot and steamy from his earlier shower because ventilation was an issue.

Kieran took a slow breath.

Against his better judgement, he'd agreed to attend the pub barbecue. A first, according to Janette.

'I'm no' really a fan of burnt sausages and those corn-on-the-cob things that get stuck in yer teeth, but wi' wee Beth in charge, I'm expectin' haute couture.'

Kieran hadn't corrected her. Nor had Alison, when they appeared at his door waving a flyer for the event.

The Jekyll & Hyde BBQ
An Afternoon of Smoke, Fire & Dual Personalities

From the Grill
Dr. Jekyll's Burgers – Beef patty, cheddar, whisky-onion relish
Mr. Hyde's Burgers – Beef patty, jalapeños, smoky chilli sauce
Split Personality Sausages – A mix of classic pork & fiery spiced
BBQ Chicken Wings – Sweet glaze or hot & smoky

Sides & Pub Favourites
Tattie Wedges – Crispy potato wedges, dips on the side
Neep Slaw – Creamy coleslaw with a Scottish twist
Grilled Corn on the Cob – Butter & herbs
Pub Chips – Thick-cut, malt vinegar & sea salt

Sweet Endings
Shortbread Bites – Buttery Scottish shortbread
Dark Chocolate Brownies – Rich & gooey, a Hyde indulgence

Kieran's mouth watered at the thought of a juicy burger and a side of thick-cut chips. The supermarket food filled a hole but lacked flavour or substance.

'You eat better than me,' he grumbled to Prom.

Prom blinked, unconcerned with human gastronomic crises.

Kieran eyed himself in the mirror. Cream linen shirt, khaki shorts, deck shoes. A look that said: *pretending to be relaxed while battling existential dread.*

Beth would approve. Possibly.

Then he recalled Peggy at the hairdresser's the day before, scissors snipping near his ear. 'If it ain't broke, don't fix it,' she'd huffed, referring to Beth's menu. 'It's a wee Scottish pub, no' a posh hotel wi' snooty waiters and no prices on the fancy menu.'

He'd bitten back a retort and swallowed his snobbery. It was easier to keep the peace than start a debate about culinary innovation while inhaling perm fumes.

'Do I pass muster, Prom?' Kieran asked. 'Will the fine ladies of Cranley swoon at the sight of my debonair charm?'

Prom stretched, yawned, and fell asleep.

'That's a no, then.'

Arriving at the pub's beer garden, Kieran sniffed the air appreciatively. Smoking charcoal, sizzling meat, and a hint of suntan lotion.

'Hello, laddie.'

It was the elderly woman he recognised as Jinnie's gran, Wilma. The one who'd banged on about his aura of sadness. In defiance, he pasted on his broadest grin.

'Are you auditioning for the role of The Joker in another *Batman* remake?' Wilma cackled, and the man next to her sighed.

'You must be Kieran. I'm Gus. Pay no heed to Wilma. Her heart is generous, but her mouth is prone to uncensored outbursts.'

'Meaning I'm an honest soul.' Wilma looked Kieran up

and down. 'Aye, yer aura's lightened. Less dark purple, more mauve.'

'Fascinating,' Kieran said, edging away before she started diagnosing his chakras.

He wove through crowds until he reached the barbecue station where smoke curled into the bright air. Two massive charcoal grills hissed and spat. Ed stood over them, tongs in hand, wearing an apron that declared: *Chillin' & Grillin'*.

'Hi, Kieran,' Angela called.

Before he could respond, Beth stepped into view, carrying a gargantuan bowl of potato wedges. Her striped apron was streaked with flour and something unidentifiable but appetising. Sweat glistened on her brow. She looked flushed and tired … but utterly in her element.

He stepped forward automatically. 'Here, let me help with that.'

'Thanks,' she said, shifting the bowl. Their hands brushed for a moment. Kieran pretended not to notice.

'Hot work, Beth.'

'It is.' She gulped from a water bottle. 'But it's nice to be outside for a change. The pub kitchen's even more like a cauldron on a day like this.'

'You summoned me with the promise of a burger,' Kieran joked. 'I couldn't refuse.'

She rolled her eyes. 'You summoned yourself: don't flatter me.'

Ed served him a Dr Jekyll burger, chips, and a spoonful of coleslaw. Kieran smothered the chips in mayonnaise.

Beth stared in horror. 'Heathen.'

He added more mayo with exaggerated relish. 'Don't tell me: you think only ketchup goes with chips.'

'Unless you're Belgian, French or Scandinavian, maybe. Which you're definitely not.'

'Scottish through and through.' He winked. 'Although I could be part Viking.'

A sudden shriek pierced the air. A woman brandished a brownie like a lethal weapon. 'Do these contain nuts? I could die if I eat even a sliver!'

Beth rushed over with calm authority. Kieran followed, half-concerned, half-amused.

'No nuts,' Beth assured her. 'No gluten, either. They do have a secret ingredient, but if I tell you, I'll have to kill you.'

The woman squeaked and grabbed shortbread instead.

Ed waved from the grill. 'Beth, we're running low on sausages and wedges. Can you grab more from inside? Jinnie should be plating up.'

'Jinnie's working too?' Kieran asked. 'Who's minding the little ones?'

Something flickered across Beth's face – a stiffness, a shadow, quickly masked. 'Sam's got them. I need to crack on. See you around.' She turned to leave.

An impulse tugged at Kieran to make her stay. His mouth operated faster than his brain. 'Beth?'

She paused, exasperation tightening her shoulders. 'What?'

'What's the secret ingredient?'

The ghost of a smile played on her lips – weary, teasing, and strange. 'If I told you,' she murmured, 'you'd never believe me.'

Before he could respond, Ed yelled something about chicken wings, Rose tripped over a crate of corn, and Wilma began loudly diagnosing someone else's aura as 'acid yellow'.

Beth vanished into the throng.

Kieran stood there, burger in hand, an odd sensation tugging at his chest.

Something warm and hopeful.

Something downright terrifying.

He took a bite of his burger, scanning the crowd and forcing himself not to acknowledge that he already knew where his eyes were drawn.

Chapter Fifteen

Every bone in Beth's body ached. She wished she could conjure up Diana for a relaxing massage, but a hot shower and a nap was the best she could manage. A nap interrupted by thoughts of the pinball machine and Kieran. They weren't related, but the word 'wish' niggled at her brain.

The barbecue had been a success, but not a moneymaker.

'I think we undercharged, but hopefully newcomers will spread the word and get more punters through the door.' Those were Ed's exhausted words before he said an early goodnight.

They'd agreed to close the pub for the evening and the next day. Back to business as usual after that. However, with fresh ideas on board thanks to a suggestion box placed at the pub entrance, The Jekyll and Hyde still had new tricks up its sleeve.

'A pub quiz. Fantastic.' Beth flung back the bedcovers. A

glance out of the window revealed an overcast sky. Rain forecast for tomorrow and the rest of the week.

Ed and Angela were spending the night with Angela's son, Jamie, in Edinburgh. 'He absolutely dotes on Ruairi and he's a genius when it comes to pub quizzes. Head full of trivia, but he's the champion of the local quiz league.'

Beth knew that both Angela and Jamie had had a tough time. As an alcoholic single mum, Angela had clawed her way back to sobriety and sanity with Ed by her side. Jamie worked in an Edinburgh clothing shop, had a steady girlfriend and was, by all accounts, a happy young man.

Beth felt twitchy and out of sorts. Part of her wanted to visit the basement. A larger part of her never wanted to set foot in the place again. Diana was right: she'd probably had a concussion which had triggered hallucinations. What other explanation could there be?

'Right, you don't need to be moping around here. Get out and explore Cranley.'

Locating a waterproof jacket in case of a shower, Beth headed towards the main street. A few locals smiled as she passed: unfamiliar faces, not that she'd got to know many people yet.

Beth paused outside the boutique, Gale Force, a floral dress with handkerchief sleeves catching her eye. The entire window display had a summery theme, with a layer of sand strewn with seashells, artfully arranged pastel T-shirts, and delicate silver bracelets and necklaces draped from pieces of driftwood.

'Hello!' An elegant older woman greeted Beth as she entered the shop. 'It's nice to see a new face. Have you travelled far, or—'

'I'm Beth. I live here.' Beth regretted her curt response, but the woman seemed unfazed.

'Oh, how lovely to meet you! I'm Alison, the owner. Jinnie mentioned that you'd moved here to run the kitchen at The Jekyll and Hyde. I'm sorry I couldn't make the barbecue, but my dog was poorly and I didn't want to leave him.'

On cue, a spaniel emerged from behind the counter, looking distinctly down in the mouth.

'This is Hector, my fur baby. Are you OK with dogs?'

Beth knelt to stroke Hector's floppy ears. 'I always wanted a dog' – *and a baby* – 'but my parents weren't keen and my… Never mind. He's adorable.'

Taking up Alison's offer of a cup of tea, Beth browsed the rails. She stroked buttery-soft leather jackets, silky blouses in jewelled hues and lightweight knitwear in a neutral palette.

'You're probably wondering how I survive business-wise in a place like Cranley,' said Alison, placing two cups of tea on the counter.

The thought had crossed Beth's mind, but she waited for Alison to elaborate.

'I took over these premises about six months ago. Before, it was Sam Addin's antiques shop. Jinnie's husband, that is.'

Beth sipped her tea. Gingery, with a hint of lemon.

'I did some advertising, word spread, and next thing I'm being featured in a Scottish magazine.' Alison beamed. 'Now, customers come from Edinburgh and beyond, or place orders online. My son helped set me up with that side of things, because I'm technologically clueless.'

'Well done you,' said Beth. 'But how do you manage on your own?'

Alison clasped her hands together in a prayer gesture. Beth noted her perfectly manicured nails, in contrast to her own kitchen-friendly stubby ones. 'You know the saying, "It takes a village"? In Cranley, people look out for one another. Rose from the pub helps, as does her sister, Caitlin. Jinnie too, and my partner, Janette. Have you met Janette yet?'

Beth stared at the dress in the window. 'Sorry, what did you say?'

Alison followed Beth's gaze. 'Oh, just that Cranley's a tight-knit community. I moved here when I lost my husband, and it's changed my life in ways I can't describe. Now, that dress you're eyeing up would look fabulous on you!'

Fifteen minutes later, Beth left the boutique with the dress – which *did* look fabulous on her – and two cute tops in pale blue and gold-threaded green.

'Not that I'll be going anywhere special to wear them,' she mumbled, climbing the stairs to her quarters.

With her purchases stowed away in the wardrobe, Beth made herself a cheese and ham toastie. She'd thought about stopping at the local café, but her reserves of polite chitchat had run dry.

Helping herself to a packet of tomato-ketchup crisps, Beth allowed herself a sly smirk at winding up Kieran. In truth, she loved mayonnaise – or to be more precise, its fancier cousin aioli, with all its garlicky goodness. Oh, and his face when she revealed that the brownies contained black beans!

Beth gave the place a perfunctory tidy. Not that it needed much since Diana's visit. Diana and Luke had a lot in common. Both were neat freaks, unable to settle until they'd rinsed the last coffee cup, wiped down every surface, straightened the towels and ensured the toilet roll faced the right way.

Are you like that, Kieran?

Beth gasped at the unexpected thought. What did it matter if Kieran liked things spick and span or dwelt in a pigsty? It was no business of hers.

With nothing else to occupy her, Beth found herself drawn to the basement. No one else was in the pub. It was a chance to lay to rest the nonsense that needed to be swept from her cluttered mind.

Beth approached the silent machine. Silent briefly, then… A faint whirr, one bulb flickering. The right flipper twitched like a dying fish.

'No. No, no, no. This isn't happening again.'

'And yet here you are. Couldn't stay away, could you?'

Beth shook her head so hard that she felt dizzy. *That bang on the head must have done more damage than I thought.*

'Poor Beth. Brain all scrambled. Shame hallucinations don't usually spit out coins.'

A coin clattered into the return tray.

Beth backed away. 'You're not real. You're … some kind of wiring fault. Dodgy electrics.'

'Wiring fault? Darling, I pre-date half the sockets in this place. Call me vintage. Oh, and the name's Gigi, in case you'd forgotten.'

Beth bent hesitantly and picked up the coin.

'Careful. Coins aren't just tokens: they bind. Spend one, and you're in my game.'

Beth swallowed hard. 'What happens if I walk away?'

Gigi gave a teasing laugh. 'I'll wait. Machines are patient. People, not so much.'

Beth watched, mouth agape, as the score display reset, letters forming slowly: B-E-T-H.

'Oh my God.' She needed to run, right now. Leave the basement, leave the pub, leave Cranley.

'Oh, we're not finished, Beth. We haven't even started.'

Then the lights went out.

Chapter Sixteen

Kieran was on the brink of throwing his laptop out of the nearest window.

Despite hours of tweaking, adjusting, and swearing under his breath, Kieran couldn't get the prototype of ClosetAura to look good enough or function anywhere near well enough for potential investors. Its Unique Selling Point had vanished somewhere between his third and fourth caffeine hit, his business model had more holes than a chunk of Swiss cheese, and the list of potential investors felt like a roll call of unattainable gods.

'Maybe I should quit and take up something less painful. Like sword swallowing.' Kieran eyed Prom, who miaowed with leisurely contempt.

'Thank you, that's very motivating,' Kieran grumbled.

His phone rang. He braced himself. Only one person he knew used that ringtone.

'How's it going, son?' bellowed his dad, Roger. Kieran held the phone at arm's length. Even so, Prom winced.

'Pretty crap, to be honest.'

'You're not still pining for that Lisa, are you?'

Ah yes, straight to the jugular. Roger never minced his words. Neither did his mum, Val, but at least she managed hers at a normal decibel level. Kieran pictured Lisa turning up her nose at Val's mince and tatties, lecturing them all about the dangers of gluten, meat and joy.

'No,' Kieran said. 'Well, a tiny bit. It's the app that's doing my head in. Maybe I've bitten off more than I can chew.'

'Nonsense!' Roger roared. 'Last time we spoke – when was that, three weeks ago? – you were all fired up. Enthusiastic. Driven.'

Guilt curled heavily in Kieran's chest. He'd let the calls slip. The visits, too. 'I'm overwhelmed,' he admitted. 'There's too much involved. I need help, but I can't afford to outsource anything.'

'I'll lend you money,' Roger declared immediately. 'Low interest rates. Pay me back when you sell it for ten million.'

Kieran smiled despite himself. 'Dad, I need to do this on my own.'

'Stubborn as a mule, just like your mother. Ouch! Val, put that tea towel down!'

A scuffle, more booming laughter, then—

'Kieran, sweetheart,' came Val's gentler voice. 'Are you eating? Sleeping? Washing your clothes properly?'

'Mum, I'm not twelve.'

'You'll always be twelve in my heart.'

He sighed. Lovingly. 'I'm eating well enough. The pub food's excellent. I escape there when I need fuel or company.'

'Anyone in particular?' Val asked innocently. Too innocently. Mother-mode engaged.

'Mum…' He rubbed the bridge of his nose. 'There's

Beth. The new chef at the pub. She's … interesting. But not like—'

'Lisa? Good. You don't need another Lisa in your life.' Val paused. 'What's Beth like?'

'Different.' He couldn't explain it. Wouldn't even try. 'I think she's run away from something. Or someone.'

'Do you think she's in trouble? Or maybe she needs a friend?'

'Maybe,' he said, throat tight. 'Listen, I've got to go. Prom's hungry.'

'Feed both of you properly,' Val admonished. 'And come visit soon.'

'I will.'

After the call, Kieran sat still for a few moments, staring out of the streaky cottage window. Wind rattled the rickety panes. Rain began to spit against the glass.

His parents, rock solid for over thirty years. That made his three years with Lisa pale into insignificance. Would he ever meet someone he wanted to spend decades with?

'How long do cats live, Prom?'

Prom, unsurprisingly, didn't reply. A quick Google search revealed that the average domestic cat lived for between fifteen and twenty years. Kieran had no idea how old Prom was – they'd never exchanged birthday cards – but the thought of hitting his forties with only a cat for company didn't fill him with joy.

Beth. Why had he mentioned her? He knew his mum dreamed of the day he turned up with a woman who made him happy. One who embraced Scottish grub and him with equal enthusiasm.

He didn't know what to make of Beth. She was stoic, guarded, with the occasional glint of wicked humour, but shadowed. Haunted. Something about her felt fragile, like fine glass with invisible cracks.

He grabbed his coat.

A plate of chips at the pub wouldn't break the bank. With mayo. Lots of mayo.

'Keep an eye on the place, Prom,' he said.

Prom blinked once. Translation: *I will continue lying here like a starfish.*

The pub was buzzing with post-barbecue energy, despite earlier rain. Ed was stacking glasses in the dishwasher. 'Hey, Kieran!' he said. 'Fancy a pint?'

'A plate of chips will do. And maybe a pint if I'm feeling reckless.'

Ed grinned. 'Beth's nipped outside. Busy day, but I reckon she needs cooling off more than the ovens.'

Kieran frowned. 'Is she OK?'

Ed hesitated. 'Between you and me, Angela caught her earlier muttering to herself about the pinball machine.'

'Pinball machine?' Kieran repeated. His brows knitted. 'What pinball machine?'

'A relic from the past. It's been down in the basement for ages.' Ed dried his hands. 'Sorry, mate, there's a queue forming. Catch you later.'

Kieran's curiosity sharpened. Beth, muttering about a pinball machine? She'd mentioned otherworldly things before, but not an ancient arcade game.

Outside, a mild drizzle dampened the air. He spotted Beth perched on a bench, hunching slightly against the mist, stroking something furry and familiar.

Kieran blinked. Twice.

'Isn't he a handsome guy?' Beth asked, running her fingers down Prom's chin, eliciting purrs of biblical intensity.

'As he's *my cat*, yes,' Kieran said. 'I can confirm he is, indeed, handsome.' *And as unpredictable as the Scottish climate.*

'Your cat?' Beth stared at Prom, startled.

Kieran nodded. 'Prometheus. Master of mischief. How did he—' He groaned. 'I forgot to lock the door again, didn't I?'

Beth shrugged. 'He's safe. Though we're all getting damp. Do you want to go inside and dry off? You can take him home afterwards.'

He hesitated. She looked pale and worn. The kind of worn that wasn't fixed by a good night's sleep.

'Sounds like a plan. Can I buy you lunch?'

'I … don't know. I'm technically on a break…'

'Prom's smitten,' he said lightly. 'Just a quick bite.'

Prom rolled onto his back and exposed his belly in agreement.

Beth's lips curved faintly. The tiniest smile.

'OK,' she said softly.

And for reasons Kieran didn't fully understand, relief blossomed in his chest.

Chapter Seventeen

'Let's go all seventies and eighties retro,' Ed had announced two days before the pub quiz, clapping his hands like an overexcited game-show host.

'The fifties and sixties might be more suited to some of our customers,' Angela teased, taking a sip of tea and raising an eyebrow at her partner.

'Well, in my humble opinion, the seventies and eighties produced some of the best films and music ever,' said Ed. 'Even if I wasn't born until the nineties.'

Beth sat at the bar, laptop open, tapping out menu ideas with the fervour of someone trying very hard to pretend she wasn't thinking of hallucinated genies. A retro theme meant retro food which, thankfully, meant uncomplicated dishes. Comfortingly naff. She typed: *prawn cocktail, creamy mushroom vol-au-vents, pork pies and pickles, cheese-and-pineapple hedgehog, Black Forest gateau, Arctic roll.*

She'd never served a hedgehog of any kind before. First time for everything.

'How's it looking, team-wise?' Rose appeared with a tray of tea and coffee.

Angela checked her phone. 'Jinnie's going to team up with Sam, her gran Wilma and Gus. They'll bring a travel cot so Dahlia can sleep in Ruairi's room, and we'll take turns checking on them. Janette, Alison, Peggy and Peggy's niece Matilda are up for it. So are Jo, Harvey, Jo's friend Carole and her husband, Austin. Plus whatever customers Janette has bullied into signing her sheet. So hopefully quite a few teams.'

'I'll be the quizmaster,' added Ed, 'and Angela will help Rose and Beth with keeping everyone fed and watered.'

'Yep,' muttered Beth. 'I'll be busy stuffing vol-au-vents and spearing hedgehogs.'

Rose shrieked.

'Not real ones, sweetheart. Oh, I just remembered, I've an old recipe book of my mum's that might provide more inspiration. I'll see if I can lay hands on it.'

She slipped away while Ed and Angela debated whether the music round should include Bowie or Bananarama. Down the stairs to the basement once again. She hadn't set foot in it since the other night. The rational side of her brain said that Gigi didn't exist. That he was a figment of her imagination, brought on by stress and a bump to the head.

'Well, lookie here!'

Nope. Not a figment of her imagination. Gigi sat cross-legged on top of the pinball machine. Or rather, hovered inches above it.

'You cannot be real.' Beth reached out her hand and he shooed her away.

'No touchie, no feelie. Them's the rules. Just gaze in awe

at my wondrousness and know how privileged you are to be chosen.'

Privileged? Many words sprang to mind. Deranged, unhinged, off her rocker, a sandwich short of a picnic, but in no way, shape or form did Beth feel privileged.

'Who, or rather *what* are you?' she stammered.

Gigi guffawed. 'Isn't it obvious?' He clutched his sizeable belly, which jiggled like a pink blancmange. 'I am a genie. But no ordinary genie. Unlike others who have passed here before. I'm the wizard of bumpers and the sultan of spin, dig?'

Momentarily distracted by Gigi's change of outfit – an unflattering combo of a glittery gold crop top and magenta velvet bellbottoms – Beth gasped. 'You're a genie? Not possible. Genies don't exist, and— What do you mean by others?'

Gigi tapped the side of his bulbous nose. 'That is for me to know and you to find out. Secrets lie beneath the surface of even the dullest of places. And Cranley is – how shall I put this politely? – duller than a silver platter that has remained unpolished in centuries.'

'That's very rude,' countered Beth, then wondered why defending her new home trumped the realisation that a mythological being was levitating before her.

'Pah. You will learn, eventually. For now, we have the small matter of wishes to deal with. Open your hand.'

Beth unclenched her fist. A gold coin, shiny and new, lay within. 'How did that get there? Oh, never mind. Daft question. Am I supposed to—?'

Gigi flicked his eyes upwards in theatrical despair. 'Put the coin in the slot. Play the game. Make a wish. It's not rocket science.'

Make a wish? Thoughts raced around Beth's skull, vying

for pole position. One streaked ahead: the wish she'd carried in her heart for so long. The one that had ultimately destroyed her marriage. She couldn't wish for that.

'Beth.' Gigi's voice softened. 'I cannot grant a wish until you play the game and say it out loud. And you must score over 300,000 to win.'

Beth cracked her knuckles: a habit that used to drive Luke mad. But he wasn't here, and probably never would be. 'Game on!' she yelled.

The flippers flipped, the lights flashed, the ball bounced, ting-ting-ting, hitting its target. Beth pushed the buttons with all her strength, her chest heaving and her heart racing. 'Come on!' she urged, watching the counter increase. 10,000. 50,000. 200,000.

A ball threatened to drop and she screamed in frustration. A close shave, but… Finally, the score passed 300,000 and her name blinked rapidly.

'Winner winner, chicken dinner!' Gigi clapped his hands in glee. 'You had me going for a minute.'

'I played to win.' Beth bent over, exhausted yet exhilarated.

'And win you did. Now – tah dah! – your wish is my command. Which is the cheesiest line ever. Why the Charter for Harmonious Upstanding Genies ever thought that slogan deserved historical status is beyond me.' Gigi's gaze spun in a tired circle of disbelief.

'Why the who … what… I have no idea what you're talking about.' Beth slumped on the floor. 'But I need to make a wish. Right?'

'Please. Because I need to shut down soon. Power levels are low.'

Beth watched Gigi fade in and out. The wish tugging at her heart wasn't one she could say out loud. So instead—

'I just … want a sign that life can still be good.'

Gigi gave a slow clap that dripped with sarcasm. 'That is the best you can come up with? Sunshine, as first wishes go, that's lamer than a three-legged camel.'

Beth conceded it lacked the wow factor, but it felt right.

Gigi rolled his eyes with such exaggerated flair Beth half-expected them to tumble out and bounce across the basement floor. 'Fine. A sign it is. But don't come boo-hooing to me when it's underwhelming.'

He tilted his head, suddenly serious. 'You've got two wishes left, sweetheart. Don't squander them.' Then he snapped his fingers, and with a fizz like a bottle of champagne being cracked open, he vanished. The pinball machine fell silent.

Beth waited, heart still thumping, wondering if she'd finally lost it completely, until a soft glow bloomed in the corner of the room.

A butterfly, luminous and impossible, shimmered into view.

Its wings glowed with shifting colours: gold bleeding into violet, violet into silver, each beat scattering motes of light like falling stars. It circled lazily above her head, then drifted down until it hovered in front of her face, as if daring her to doubt it.

Beth held her breath as it floated inches from her nose. Then it drifted upwards and slipped through the tiny basement window, dissolving into the dark.

Beth let out a shaky laugh. 'A butterfly. Indoors. Glowing. Why not?'

And though her rational brain fought to explain it away, she realised she was smiling. Not a brittle, forced curve of her lips. A real one, that felt like it belonged to her again.

Chapter Eighteen

'You have to help, laddie,' begged Janette, grabbing Kieran's forearm with the same grip she used on her customers when extracting their deepest gossip. 'Peggy's niece has come down with the lurgy, so we're one down. And I've already promised Ed a full team.'

Kieran's evening plans had been blissfully simple: nachos, beer, telly, solitude. Maybe a bit of coding, if he could summon the energy to stare disappointment in the face again. Now he was being conscripted into a village pub quiz by a woman whose persistence could rival a bulldozer.

'Fine,' he said. 'Whatever.'

Janette performed a triumphant jig, a cross between a ceilidh and a Morris dance. Kieran smothered a smile. He told himself his willingness had nothing to do with wondering whether Beth would take part. Absolutely nothing.

Inside the bar, Ed greeted him with a hearty grin and a pint. 'Thanks for stepping in at the last minute, Kieran.

Tickets are fifteen quid, which includes one drink and some themed nibbles, courtesy of Beth.'

'And the winning team gets the inaugural quiz trophy,' Angela said, pointing to a pint-sized pewter cup that looked as if it had been freshly polished or possibly salvaged from a charity shop.

'Let the fun begin,' Kieran said drily, handing over the cash. 'Bit quiet, though.'

Ed nodded, his smile slipping. 'After the initial buzz of the new menus, I think we need to keep the momentum going. We've got plenty of ideas. Open mic, karaoke, bonfire—'

'Health and safety nightmare,' Angela interjected.

'We'll iron out the details. Point is, we're trying.'

Kieran took his place with Janette, Alison, and Peggy. Alison greeted him warmly; Peggy stared at her pencil as if it might explode.

'I'm not sure I'll be any good at this,' Peggy murmured. Her left eye twitched.

Alison patted her arm. 'Relax: it's just for fun, not University Challenge. No fingers on the buzzers here.'

Each table held scoresheets, pencils, jugs of water. The room was alive with chatter and anticipation. Kieran glanced around, half-expecting Beth to emerge from somewhere, but she wasn't in sight.

Before Ed could officially begin, a disgruntled man in a three-piece tweed ensemble interrupted, eyebrows bristling with indignation. 'Excuse me, is there any actual food tonight? My wife and I drove here on recommendation, only to find pork pies and cheese-and-pineapple … monstrosities.'

Beth materialised as if from nowhere, cheeks flushed, jaw clenched. 'We have a special event tonight,' she said, her voice controlled. 'However, we can offer you venison and wild mushroom stew or fish and chips. Desserts on the house. Apologies for the limited choice.'

The man harrumphed but retreated with his wife to a distant table.

Kieran leaned in. 'Nice save,' he murmured. 'Are you planning to lace his food with laxatives?'

Beth giggled – an actual giggle – and Kieran's stomach did a ridiculous little flip. 'Tempting,' she said, 'but I'd like to keep my job.'

Ed called the room to order and switched on his microphone. 'Right, folks. We're keeping it short and sweet.'

'A bit like me,' heckled Janette.

Pens and paper at the ready, the teams huddled together as Ed announced round one, related to pop and rock anthems.

'Question one. Who had a 1977 hit with the album *Rumours*?'

'Easy peasy,' announced Wilma.

'Keep your voice down,' hissed Jinnie. 'You don't want to give the answer away.'

Wilma scribbled on the paper, then fixed Jinnie with a stare. 'I'm old, pet, not stupid.'

Kieran concentrated, forcing himself to focus on the quiz. He caught Alison writing *Fleetwood Mac*.

'OK,' said Ed, 'is everyone ready? Next question. In what year did ABBA win Eurovision with "Waterloo"?'

At Kieran's table, Alison frowned, counted with her fingers, then wrote *1974*.

As the quiz continued, the contestants got rowdier as they downed beers and wine.

At Jo and Harvey's table, a debate raged over the identity of a yellow arcade character.

'I'm sure it's Mario,' said Harvey, under his breath.

'Lucky I didn't marry you for your brains,' Jo retorted, writing down *Pac-Man.*

Ed moved on. 'TV and Film. Who shot J.R. in the TV show *Dallas*?'

A low rumble of disquiet echoed around the room.

'Wasn't it his brother, Bobby?'

'No, it was definitely a woman. Sue Ellen. She had plenty of reasons to shoot the slimy bastard.'

'Wait! I think it was the wee blonde one. Remember, Terry Wogan on the radio called her The Poison Dwarf.'

'Time's up,' called Ed. 'This one seems to have slipped in under the radar. I think it's from the nineties but never mind. Brain cells at the ready.'

Kieran turned instinctively and spotted Beth walking in with a tray of pork pies.

'Who voiced the Genie in Disney's 1992 animated film *Aladdin*?'

She froze. The tray tipped. Her entire body listed sideways.

Kieran sprang up and took the tray before it upended. He set it on an empty table and slipped an arm around Beth's shoulders, surprised by how unsteady she felt. 'Sit down,' he urged quietly.

Across the room, faces showed concern. Jo's hand clutched her throat; Sam's eyes narrowed, with a gleam of something like recognition. Wilma looked spooked. Jinnie's fists clenched.

Angela hurried over with a glass of water. 'Beth, you're as white as a sheet. Do you need me to call a doctor?'

Beth took a sip, her hand shaking. 'No need. I'm fine.'

She wasn't fine: anyone could see that. Kieran raised his hand. 'Maybe let's take a break?'

A tipsy chap leapt up. 'Charades? Have we moved to charades?'

Ed gave Kieran a thumbs up and switched off the mic. Conversations resumed at a muted level, but tension laced through the room.

Kieran guided Beth towards the stairs.

She protested. 'I'm fine, I said.' The colour had returned to her cheeks, but something behind her eyes didn't match her insistence.

He tried humour. 'Hey, I know Robin Williams's death hit people hard, but…'

It fell flat. Spectacularly. Beth opened her door, stepped inside. 'You can go back,' she said. 'I'll come down in a bit. Rose can hold the fort.'

He hesitated. Something was wrong. Really wrong. But Beth's tone made it clear his presence might push her further into whatever storm she was weathering.

'All right,' he murmured. 'But I'm not leaving until you tell me who shot J.R.'

Beth's voice was small, tired, but clear. 'Kristin Shepard. His sister-in-law … and mistress. My mum loved the show.'

Kieran let out a low whistle. 'Messy families.'

Beth didn't laugh. Her hand gripped the edge of the door, knuckles white.

He wanted to reach out.

He didn't.

She closed the door gently, Kieran was left staring at the wood grain, a cold tightness settling in his chest.

Whatever was going on with Beth wasn't just stress.

But he wasn't ready to walk away.

Chapter Nineteen

After a lie down and a splash of cold water, Beth returned to the pub just as Ed was preparing to announce the final quiz round.

'Erm, there's something wrong with the microphone,' he said, tapping it experimentally. It rewarded him with a high-pitched squeal, followed by what sounded suspiciously like a mischievous giggle. Beth's insides did an uncomfortable somersault.

She glanced across the room. Kieran caught her eye and shrugged, his expression saying *I heard that too.*

'Did the mic fall off the back of a lorry?' quipped Harvey, which drew a ripple of chuckles.

Ed, refusing to be flustered, flicked the switch off and on again. 'Right,' he said. 'Moving swiftly on. This is the wild-card round, folks!'

Groans, cheers, the rustle of scoresheets.

Beth stayed long enough to hear the first question before ducking behind the bar. She poured herself a glass of water and perched on a stool.

'Only two questions to go. Ready? Which popular UK fizzy drink brand launched its famous "The Totally Tropical Taste" advertising campaign in 1975?'

Murmured debates filled the room. Beth took a sip from her glass – and froze as the skirl of bagpipes drifted faintly through the air. No one else reacted. The sound evaporated as quickly as it came, leaving her pulse thudding.

'No cheating, Wilma!' Ed called.

Wilma huffed, stuffed her phone in her handbag, and muttered about quiz fascism.

Beth shook her head and raised her glass again, only to choke back a gasp. The clear water was now fizzy yellow. Pineapple, grapefruit. Sweet and sharp. She tipped it down the sink with a muttered curse.

A voice shouted, 'No, it's not the one made from girders!'

'Shut up, stop giving people hints,' snarled their teammate.

Beth scowled. She wasn't angry at the quizzers. She was angry at *him.*

The trickster. The sequinned pest. The self-proclaimed sultan of spin.

Ed was reading again. 'OK. Final question, which again I don't remember reading before.' He scratched his head, then carried on. 'Which 1975 film, starring Elton John in oversized boots, featured the song "Pinball Wizard"?'

The room erupted in delighted murmurs and a lot of frantic scribbling.

Beth, meanwhile, went cold. *Of course.*

Because why wouldn't he meddle? Why wouldn't he turn her night into a cosmic joke?

Slipping away unnoticed, she hurried down to the basement, her pulse a drumbeat of fury and disbelief.

'What are you playing at?' she snapped, slamming her palms on the pinball machine. The sound echoed around the empty room.

Nothing. No shimmer, no wisecrack.

And then a flicker of golden light.

The butterfly.

It drifted down from nowhere, luminous wings shimmering violet and silver. Beth watched it land delicately on her hand, its tiny feet tickling her skin. Her breath caught.

Life can still be good.

The butterfly rose, circled once and vanished into the air with a faint metallic clink. Beth looked down.

Another coin.

Beth stooped to pick it up, turning it over in her fingers. Her reflection rippled on its surface – tired, confused, defiant.

She sighed. 'Fine. Let's do this.'

The coin dropped into the slot.

Instantly, The Wish Master sprang to life – lights flashing, bells ringing, Gigi materialising mid-spin, his outfit a chaotic clash of glitter and velvet.

'Well, well,' he drawled, reclining mid-air. 'If it isn't my pinball wizard. Or should that be witch? No, wait – enchantress!'

'I prefer Beth,' she said flatly. 'And I want to know what game you're playing. Because this is well beyond three wishes, Gigi. You're interfering.'

'Moi?' He pressed a hand to his chest in mock offence. 'As if I would meddle. I'm subtle, discreet—'

'Turning my water into Lilt and throwing in quiz questions about a genie and *Pinball Wizard* is your idea of subtle?' she said. 'You're about as discreet as a glitter bomb.'

Gigi gave a sheepish grin. 'Ah. You wound me. But perhaps I got carried away. Just a little fun, that's all. It's been *ages* since I had such a promising protégée. Play, darling, and all shall be revealed.'

Beth glared, but the machine was already alive again, its lights pulsing, the ball released. Against all common sense, she set her hands on the flipper buttons.

She played hard. Harder than she ever had before. The ball danced, rebounded, spun. Every metallic ding echoed in her chest. Her fingers burned, her wrists ached. Somewhere between the flashing lights and the noise, she thought she heard Luke's voice – soft, amused, distant. *You're overdoing it again, Beth.*

'Beth,' came Gigi's voice, quiet now. 'You can stop.'

She blinked through tears she hadn't noticed forming. 400,000 points.

'Your wrist is impressive,' said Gigi solemnly, then spoiled it by waggling his eyebrows. 'One of the best I've ever seen. But your heart … well, that's heavier than any jackpot.'

'You don't know anything about me.' Her voice cracked and she dashed away tears. 'You're just a stupid genie trapped in a box, tormenting people for fun. I wish you'd disappear and let me live my boring life.'

'Uh-uh.' Gigi wagged a glittery finger. 'That wish doesn't count. Only I decide what's official. And there's a difference between a formal wish, which requires you to play the game, and me being given free rein to … help.'

'You mean meddle,' retorted Beth. 'Surely there are strict rules in the genie world?'

Gigi looked heavenwards as if searching for patience in the rafters. 'Rules are for fools, sugarplum. And your life isn't boring. You're standing on the edge of something marvellous. You just don't believe in it yet.'

Beth groaned. 'I'd rather believe in an early night.'

'Then go. Sleep tight, dream loud. Magic never rests.'

Her phone buzzed in her pocket.

'Shouldn't you check that?' Gigi asked. 'You humans live for your little glowing rectangles. It could be something life-altering. Or it could be a pizza ad. Fifty-fifty.'

'I'll check later,' she muttered. 'Goodnight, Gigi.'

'Nighty-night, doll face,' he called, fading into a swirl of violet mist.

By the time Beth went back upstairs, the pub was vibrating with laughter and cheers.

'We won!' Jinnie shouted from across the room. 'Only by two points! Janette's team got the ABBA and *Dallas* questions wrong!'

'Congratulations,' Beth said, managing a smile. 'I'll just check on Rose and—'

'No need,' said Angela, gently touching her arm. 'All under control. Go get some sleep.'

Wilma sidled up to Beth, tapping the side of her nose. 'Your aura's interesting, pet. No' as dark as Kieran's. More playful. Like a wee rainbow, with a bag of gold under it.'

Beth nodded, unsure what that meant. The noise, the warmth, the weight of everything drained her energy. She slipped away, her feet heavy on the stairs.

In her room, she kicked off her shoes and pulled out her phone.

One message. From Luke.

Beth. We need to talk. Sorry it's been so long. Sorry for so many things.

I think of you all the time, but life has a funny way of turning things upside down.

Call me.

Luke x

Beth stared at the screen until the words blurred.

Somewhere deep in the pub below, the pinball machine gave a faint, satisfied *ding*.

Chapter Twenty

'Well, that was all a bit weird, Prom.'

Prom, perched on the windowsill, yawned, stretched, and began washing his paw with exaggerated indifference. His earlier contribution to the day – depositing a dead bird on the rug – had clearly met his definition of a productive shift.

'Yeah, thanks for your input,' Kieran said drily. 'Something's definitely off about this village. It gives off the whole sleepy rural chocolate-box vibe, but there's … something bubbling underneath. And it's all connected to Beth. She's the key.'

Kieran rambled on for a few more minutes, trying to piece together the events of the quiz night. The mischievous laughter. The unmistakable sound of bagpipes.

Prom turned, arched his back, and padded out of the room, tail flicking like a punctuation mark of disdain.

'I'm going to trade you in for a gerbil,' Kieran called after him. 'You ungrateful, bird-murdering layabout.'

He lobbed a trainer vaguely in Prom's direction. It landed nowhere near him. Kieran sighed.

'Maybe moving here was a mistake. I've demolished more of the cottage than I've fixed, my app is appalling, and now I'm developing feelings for someone I barely know.'

He paused. 'And I'm talking to myself. Classic sign of madness. Or loneliness. Take your pick.'

He needed to clear his head. A run, that was it. Get the blood moving, burn off the mental static. He pictured himself in glorious slow motion – a *Chariots of Fire* moment, Vangelis swelling in the background, sea breeze ruffling his hair.

Reality: he hadn't run since sprinting for a bus in Edinburgh last year.

Still, he laced up his trainers, stretched half-heartedly, and headed out. With no beach in sight, he settled for the country lanes looping around Cranley.

The first few minutes were glorious. His stride smooth, breathing steady, arms pumping in something resembling rhythm. Then came the chest burn. His lungs shrieked in protest. By the ten-minute mark, his legs felt like overcooked spaghetti.

He slowed to a walk, pretending to admire the hedgerows so anyone watching wouldn't think he was dying.

'Morning!'

He looked up. Alison from the boutique, immaculately put-together, her Cavalier King Charles spaniel trotting ahead like canine royalty.

'Training for a marathon?' she asked, all cheerful curiosity.

'Something like that,' he wheezed. 'More of a short film than a feature-length effort.'

She smiled. 'Well, keep at it. It's a warm day, so make sure you hydrate.'

The dog gave him a pitying glance before they continued on their way.

'Cheers,' Kieran muttered, jogging on out of sheer pride.

By the time he reached the pub, several people were already outside, enjoying drinks in the sun. Desperate not to be spotted gasping like a landed fish, he tried to jog past with forced nonchalance.

'Steady on!'

He swerved just in time to avoid colliding with the sandwich board outside A Bit of Crumpet. Jo, the café owner, was watching him with a blend of amusement and concern.

'Hey, Kieran! Everything all right?'

'Peachy,' he panted. 'Just out for a quick 5K.'

Jo's eyebrows lifted. 'In jeans?'

'Experimental training technique,' he said, and carried on before she could reply.

By the time he stumbled to the edge of the village, his T-shirt clung to him and his legs screamed betrayal. The track curved down towards a stream, shaded by oaks and lined with wildflowers. He slowed, grateful for an excuse to stop.

And then he saw her.

Beth stood on the little wooden bridge, a basket over one arm, leaning on the rail and watching the water slide beneath. Sunlight caught her hair, turning it copper bright. She looked so still, so quietly intent, that for a moment he forgot to breathe.

Of all the people to bump into when he looked like he'd lost a fight with a treadmill.

He considered sneaking away. Too late: she'd seen him. Her face lit up. 'Kieran! I didn't know you were a runner.'

'I'm not,' he admitted, wiping sweat from his brow and trying for nonchalance. 'Just clearing the cobwebs.'

'Looks like they're putting up a good fight,' she said, laughing, and the sound hit him right in the chest. It had warmth, and a lightness he hadn't heard since the barbecue.

'Yeah, well. I'm not built for speed. Or stamina. Or self-respect, apparently.'

Beth smiled faintly. 'Still, good for you. Most people in Cranley get their exercise through dog walks and pub quizzes.'

'The quiz was certainly, um, lively,' he said. 'I hope you're feeling better.'

Beth's eyes flicked towards him then away. 'I am. Sort of. It's just—' She hesitated. 'Someone I haven't heard from in a long time got in touch.'

The careful phrasing made him tread softly. 'A bad kind of hearing from, or a good one?'

'Complicated,' she said. 'He's my husband. Or was. We're separated.'

Kieran's stomach dropped. Then righted itself when she added, 'We've been apart for a while.'

'Ah,' he said, too neutrally. Then, before he could stop himself, 'Did he hurt you?'

Beth gave a half-laugh, with a smile that didn't reach her eyes. 'We hurt each other, I think. It's … a long story. I moved here to start again. But last night he sent a message.'

'Saying what?'

'That he wants to talk.' She looked down at the water, her voice almost lost to the murmur of the stream. 'And I don't know if I can. Or if I should.'

Kieran's instinct was to make a joke. Something light to

deflect what he was feeling. Instead, he heard himself say, 'If it helps, sometimes the only way to stop a story haunting you is to let it end properly. Even if it hurts.'

Beth's mouth curved: sad, grateful. 'That's surprisingly wise.'

'Don't sound so shocked.'

'No, I just didn't have you down as the introspective type.'

'Me neither,' he admitted. 'Must be the oxygen deprivation.'

That earned him a soft laugh.

They stood in comfortable silence for a while, watching sunlight shatter across the water. Then Beth gestured at her basket. 'I was picking wild herbs for tonight's menu. Want to walk back with me? You look like you've earned a cool-down.'

'Definitely,' he said, eager for an excuse to stop pretending he was an athlete.

They walked side by side through the lanes, her stride light, his more of a trudge. She talked about food – lemon thyme, trout, how freshness changed everything. He barely heard the details, too busy watching her hands move as she spoke, the way her eyes brightened when she mentioned flavours.

After a pause, she glanced sideways. 'So, what made you take up running, anyway?'

'A misguided belief that I could outrun my thoughts,' he said. 'Turns out they've got more stamina than me.'

Beth smiled. 'Well, for what it's worth, I think it's brave. Starting again. Running. All of it.'

'You too,' he said quietly. 'You're doing it too.'

When they reached the pub, Beth turned to him with a faint, knowing smile. 'Thanks for the walk. And the talk.'

'Anytime,' Kieran said. And he meant it.

As she disappeared inside, the sun slipped behind a cloud, and Kieran found himself grinning at nothing.

Maybe he hadn't come to Cranley by mistake after all.

And maybe – just maybe – running wasn't such a bad idea.

Especially if it kept leading him back to Beth.

Chapter Twenty-One

'Hi, it's me.' Beth tried to sound brisk and businesslike, but her voice betrayed her.

'Beth! I'm so glad you called. How are things?'

Completely normal. Just trying to rebuild my life after you walked out. Oh, and trying to coexist with a pinball-machine-inhabiting genie.

'I'm doing OK,' she said instead, her tone clipped. 'I rented out Bilberry Cottage, by the way.'

Luke cleared his throat: a habit he'd had for years. Beth used to find it endearing, but now it irritated her.

'Yes, I dropped by the other week. The tenants said you'd left. It would have been nice if you'd told me.'

Beth fought the urge to smash her phone to smithereens.

'It would have been nice if *you* hadn't vanished off the face of the earth, Luke. You left me when I could barely stand. It's been a bloody battle getting back up.'

'I know, I know.' His sigh rattled down the line. 'I messed up, Beth. It just felt as if the baby thing drove a wedge between us and that we – you and I – weren't enough.'

The baby thing. Beth's hand went white around her phone. The *thing* that had broken her heart several times over, reduced to a convenient euphemism.

'Correct me if I'm wrong,' she said, her voice shaking with fury, 'but didn't we both want a child? You certainly gave that impression.'

A silence stretched, then another of his nervous throat-clears. 'I did want a child. I wanted it so much it hurt. But every time we lost one, I felt I'd failed you. That loving you wasn't enough. That you'd be better off without me.'

'So your solution was to disappear?' Her tone turned icy. 'How incredibly thoughtful of you, Luke. Truly.'

She'd imagined this conversation a hundred times – civil, calm, maybe even cathartic. A chance to find closure. Instead, she could taste bitterness on her tongue.

'By the way, do you still have that plant stand and those picture frames I carved? You know the ones. I gave them to you on your birthday and at Christmas.'

Luke's words hit like hammer blows. Of all the things she'd expected him to bring up… 'I think I binned them,' she said. In truth, they were still packed away in a box in the basement, probably next to Gigi's domain. Maybe the genie could make use of them. Or Ed could burn them next time he lit a bonfire.

'That wasn't very nice.' Luke huffed. 'I'd have picked them up if you'd let me know you were moving to Cranley.'

Beth froze. So he *knew* where she was. She, however, had no clue where he'd been hiding. And at this point, she wasn't sure she cared.

'Can we get to the point, Luke? You asked me to call. What's on your mind?'

The silence stretched again, and somewhere in the back of her brain, Taylor Swift started singing 'We Are Never Ever Getting Back Together'. Except this version had a distinctly Middle Eastern vibe – and the unmistakable *ding-ding-ding* of a pinball machine underneath it.

Beth slapped her forehead. 'Oh, for—'

'Sorry?' Luke said. 'Line's gone funny. I just needed to tell you I'm moving again.'

'From where? You never said where you were in the first place.'

'Be there in a minute, Mum,' he called to someone in the background.

Ah. *Mum*.

Of course. Back to the nest. His parents' house: a six-bedroom Essex palace with a kitchen the size of Bilberry Cottage. She could picture him there, being plied with sympathy and shepherd's pie. 'It's not your fault, darling,' his mother would coo. 'You married beneath you.'

Beth's jaw tightened. 'So where are you off to this time?'

'I'm moving to Eilean Driftach,' he said, his voice lifting with excitement. 'You've probably never heard of it, but it feels like my spiritual home.'

What? He'd wanted to talk to her about moving to some remote Scottish island? Not that Beth *knew* it was an island, but the name conjured up images of a craggy coastline, sheep and fishermen in sou'westers. Well, maybe not the *sheep* in waterproofs.

'It's off the west coast. Beautiful, wild, full of artists. The locals make furniture out of driftwood. Even boats! It's a whole community built on craftsmanship.'

'Fascinating,' said Beth, though her tone suggested she'd rather discuss root-canal surgery.

'Listen, Beth, I'd like to see you before I go.'

A silky whisper rippled through her ear, unmistakably Gigi's voice. *Tell him to take a long walk off a short cliff, sugarplum.*

Beth clenched her teeth. 'Luke, I'm not sure there's much point. Unless you want to discuss a divorce.'

He inhaled sharply. 'Divorce? Beth, I don't think we need to go down that path yet.'

'Really? You've made no move to come back, no suggestion we try again. What exactly are we waiting for? The moment you meet some winsome islander with a fully functional womb?'

'That's a cheap shot,' Luke snapped. Then, louder, 'Mum, I'm coming, all right?'

And then he was gone, the call ending with a mumbled apology and a beep that left Beth staring at her phone in disbelief.

He hadn't asked about her job. Hadn't asked if she was happy, or safe.

He just wanted to announce his next reinvention and collect his bloody picture frames.

'Selfish pig,' she muttered, shoving the phone into her pocket.

Anger coursed through her as she stomped downstairs to the bar, desperate for a distraction. Ed and Angela were huddled by the counter, heads close, expressions grim.

'What's up?' she asked, seizing the chance to put Luke out of her mind.

'Look around, Beth,' said Ed, his voice heavy.

Beth turned. The pub was empty, apart from an elderly couple nursing Diet Cokes in the corner, staring into the middle distance as if life had personally offended them.

'There's hardly anyone here,' she said.

'Exactly,' said Angela. 'It's like a morgue. We've barely covered costs this week.'

Beth felt the optimism drain out of her. Maybe she'd been too ambitious, too quick to change things. Maybe Cranley didn't *want* modern menus or quirky cocktails.

'Things'll pick up,' she said, forcing cheer she didn't feel. 'Once word spreads.'

'Let's hope so,' said Ed. 'But unless a coachload of tourists appears in the next ten minutes, you won't be serving much food today. Rose is in the kitchen, leave her to it for now.'

Beth nodded, trying to look grateful rather than defeated, and trudged back upstairs.

Halfway up, she paused, hand on the banister.

If business didn't recover, she could lose this job – the one stable thing she had left.

Her thoughts drifted inevitably to the pinball machine.

Its shimmer. Its promises.

The genie's words.

You've got two wishes left, sweetheart.

Beth sat on her bed, staring at her phone as if it might offer an answer.

'Should I?' she whispered into the stillness.

Down below, she could almost hear the faint, teasing jingle of bells and bumpers. And the softest of voices, half amusement, half challenge:

Make it count.

Chapter Twenty-Two

Finally, some progress.

Kieran leaned back and admired his laptop screen. The ClosetAura prototype was still rough round the edges but beginning to shine. The code worked, the interface almost looked professional, and for once he could see a potential glimmer of success.

'Cooking with gas, Prom,' he declared. 'This app's going to be a game-changer. All I need now are backers, beta testers, a sprinkle of magic and' – he grinned at his own joke – 'a few unicorn tears.'

He waited for a sarcastic *miaow*. Silence.

'Prom?' He looked around. No sign of the cat. Not on the sofa, not under the table, not even pretending to be dead in his food bowl.

'You're kidding me.' The front door, of course, was ajar. 'For God's sake.'

Kieran shoved his feet into his trainers, wincing at the blister still healing from his last ill-fated run. 'Why does that bloody cat think he's got diplomatic immunity?'

He sprinted – jogged – the short distance to The Jekyll and Hyde. He'd find Prom, threaten him with castration, and bring him home.

When Kieran stepped into the beer garden, it was empty. Not a soul in sight, and eerily still for a sunny afternoon. But music thudded from inside. Not pub music. *Party* music.

He pushed open the door and blinked.

No. Way.

Jinnie's gran, Wilma, was spinning across the floor, her floral skirt fanning out like a maypole in motion. A bearded folk band sawed away at a fiddle, plucked a mandolin, played something with strings that defied classification. The place was heaving – a whirl of colour, movement, and absolute lunacy.

'Come on, join us!' Jinnie shouted, baby Dahlia balanced on her hip, both beaming.

'We are family!' Jo bellowed into a microphone that had definitely not existed five seconds ago.

Before Kieran could retreat, a familiar voice cut through the chaos.

'Your cat's got all the rhythm!' Ed yelled over the din. 'Busting the moves and acing the grooves!'

Kieran stared. There, in the middle of the pub, was Prom. *Dancing.*

Not the random skittering of a startled animal. Oh no. This was full-blown, paws-in-the-air, spin-on-his-back, tail-in-time choreography.

The crowd whooped and clapped.

'Aww, he's adorable!' Angela appeared beside Kieran, shimmying in sequins he could have sworn she hadn't been wearing earlier. 'Fancy a foxtrot?'

Before he could protest, she'd seized his hand. Suddenly,

Kieran was twirling across the floor like a contestant on *Strictly Come Dancing: The Full-On Madness Edition*.

'I don't dance!' he gasped, his legs apparently possessed.

'You do now!' Angela grinned, dipping him with surprising strength. 'And look. People are eating!'

She was right. Every table was full – diners tucking into plates piled high, glasses clinking, laughter ringing off the walls. Rose led a conga line past the bar, trailed by Jo, Harvey, and Gus, all grinning like children at a school disco.

And just beyond the madness stood Beth.

She was in the doorway, hands covering her mouth, shoulders shaking. Was she laughing? Crying? Both?

'This can't be real,' Kieran muttered. 'This is a hallucination. Some kind of mushroom-induced fever dream.'

He disentangled himself from Angela and forced his way through towards Beth, but she'd vanished like smoke. Prom, meanwhile, had finished his breakdancing routine and sat licking his paw, tail flicking smugly.

'Prom, come here,' Kieran said, half-command, half-plea.

The cat ignored him, obviously.

Then the music shifted. The folk band, joined by other musicians, launched into something completely different – a brass-heavy number with trumpets, trombones, and unmistakable familiarity.

'Is that "Friend Like Me"?' Kieran said aloud, his voice barely audible over the tune. 'What – how—?'

A booming voice echoed through the room, though Kieran couldn't tell where it came from, 'Ladies and gentlemen, it is time to wind things down.'

The music faltered. The crowd stilled.

'You have had fun, yes?' the voice continued, smooth

and lilting. 'Tell your friends. Spread the word. The Jekyll and Hyde is the hip, hop, happening place to be!'

And just like that, the spell broke.

The energy drained out of the room. People blinked, muttered to each other, gathered coats and handbags. Within moments the pub was half-empty, the chatter replaced by the faint hum of the fridges.

Kieran stood, gripping a chair for balance. The air still crackled faintly, like static after a storm. He wanted Beth to appear again, to tell him it was some elaborate themed event, a fundraiser, a local tradition – *anything* logical.

Instead, Jinnie came over, flushed and grinning. 'That was wild, wasn't it? Oh, here.' She handed him something small and papery.

A crown. Pink, crinkled, with *King of the Cat Disco* scrawled in glitter pen.

'Er … thanks?'

'For your cat,' she said, and left before he could reply.

The door swung shut behind her. Silence. Just Kieran and Prom.

'Miaow,' said the cat, perfectly serene.

'What's going on?' Kieran whispered.

Prom blinked, let out a louder miaow, and began grooming his tail.

Kieran laughed, a dry, incredulous sound. 'You're enjoying this, aren't you?'

No response. Just another smug tail flick.

The room felt wrong now. Too empty, too still. He needed air. He scooped up Prom, jammed the paper crown onto his furry head, and stepped outside into the fading light.

They'd barely made it ten paces when someone called

his name. Jo was jogging up the lane, eyes wide with concern. 'Wait! Are you all right?'

He blinked at her. 'Define "all right." I've just watched my cat out-dance half the village to Sister Sledge.'

'Ah,' Jo said softly. 'It's happening again.'

'What is?'

'You're new,' she said carefully. 'You don't know Cranley's history.'

'What, witch-burnings? Goat sacrifices?' He tried to laugh but it came out shaky.

'Not quite,' Jo said, managing a thin smile. 'But… Strange things happen here. They always have. We thought it had stopped.'

'What had stopped?'

She shook her head. 'Not now: you need rest. I'll speak to the others.'

'The others? Who are—' But Kieran's words slurred, and his head was suddenly heavy.

Jo caught his arm, guiding him forward. 'Come on,' she murmured. 'Nearly home.'

The walk back was a blur. Streetlights smeared into gold streaks. His limbs felt like lead and his mind fizzed with fragments of music, light and laughter.

When he collapsed on his bed, Prom was already curled beside him, paper crown still perched at a jaunty angle.

'Sleep,' Kieran muttered. 'Need to sleep.'

As his eyes fluttered shut, words drifted through his half-dreaming brain, spoken by the same silky voice that had haunted the pub.

Sweet dreams, darling boy. You're part of the story now.

And then he fell asleep.

Chapter Twenty-Three

'I did *not* wish for that to happen!'

Gigi didn't even look up. He was busy buffing his already pristine fingernails to a mirror shine.

'Oh, but you did, naughty girl. I heard the words as clear as a bell. "I wish the bar would come to life."' He waggled a sequinned finger at her.

Beth folded her arms. 'Hah! But I said that privately, in my head. Not here. And I thought I actually had to *play* the pinball machine for wishes to come true.' She glared at him. *Wriggle out of that one, you barrel-bellied buffoon.*

Gigi pouted theatrically. 'As you *obviously* know, I can tune into your thoughts. I must say, they're very hurtful.'

'Sorry,' she muttered. 'But it's not fair. The sign says *three* wishes, and I've only had one.'

So here I am, arguing with a genie about wish regulations, while my almost-ex-husband goes off to hew driftwood into artisanal nonsense and the village descends into dance fever. Just another perfectly ordinary day in Cranley.

'Hmm. Perhaps the FBI has done an update. Let me

check.' Gigi whipped something out of a pocket Beth hadn't seen before. A wand-like instrument, emitting a high-pitched beep and flashing like a Christmas tree on steroids.

'What on earth is that? And what does a US law-enforcement agency have to do with anything?'

'This,' Gigi said, waving it about like a conductor's baton, 'is a Wish-Instigating Finder Instrument.' He beamed, ridiculously proud of himself. 'WIFI for short.'

Beth blinked. 'Of course it is.'

'The FBI,' he continued breezily, 'isn't that dreary human lot with badges and bad suits. It's the Federation of Benign Intelligent Beings. Along with CHUG – the Charter for Harmonious Upstanding Genies – they have ultimate power over our existence. Meaning other genies.'

Beth considered herself intelligent. OK, she might be crap with numbers and foundation colour choices – Trump orange, anyone? – but this was way beyond dodgy counting skills and needing to blend something hideous at the jawline. 'Explain, please, in layman's terms. Including how this affects me.'

Gigi fiddled with the wand. 'Stupid useless WIFI,' he muttered. 'Some genies think this is cool to the max, but… Oh, fiddlesticks. It is granting wishes it has no right to grant. Which makes a mockery of my preferred modus operandi.'

Beth had had enough of Gigi's gibberish. And what did he mean by *some genies?* 'Are there others like you?' she whispered. 'Here, in Cranley?'

Gigi guffawed. 'There ain't nobody like me around here, darlin'. In the past, yeah, but they wriggled back into their lamps and vamoosed. Poof! Gone, just like that.' The ridiculous crushed-velvet turban on his head rotated, its disco-ball centrepiece flashing incessantly.

'You said Cranley was dull!' shrieked Beth. 'I don't see

anything dull about a village that's housed a horde of genies.'

Gigi shrugged. 'Every village has its secrets. It's a sort of … hotspot, if you will. Like Ibiza for stag dos, only with less vomit and more metaphysical chaos. A long time ago, Cranley was designated a Holding Zone. A waiting room for wayward wish-granters who couldn't keep their turbans on straight.'

Beth blinked. 'A Holding Zone? For genies? You're telling me this sleepy corner of Scotland is basically a halfway house for magical misfits?'

'Correctamundo.' Gigi stroked his stomach with exaggerated elegance. 'Some villages get Roman artefacts. Cranley gets us.'

'But why here? Why not somewhere exciting? London, Paris, even Milton bloody Keynes?'

'Because Cranley is boring, darling.' Gigi sighed as though the very word induced ennui. 'The perfect canvas. Genies were never meant to hog the spotlight. Stick us somewhere with glitz and glamour and we'd have punters queuing around the block for free iPhones and eternal youth. But Cranley? The most thrilling thing that happens here is a Bake Off at the church hall. You couldn't get more beige if you spread the whole place on a digestive biscuit. Ideal for containing magical overflow without causing global panic.'

Beth chewed her lip. Beige Cranley. Yes, that rang depressingly true. But there was still one shiny, flashing, noisy elephant in the room.

She pointed at the pinball machine. 'Then why, pray tell, are you stuffed inside this tacky contraption instead of a lamp? Isn't that genie law? Oil lamps, mysterious smoke, belly dancing at the drop of a fez?'

Gigi puffed out his chest. 'Tradition is such a bore. Do you know how cramped lamps are? You try folding yourself into a brass teapot for a few centuries. Crippling sciatica, darlin'. When the Federation of Benign Intelligent Beings offered upgrades, I jumped. Literally. My options were lava lamp, snow globe or pinball machine. And I thought, "Hey, who doesn't love pinball?" Bright, noisy, addictive. Much like me.'

'You chose this?' Beth squawked. 'You could've been in a lava lamp, swirling about seductively in neon pink, but no – you opted for this infernal bleeping monstrosity? And now I'm stuck wishing for things with the finesse of a toddler on a sugar high?'

'Oh, don't be melodramatic,' said Gigi, though his pout deepened. 'Pinball is culture. Retro chic. And besides, the Federation insisted I remain in constant proximity to humans. Lamps, snow globes, they get put away. Pinball machines? They live in pubs. Pubs mean chatter, ale, confessions, arguments – plenty of wish-fuel. I feed on intent, darlin', not just words.'

'But you're not *in* the pub! You're in a dusty old basement surrounded by clutter. Or hadn't you noticed?'

Gigi nodded, his jowls drooping. 'Which is why I'm so grateful you dropped by. In fact, if you could arrange for me to take centre stage, I'd be made up to the max.'

Not happening. 'So you're saying that every daft thought muttered into a pint glass might turn into … into whatever disaster you fancy?'

'Not quite,' said Gigi, smoothing his sleeve. 'I'm selective. Or I used to be. That's where this blasted WIFI gadget is cocking things up. It's leaking wishes without my permission. Which is why you've had one-and-a-half granted already. Very sloppy business. Makes me look like a budget children's entertainer.'

Beth clutched her head. Cranley, soporific little Cranley, a genie Holding Zone. Gigi, self-styled hipster of the magical world, trapped in a pinball machine. And now, dodgy wishes bleeding out and coming true, thanks to some malfunctioning genie tech.

'I need a drink,' she muttered.

Later that evening, after a decent number of hungry and thirsty customers, Beth perched on a stool nursing a white-wine spritzer. She caught Angela's eye and waved her over.

'You all right, Beth?' Angela slid onto a stool, wiping her hands on a cloth that had seen better days. Like everyone else, she had no memory of the madness of the previous night. And although Beth itched to tell someone about Gigi, thoughts of Luke kept bubbling to the surface.

'Not really,' she said quietly. 'It's Luke.'

Angela raised her eyebrows. 'As in estranged Luke?'

'The very same. He rang me. Well, he asked me to call him. Apparently, he's moving to some godforsaken island off the west coast. Wants to carve driftwood into art.'

Angela frowned. 'Is he a carpenter? Ed can barely carve a Sunday roast without supervision.'

Beth gave a weak smile. 'It's his hobby. He's an architect by profession but he's always dabbled. He kept talking about salt spray and solitude and "finding his true self". Like his true self has been hiding in a pile of wet sticks all this time.'

Angela sipped a lemonade and clinked her glass gently against Beth's. 'So what's bothering you more? That he'll vanish completely? Or that he'll succeed?'

Beth stared into her fizzing drink. 'Both. I haven't told you why we split up, and I'm not ready to. Not yet.'

Angela gave Beth an encouraging smile. 'You don't have to. But when you *are*, I'll be here.'

That kindness cracked something in Beth. The words came in a rush. Brittle at first, then unstoppable.

'It was perfect for so long. Or it looked perfect. The house, the plans, the everything. Then it fell apart. I thought if I just stayed strong, maybe one day we'd fix it. But if he disappears to some island, that's it. No more "maybe". Just driftwood and silence. And I can't tell if that's a relief or a loss.'

Angela reached out, squeezed her hand. 'Maybe you've carried him long enough. Let him drift, Beth. If he wants to play Robinson Crusoe with a chisel, that's his business. You deserve something solid. Something that stays.'

Beth let out a fractured laugh. 'That's an interesting way of putting it.'

Angela smiled. 'Trust me. Focus on *you*. The bar. Your friends. Whatever it is you've got going on in that basement.' Her tone was casual, but her eyes were sharp.

Beth froze, her cheeks warming. 'What makes you say that?'

Angela just grinned. 'Call it intuition. Around here, secrets don't stay buried for long.'

Beth managed a weak smile. Maybe she was right. Maybe Cranley had its own strange rhythm – part gossip, part magic, part madness.

'I'll try,' she whispered.

The bar hummed around them, alive in ways she didn't fully understand. Gigi was somewhere in the shadows. No doubt preening, plotting and waiting for another careless wish to slip through her lips.

And Luke? Luke was already halfway gone, lost to tides, timber and the ghosts of what they'd been.

Beth raised her glass, the bubbles catching the light.

'To survival,' she murmured. 'And maybe … to something better.'

The faint sound of a pinball flipper echoed from below.

Somewhere, Gigi chuckled.

Careful what you wish for, sweetheart.

Chapter Twenty-Four

Kieran needed paracetamol. Urgently.

His head pounded as though a herd of elephants in hobnailed boots had started a ceilidh in his skull. He rummaged through cupboards, drawers, under the sink – even the freezer, in case some crazed version of past-him had hidden a packet among the peas. Nothing.

'Drugs,' he croaked. 'I need drugs.'

Prom yawned from the sofa, stretched luxuriously, and gave him a look of pure feline smugness.

'Glad you're happy,' Kieran muttered. 'Meanwhile, my head's hosting the Elephant Olympics.'

There was no avoiding it. He had to venture out.

The bell above the door of Janette's shop gave a half-hearted jangle as he entered. The shop smelled of old wood, mint humbugs and disinfectant. Shelves bowed under the weight of tinned goods, lurid cleaning products and novelty mugs bearing slogans like *Keep Calm, It's Only Cranley*.

Janette sat behind the counter engrossed in a copy

of *Take a Break*, her reading glasses perched halfway down her nose.

'Morning, laddie,' she said, giving him a cursory glance. 'You look like death reheated in a microwave.'

'Thanks,' Kieran rasped. 'Got any paracetamol? I'm dying.'

'Only the cheap ones,' she said cheerfully. 'Sixteen tabs for fifty pence. They taste like chalk scraped off a gravestone. You want them or not?'

'Yes.' Kieran reached for his wallet, but Janette slapped his hand away.

'Don't be daft. Family discount. You can pay me in tech support.'

'Tech support?' He eyed her suspiciously.

Janette smiled sweetly, always a worrying sign. 'Alison needs some help with the website for her boutique. You'll help, won't you?'

Kieran groaned. Not at the task itself – though the thought of teaching Alison how to upload product photos filled him with dread – but because bending his brain around HTML while it pulsed like a bass drum sounded like torture.

'Can't she just use Etsy, or Shopify, or… I don't know, one of those plug-and-play sites?' he ventured.

Janette snapped her magazine shut. 'If I had the faintest clue what that meant, I might agree. As it is, Alison wants her boutique to stand out. Says Cranley deserves couture online. Not just another shop front: *a boutique experience.*' She air-quoted extravagantly.

'Brilliant,' Kieran muttered. 'That'll definitely cure my headache.'

Janette slid a packet of bargain-basement tablets across

the counter. 'You'll be grand. Alison's excited to work with you. Says you've got flair.'

'Flair,' he repeated flatly.

'And nice eyes. Although right now they look like piss-holes in the snow.'

Kieran grabbed a bottled water, downed two tablets and insisted on paying anyway.

'Freshen up,' Janette said as he turned to go. 'Drop by the boutique in an hour or so. I'll tell Alison you're on your way.'

By the time he got home, the pain had retreated from stampeding elephants to tap-dancing mice, albeit large ones. He collapsed on the sofa with a groan. 'How do I feel this rough after two pints?' he muttered.

He stared at his sideboard, where a half-empty bottle of whisky glinted reproachfully. Had he had a few shots when he got home? He didn't think so.

Images flickered at the edges of his memory. Music. Dancing. Angela's perfume. Prom spinning on his backside to applause.

Ridiculous. Impossible. Probably a dream.

'Did you dream it too, Prom?' Kieran asked.

Prom blinked, stretched, and promptly went back to sleep.

'Thought so,' he sighed.

An hour later, Alison greeted Kieran with a warm smile. 'I can't tell you how much I appreciate your help,' she said. 'Janette mentioned you were under the weather.'

'I'm sure her phrasing was less polite,' Kieran said. 'But I'm recovering. Let's see what we can do.'

To his surprise, Alison already had a basic website up. Rudimentary, sure, but not bad. They set up at a small table in the back room, surrounded by rails of colour and the faint scent of upmarket perfume.

Alison spread out a folder of photographs: dresses on mannequins, handbags in all shapes, floaty blouses styled in a multitude of ways. 'It needs to feel personal,' she said earnestly. 'A digital boutique, not just … buttons to press.'

'Got it,' said Kieran. 'Simple navigation, clean design, minimal chaos.'

For the next two hours, they resized images, debated colour palettes and argued over fonts. Kieran steered Alison away from Comic Sans and neon pink and gave a mini lecture on user experience.

'The average punter's got the attention span of an amoeba,' he said. 'Social-media users scroll the equivalent of one and a half Eiffel Towers every day.'

Alison blinked. 'Good grief. I check Facebook twice a week. Don't do TikTok. Instagram frightens me.'

'Keep it that way,' Kieran said. 'You'll live longer.'

By the second cup of tea and the third ginger biscuit, the site was beginning to look … not half bad.

'It's perfect!' Alison declared, clapping her hands. 'You're a genius!'

'Flatterer,' Kieran said, smiling despite himself. 'Let's just say it's functional.'

Alison flipped the sign to *OPEN* as Wilma breezed in, clutching her handbag like a weapon.

'Hi, Wilma!' Alison called. 'Give me a few minutes and I'll be right with you.'

Kieran nodded a polite greeting and started to leave, but Wilma caught his arm. Her grip was surprisingly firm. 'You remember something,' she said, her voice low.

Kieran blinked. 'Sorry?'

'Last night. At The Jekyll and Hyde.'

He forced a laugh. 'Can't say I do. I was probably home watching *Gardener's World*.' Although he knew he hadn't been.

Wilma shook her head, her eyes narrowing. 'Your aura's off again. Muddy grey. Very cloudy.'

'Are you sure you're not talking about the weather?' he said lightly, although a faint prickle crept down his spine.

She wagged a finger in his face. 'You can't hide the truth from those who know.'

'I don't *remember* anything,' Kieran insisted. 'Seriously. My brain's more scrambled than a plate of eggs.'

Wilma studied him a moment longer, then sighed. 'Maybe that's for the best.'

Kieran frowned. 'What's that supposed to mean?'

She hesitated. 'Let's just say Cranley has … traditions. Quirks. You're not the first outsider to get swept up.'

A chill ran down his spine. Jo had said something similar. 'Traditions like what?'

Wilma tapped the side of her nose. 'I've said enough. Get yoursel' home, laddie and have a rest.'

Back home, Kieran sank into the sofa, eyes fixed on a TV show he didn't remember putting on. His temples pulsed again, faint but insistent.

Prom leapt into his lap, tail curling neatly, purring like a small, self-satisfied engine.

Kieran rubbed his forehead. 'What is going on in this village?'

Prom's eyes gleamed. Too bright, too knowing. And for a heartbeat, Kieran could have sworn the cat smiled.

Chapter Twenty-Five

'Nooo.' Beth stared at her phone as if sheer willpower might vaporise the message. Deleting it would only erase pixels, not the words already tattooed on her brain.

I'm all packed up for Eilean Driftach but I'd like to drop by today. Or tomorrow, whichever suits you best. Luke xx

Two kisses. She fought the urge to reply with a selection of 'up yours' emojis, if such a thing existed.

The previous message, from Diana, had been far easier to deal with:

Right, I've gathered the girlie gang – me, Kit and Nina – and we're cordially inviting (telling) you to get your bumpkin arse over to mine on Friday for a night of debauchery.

Beth had tomorrow evening off ahead of Ed and Angela's latest 'drum up business' brainwave: a pub tombola where punters brought wrapped, vaguely Scottish-themed tat, bought a ticket, and won someone else's daft offering. Beth had been tasked with deep-fried everything – Mars Bars, pizza, black pudding, Scotch eggs. She feared the defibrillator might earn its keep.

She typed before she could overthink:

Come this afternoon. After three, as I'm working lunchtime. Let me know what time. The Jekyll & Hyde.

She pressed Send. Then she messaged Diana to confirm Friday night, not mentioning Luke. That was a hill she had to climb alone.

Then work. The kitchen had no time for melodrama.

'We've actually got a few bookings,' said Rose, whisking batter like a woman possessed. 'I told Ed and Angela relying on walk-ins isn't a strategy, it's a hobby.'

'I agree,' said Beth, tugging open the fridge. 'Ed's looking at TableTap or SeatSavvy. Hopefully that'll help.'

They fell into their rhythm. Rose chattered about her new boyfriend – 'super cute, also cooks' – while Beth listened, her mind ricocheting between Luke and a certain sequinned squatters' rights genie.

Lunch brought a welcome buzz. A family of six loved the Cauldron Mac and squealed when Rose brought out sticky toffee pudding with sparklers.

Beth's phone buzzed and she checked it. Luke: *3.30.* Fine. She scrubbed down every surface, then nipped upstairs.

At the small dressing table, she scraped her hair into a scrunchie, dabbed on lip gloss, then wiped it off. She didn't need to impress Luke. She just needed to hear him out.

'Angela,' she murmured at the bar, 'Luke's due any minute. I'll wait in the beer garden.'

'No worries.' Angela lowered her voice. 'Remember what I said – focus on *you*. What *you* want.'

'I will.' Beth tugged on a fleece and stepped into the chill. The good old Scottish weather as fickle as always.

Seconds later, a sleek black Lexus glided into the tiny car park. *Daddy's car,* Beth thought, uncharitably.

Luke got out, dressed in faded jeans, a checked shirt and a puffer jacket. Familiar, except for the beard – not full lumberjack, more deliberate neglect. Annoyingly, it suited him.

'Hi,' he said, stopping before her.

'Hi yourself.' She patted the bench and he sat.

'You sure you're all right here?' He exaggerated a shiver. 'No roaring fire indoors?'

'It's July, Luke. Scottish summers are as unpredictable as husbands.'

'Ouch.' He clutched his chest, but his eyes were sad – a mirror to her own.

Beth took a breath. 'I said yes to you coming because I thought we needed … closure.' She pulled a face. 'Hate that word. Along with "reaching out" and "vomit".'

Luke raked a hand through hair that now brushed his collar. 'I know I handled things badly. I'm sorry.'

'And now you're off to an island to – what? Find yourself? After leaving me to pick up the shattered bits. Every time we lost a baby my heart broke, Luke. You didn't have to take a sledgehammer to the fragments.'

He reached for her hand. She wanted to slap it away. She wanted to slap *him*. Instead she let the feeling sit there, weighty and familiar.

'Beth, I'm not here to hurt you. I've never stopped thinking about you. I've … never stopped loving you.'

Air left her lungs in a stutter. How many nights had she wished to hear those words again?

Gigi, she warned silently, *stay out of this.* But no. This wasn't genied-up. This was Luke. He sounded as if he meant what he said.

But how do I feel?

'I'm not sure there's a way back for us.' As she spoke,

something shifted inside. Nothing seismic: more like a catch releasing. Not healed, but healing.

'Don't write us off,' he pleaded. 'I won't be on Eilean Driftach long. We can keep in touch, can't we?'

'We *can*,' said Beth, 'but maybe it's better we don't.'

His face crumpled and her resolve wobbled. She steadied it.

'Being here is what I needed,' she went on. 'It's … odd sometimes' – (*do not mention a pinball-machine-dwelling genie*) – 'but it's helping. Even with two adorable babies around. Which—'

'Oh, Beth.' He pulled her into an embrace. She let him, briefly. 'You'd have made a brilliant mum.'

Past tense.

'I haven't given up,' she said, gently untangling herself. 'We could have looked at fostering, or adoption. I wanted my own child so much, but we never even *talked* about other ways.' In the end, the silence between them had been louder than any argument.

Luke's shoulders shook; his eyes shone. 'Please don't say it's over. Please.'

Beth stood. The cold seeped through the fleece, but warmth – safety – waited inside. *Home is where the heart is*, they said. Right now, Cranley held hers: dented, stubborn and still beating.

'Bye, Luke.' She pecked his cheek. 'I wish you well.'

She didn't look back as she strode into the pub. Tears came anyway. Angela and Ed clocked her: kind eyes, no questions. A couple of late-afternoon regulars glanced up before returning to their drinks.

Beth headed straight for the basement. 'Gigi, are you there?'

'Always, sugarplum.' He shimmered into being, today

channelling glam rocker: silk trousers, a lamé kimono and platform boots that flashed like disco traffic lights.

'I just spoke to my husband. But you probably already knew that.'

Gigi nodded, solemn for once. 'My left foot gave me a sign. Mainly one that said, "kick him into touch". Is that a football term?'

'Rugby,' Beth murmured. 'And I think I sort of did. Which confuses me, because he is – *was* – the most important person in my life.'

Gigi perched on the glass, surprisingly gentle. 'Darlin', the most important person in your life is *you*. Mortals get far too hung up on people-pleasing. "If I make you happy, I'll be happy. If I iron your shirts and cook your favourites, I'll be fulfilled. If I sit through shows I loathe to prove a point, I'll be rewarded."' He fluttered a hand. 'Enough already.'

Beth blinked. 'How did you know I only watched *Antiques Roadshow* because Luke was obsessed with old junk? Fine, he probably fancied Fiona Bruce, but still…'

He smiled, soft as silk. Of course he knew. He heard the thoughts she didn't say aloud and stitched them into something she needed.

'I don't think you're here to play tonight,' Gigi said. 'Save your wishes. The dead weight of the past will crush them if you let it.'

She didn't entirely understand, but the sense of it settled her. Save your wishes. Choose carefully. Choose *yourself*.

Beth nodded, sudden exhaustion washing over her. 'Goodnight, Gigi.'

She climbed the stairs to her little room, closed the door and leaned against it. Below, the pub murmured on. And for the first time in a long while, the ache in her chest felt like space being made, rather than something being torn out.

Chapter Twenty-Six

'Penny for them,' said Kieran with a grin.

'Aren't they worth more than that these days?' retorted Beth.

They were both outside Janette's shop – pure chance, though in Cranley, "chance" was stretching it. There weren't exactly crowds to bump into.

'You just seemed miles away,' he said. 'Wishing for somewhere less … Cranley?'

'Duller than a silver platter left unpolished for centuries,' said Beth, then let out a small croaky laugh. 'Sorry, I don't mean that. This place has helped me deal with … stuff. It's good, really. Don't you feel it too?'

Kieran, who had only come out for sardines and shaving gel, nodded. He'd noticed the weirdness here, but hadn't every small village got its ghosts and oddballs?

And one extremely attractive woman right in front of you.

'Yeah,' he said. 'It's been a decent bolthole since the breakup with Lisa.' He paused. 'Not sure why I just blurted that out.'

Beth's brow softened. 'I'm sorry. Breakups are hard. That's a song, isn't it? Something from way back.'

'Neil Sedaka,' Kieran said automatically.

'Not Neil Young?'

'Nope. Pretty sure only one singing Neil wrote about heartbreak that bluntly.'

He didn't want to talk about Neils. He wanted to know why Beth's face kept flickering between calm and sorrow. What she'd lost, and why she'd ended up in Cranley too. But confidences couldn't be forced.

'Fancy a walk?' he said, instead. 'After we brave Janette's emporium of culinary wonders. Unless you're buying a sack of tatties, or something equally cumbersome.'

'No, just toothpaste and instant coffee.'

They stepped inside. Janette was behind the counter, armed with a sticker gun and fierce concentration.

'Hello!' she said, beaming. 'Lovely to see actual customers. It's been deader than a Monty Python parrot today. Bargains galore, if you're quick.'

Kieran picked up a dented ginger cake and put it straight down. Beth snorted at a stack of Christmas mince pies.

'I'll have you know I ate two with my cuppa last night and I've no' keeled over yet,' said Janette indignantly.

Declining the delights of expired pastry, they gathered their shopping. Janette eyed them both, mischief lighting her face. 'Call me nosy – plenty do – but are you two an item, like?'

Beth flushed scarlet.

'No, absolutely not,' said Kieran – too fast, too loud – and immediately regretted it. He'd made it sound as if being with Beth would be some unspeakable disaster.

'Beautiful day,' Beth said quickly, as they stepped back

outside. The air had warmed, the sky turned clear as blue glass.

'Yeah,' he said. 'I'm sorry for what I said. To Janette.'

'What, that we're not an item?' Beth nudged his arm. He nudged back. She retaliated. Soon, they were shoulder-bumping like five-year-olds.

'This is ridiculous,' she said, through laughter. 'Two mature adults— Ow! That one *hurt!*'

He froze, about to apologise, until her shoulders started shaking with giggles.

They kept walking. Beth teased him about his running, confessing she'd once tried Couch to 5K and quit immediately. 'I was fine with the *couch* part. It's the 5K that got me.'

'I get you,' Kieran said, then jogged ahead. 'Come on, let's burn a few calories.'

'I'm wearing wedge sandals and carrying toothpaste. Not ideal running gear.'

'Excuses. Last one to the bus stop's a loser!'

He ran fast and far enough for his lungs to stage a protest. Glancing back, he blinked as Beth passed him. She had kicked off her sandals and was sprinting barefoot, hair streaming behind her.

'You didn't mention you were a finely tuned athlete and a master chef!' he puffed.

Beth ran harder and reached the bus stop first. She turned and grinned at him. 'Admit it,' she gasped, as he reached her. 'I totally thrashed you.'

'You … may … have.' He doubled over, hands on knees. 'I'm just … pacing myself.'

'Sure you are.' She leaned on a low wall, catching her breath.

They stilled a moment in the soft afternoon light, laughter fading into quiet. For once, neither of them carried their usual weight – no grief, no ghosts. Just two people feeling alive again.

'So,' said Beth, slipping her sandals back on, 'what now?'

'Depends. You free for a coffee that isn't instant?'

'Where exactly? Cranley's café scene is…' she gestured vaguely, 'limited.'

'Then tea at yours,' he said, before thinking.

She hesitated. 'I don't usually invite people over.'

'Why? Because the place is a mess? Or because you're hiding bodies under the floorboards?'

Her laugh was sharp, nervous. 'Something like that.'

'Now you *have* to invite me. Otherwise I'll assume the worst.'

'You really don't want to see my basement— I mean my quarters,' she corrected.

'Aha.' He grinned. 'You've got a dungeon. That explains everything.'

'You're impossible,' she said, shaking her head but smiling.

They strolled on. The pub came into view, doors shut and lights low. Ed and Angela had closed after another problem with the beer pump.

'So,' Kieran said, 'are we off to the dungeon? Or can we agree that torturing a man for being a bad runner's a bit much?'

'We'll have a coffee here,' Beth decided, moving behind the bar. 'But don't expect latte art. Best I can do is something drinkable.'

'That's a low bar, but I'll take it.'

Beth busied herself with the machine. Her movements were brisk but a little jittery. Kieran leaned against the counter, watching. She covered nerves with banter: he recognised the trick. He used it too.

'So,' he said lightly, 'is this where you interrogate all your customers? Local folklore, favourite biscuits, deepest fears?'

'Only the good-looking ones.' The words were out before she could stop them. Colour rose in her cheeks. 'I mean… Forget I said that.'

'Too late,' he said, smiling. 'All right then. Favourite biscuit?'

'Custard cream. Classic. You?'

'Hobnob. Obviously.'

'Oaty and reliable. I can see that.'

'Reliable?' He raised an eyebrow. 'That's code for boring.'

'You said it, not me.'

Their laughter softened into something quieter.

'Lisa hated Hobnobs,' Kieran said suddenly.

Beth glanced up. 'Your ex?'

'Yeah. Said they were over-processed rubbish. She said that about most things I liked.' He rubbed the back of his neck. 'No idea why I brought that up.'

'Maybe because it still hurts,' she said simply.

He met her eyes. No pity was there, just understanding. 'Yeah,' he admitted. 'Maybe.'

The machine hissed. Beth poured two mugs and slid one across. Her hand trembled slightly. 'I lost…' She stopped, swallowed. 'I lost a lot, too.'

Kieran didn't fill the silence. He waited.

'I don't want to burden you,' Beth said softly. 'Some things are hard to talk about. Let's leave it there.' She managed a small, fragile smile.

They sat. All was quiet, except for the tick of the old clock and the sounds of unseen machinery.

Then Kieran forced a grin. 'So this is where you show me your terrifying basement, right?'

Beth froze. He'd meant it as a joke, but the way her face shut down—

'You really don't want to see it,' she said, too quickly.

'Now I definitely do.'

'Kieran…'

A low hum rolled through the floorboards. Not pipes. Not plumbing. Something electric and alive.

'What's that noise?' he asked.

'Boiler,' she said. 'Old thing. Always makes a racket.'

But Kieran knew the sound of a boiler. This wasn't it. This had … rhythm.

Beth pushed her mug aside and stood up. 'I've things to do. You should go.'

He stood too. 'You're hiding something.'

Her chin lifted. 'Everyone's hiding something.'

The hum grew louder. His gaze flicked towards the basement door: old wood, padlock dangling loose.

'Beth,' he said quietly. 'What's down there?'

She swallowed. Her knuckles whitened.

And then, as if on cue, a metallic clang from below. Followed by a voice, muffled but unmistakable. 'Oi! Don't keep me waiting, Beth!'

Kieran's jaw dropped. 'Was that— Was that someone in your basement?'

Beth closed her eyes. 'It's not what you think.'

'I hope not. Because what I think,' he said, carefully, 'is that you've got a bloke chained up down there.'

Her eyes snapped open. 'It's not that. It's … it's an old

pinball machine that…' She exhaled, defeated. 'That talks sometimes.'

'And calls out your name?' Kieran stared at her. 'You realise that sounds insane, right?'

The silence was absolute.

Then, faintly, from the basement: *'I'm waiting…'*

Beth groaned, pressing her palms to her temples. 'Oh, bloody hell.'

Chapter Twenty-Seven

Beth squared up to Gigi. 'He can't know about you! Why did you do that?'

'Because I can,' said Gigi, as if that ended the discussion. Tonight's outfit looked like an explosion in a psychedelic paint factory: swirls of mango, teal and fuchsia that made Beth's eyes water.

'You've no idea how hard it was to make him leave,' she hissed. 'He wanted to come down here and see for himself.'

'Oh, my little Bethikins.' Gigi sighed theatrically. 'You've no idea how bored I am, stuck here with no one but you to play with. It was a teeny tiny tease. No biggie.'

Gigi's 'no biggie' lived a million miles from Beth's. Seeing Luke had torn at old stitches; talking to Kieran had felt safe until a pinball machine hollered from the bowels of a Scottish pub.

'Then wipe his memory,' she pleaded. 'You're a genie. Memory-erasing should be a doddle.'

Gigi stroked his chin. 'Pah. Easy peasy, lemon squeezy. But where's the fun in that?'

'It isn't about fun, Gigi. It's about not messing with people's lives, which are complicated enough without you sticking your' – she eyed his slippers – 'size sixes in.'

He looked affronted. 'Small feet, large … potential. Or did I get that one backwards?'

'Aargh.' She pressed her palms to her temples. 'At least I've a night at Diana's coming up. Normality. Cocktails, pyjamas, eggy bread.'

'What is it like to have friends?' he asked, so quietly that she almost missed it.

Beth's irritation diminished. He might not be human, but he'd just put a finger on loneliness. 'It's like having family,' she said. 'Except you choose them. Or they choose you.'

'And your family?'

'Gone. My parents died in my twenties and I have no siblings. Maybe that's why… When I married Luke, I wanted a child so badly. Children. Two, three—' She bit the rest back.

Gigi dabbed at the corner of one amber eye with a kaftan sleeve. 'That is sad. Perhaps you could wish, like Jo did. One last time with your parents.'

'Like Jo?' Beth stared. 'What do you mean, like Jo? Who else in Cranley has met … someone like you?'

'Oh, sweetling.' Gigi brightened, as if he'd been waiting for the question all his life. He rearranged himself on the glass, sequins rattling. 'You'd be surprised. Little Cranley is a hotspot. Jinnie, Jo, Wilma: three very different encounters. And Sam.' He pursed his lips. 'Well, that's a story with bells on.'

'Jinnie? Wilma?' Beth blinked. 'They seem … normal. What do you mean by "encounters"?'

'Jinnie met a wish-giver with a taste for theatrics. Not

like me. Too fond of hissy fits and an abominable disregard for the rules. Ever noticed her hair?' He waggled his brows.

Beth frowned. Jinnie's hair was always immaculate. 'She didn't wish for—'

'Multiple wishes, darling. A magic carpet may have been involved. And love, naturally. It *always* turns up on the wish list.' He tapped the side of his nose.

'Now, Jo,' he went on, 'she had a handful. Her genie was a self-absorbed nightmare. It's a marvel she didn't cram her back in her lamp. Then Jo's genie and Jinnie's genie… Let's just say there was chemistry. Poor boundaries. Soap-opera stuff.'

Beth's head felt as if it might come off. 'And Wilma?'

'Wilma got more than she bargained for,' Gigi said, eyes twinkling. 'An itsy-bitsy baby genie with growth spurts. Imagine changing an elephant's nappy. There you go.'

A cold ribbon slid down Beth's spine. She felt she'd reached a whole new level of insanity.

'It's random,' Gigi said, palms out in mock innocence. 'Different strokes for different folks. I'm not like them: I'm me. Mischief with a conscience, wrapped up in a glorious bubble of gorgeousness.'

'So genies have been here before,' Beth reflected, refraining from mentioning Gigi's lack of modesty. 'Why us? Why now? And what about Sam?'

At Sam's name, Gigi's brows knitted. 'Ah. That's the interesting bit. Sam is … special. Sensitive to our kind. Which means he has a sort of … leverage. A way of noticing that tugs at our threads.'

'Does he have power over you?'

'Hmm.' Gigi tilted his head. 'I don't know. He's not the key – not yet. He's more like a bell someone might ring without knowing what it does. Perception can be as dangerous as a wish.'

Beth remembered Sam at the quiz, shock flaring across his face when Ed asked about Disney's genie. Wilma, Jinnie and Jo. All of them had been on alert, like dogs hearing a frequency no one else could.

'And my part?' she asked, surprised by how small her voice sounded.

Gigi's expression softened. 'You, Beth, must remember that people are complicated. You don't treat wishes as cures; you treat them as pathways. You can play when you want to play. You will find the answers, even if right now you're not sure of the questions. Love burns inside you. Never extinguish the flame.'

Beth exhaled. The words didn't make a lot of sense, but they settled her muddled mind. 'I need to draw a line under my marriage,' she said, aware of how final it sounded. 'Luke isn't a bookmark I can slide back into place. I loved him. I probably always will, in the way you love someone who once made you whole. But I can't live waiting to mend what's broken. I need to *live*.'

'Delicious,' Gigi said, half cheer, half sigh. 'New beginnings are a joy to behold.'

Beth thought of Kieran. The way he listened, his gentle humour. The way she'd wanted to tell him everything and nothing. 'There's someone else,' she admitted, as if naming it might shrink it to a manageable size. 'Kieran. He's … kind. I like him. More than like. I don't know what to call it.'

For once, Gigi was grave. 'Then be careful. People who listen are rare. They can be challenging, too, because they make you see yourself clearly. Are you sure you're done with waiting for the past to surprise you?'

'I think so,' Beth said, a quiver in her voice.

Gigi touched two fingers to his forehead in an oddly courtly gesture. 'All right. For now, I'll smooth out the crease. Simples. He won't remember a voice calling from the basement, won't come sniffing around because of me. His life will be as it was; yours will follow its natural pace.'

Gratitude rose so fast that Beth had to sit down. 'Thank you,' she whispered.

'Don't mention it. Consider it my good deed of the day.' His grin turned wicked. 'I shall keep a few slivers of mischief in reserve. Life is very dull without it.'

The pinball machine chimed, a bright, pleased jangle. It sounded, ridiculously, as if the basement itself was applauding ordinary human bravery.

'One promise,' Gigi added, softer now. 'If you're tempted to make a wish you don't understand, come and find me.'

Beth rolled her eyes, smiling despite herself. 'I'll come and find you when I'm ready to be entertained. For now, no memory rearranging beyond the crease-smoothing, please.'

He winked. 'As you wish.'

Chapter Twenty-Eight

Another day, another pounding headache. Kieran dry-swallowed two chalky tablets and glared at his reflection. Dark crescents under the eyes, hair doing its own interpretative dance, and a general air of 'man who's slept on a park bench'.

'I don't know what's going on, Prom,' he told the cat weaving round his ankles. 'That's the second skull-crusher in a few days. I never get sick.'

Prom answered with a meaningful miaow, which Kieran translated as: *and yet my bowl is half empty*.

'You're on your own for a few hours, you furry free-loader.' He topped up Prom's bowl with the least-favoured kibble in a fit of pettiness. 'No wandering. No pubs. No … whatever it is you do when my back's turned.'

A train and a bus later, he was at his parents' place. The same unassuming house they'd had for nearly forty years. New conservatory, same squeaky gate; a place he called home.

'Kieran!' His mum, Val, opened the door, nose dusted with flour as if she'd face-planted a Victoria sponge.

'Hi, Mum.' He hugged her, then braced himself for—

'Son!' Roger boomed from the hallway like a foghorn with volume issues, crushing Kieran in a hug that threatened spinal damage. Roger Davidson did nothing by halves: voice, hugs, opinions on government and gravy.

'How was the journey? Is the app going well? You've lost weight. Good thing I did the chicken the way you like it – a lemon up its bum and loads of garlic. And I got an air fryer. The roasties! Magnificent. And—'

'Darling,' Val said, with the fond resignation of a woman who'd bought her husband a volume control and found it was purely ornamental. 'Let him in.'

By the time Roger had tamed a stubborn cork, Kieran was at the kitchen table, the little universe where his life had unfolded: fractions homework, the day Beverley with pigtails had told him his nose was weird, the night he'd brought Lisa home, so sure the bubble would never pop.

'You all right, love?' Val asked, fingers working butter into flour for a crumble.

'Yeah. Just … memory lane.'

'Dangerous path,' Roger declared, finally freeing the cork with a victory whoop. 'Last time I took it, your mum had me up for thought crime over Barbara Silverwood.'

'You should have heard him,' Val said, sliding stewed apples into a dish. 'Barbara this, Barbara that. He's lucky I didn't put the frying pan through his skull.'

Roger snorted. 'Pay no heed. Barbara's still lovely, but if I'd married her, I wouldn't be here with this astonishing woman and her superior crumble.'

'Speaking of which,' Val said, prodding the chicken and

shaking the air-fryer basket like maracas. 'How's things with your lady friend at the pub? Beth, right?'

'She's not my lady friend,' Kieran said quickly, shoving the small warm jolt of her name back where it came from. 'She's … the chef.'

'We're just interested,' Val said mildly, shutting the oven.

Roger clinked glasses. 'To health, happiness and full stomachs. Now, this app.'

Kieran reeled off the pitch he could now do in his sleep. 'ClosetAura is the smart, sustainable wardrobe in your pocket. Curates what you wear, suggests outfits, steers you to UK brands that match your style and values, nudges against impulse buys. Part stylist, part sustainability coach, part community.'

Val heaped roasties onto Kieran's plate as if they were the ultimate proof of love. 'So I should stop buying bargain tees at Primark?'

'Pretty much, Mum,' he said gently. 'It's the cheap labour and the landfill.'

'I've a wardrobe of suits I never wear,' Roger added. 'Seems a waste.'

'Donate. Someone will snap them up. Money to charity. Boom.'

'Keep the nice navy for your funeral,' Val said briskly. 'Stripes make him look slimmer.'

'Mum!' Kieran inhaled a roast-potato fragment and dislodged it with a swig of water.

'Practicalities, son,' Roger said, getting up to stir the custard. 'She's planned the music, too. Though I've vetoed my coffin gliding away to a song about swingers. Sends the wrong message.'

They moved to the lounge, where Kieran admired the new telly and linen curtains, before heading into the garden for shade beneath the weeping willow. Roger produced sangria, like a magician with a fruit addiction.

The headache lurked, a grey smudge at the edge of his vision. 'I might skip the booze,' Kieran said. 'Bit of a headache.'

'One wee glass,' Roger insisted, tipping half a jug into a tumbler.

'Are you taking care of yourself?' Val asked, spearing an orange slice. 'Holiday, maybe? Sunshine? A week of doing nothing?'

'I've got sunshine here and a cottage falling apart. And work.'

'Have you named it yet?' Val's eyes lit up. They'd christened their own house *Thistle Doo*, purple ceramic sign and all.

'Not yet,' Kieran said. 'At the minute it's *The Wee Scruffy Hoose*, but only in my head.'

When he finally left, smelling faintly of garlic and parental concern, Val hugged him long and tight. 'Call it motherly instinct, but something's off. You know you can tell me anything.'

Weird gaps in my memory. Dreams like confetti. A woman with auburn hair who has me completely bamboozled. And a cat who might be the Antichrist.

'I'm fine, Mum. Love you. Hide the sangria before Dad chugs the lot.'

On the bus back, he rested his head against the rattling window and watched fields smear into green brushstrokes. The headache ebbed. Relief should have followed. It didn't. He had the distinct, uncomfortable sense that a knot inside him had tightened another notch. And that whatever had caused it, he wouldn't untie it alone.

Chapter Twenty-Nine

'So, we have cocktails. We have snacks. We have onesies that make us look like Teletubbies. But what do we say when the blubber makes us blub?'

'Roll with it!' Kit jiggled her midriff, although there wasn't much to jiggle.

'All the more to grab on to!' Nina cackled, raising her glass.

'We are all truly flabulous,' declared Diana, stuffing a spring roll in her mouth. 'And who gives a fuck what anyone else thinks?'

Kit snorted and grabbed a fistful of Bombay mix. Nina followed with a corn chip smothered in hummus. Beth, however, sat quietly, the waves of their laughter washing over her.

She adored these women. Their loyalty, their easy banter, the way they filled a room with humour and affection. But her story… Well, her story didn't fit into an evening of cocktails and carbs.

Hey, guys! I've met a genie – bear with me – who lives in a pinball machine and dresses like Elton John's laundry basket exploded. Oh, and he grants wishes. Naturally. And then there's Luke. And Kieran.

'Beth, hon,' said Diana, waving a hand in front of her face. 'You haven't touched your drink, your favourite samosas are going cold, and that legendary Beth smile has gone walkabout. Spill.'

'It's Luke.' She said it calmly, surprised at her own steadiness.

'What about him?' Diana frowned, nudging Beth's neglected negroni closer.

'He came to see me and—'

'WHAT?' Diana shrieked. 'You didn't *tell* me? Am I not your bestiest bestie in the entire world?'

'And we're the bestie bridesmaids,' slurred Kit, halfway between a giggle and a hiccup. The cocktails were clearly kicking in.

'I needed time to think,' Beth said, taking a cautious sip. The negroni was punchier than she remembered. Or maybe her nerves were shot to pieces.

'Did he just appear out of the blue?' Nina demanded. 'I hope he threw himself at your feet and begged forgiveness. He's got a bloody cheek, that one.'

'He messaged first,' Beth said. 'Then showed up at the pub.' The memory still felt distant, like a film she'd watched rather than lived.

Diana slid an arm around her shoulders. 'If it's too much, hon, we can leave it.'

Beth shook her head. 'No, I need to talk about it.'

So she did. About Luke's apologies, his sudden yearning to make amends, his plan to retreat to some windswept island with a name she couldn't pronounce, to carve driftwood into art and maybe himself into someone new.

'I'd carve his *heart* out and mount it on a spike,' Nina hissed. 'Only in my imagination, mind. But still.'

'He's hurting, too,' Beth said softly, remembering his face when she'd told him she couldn't see a way back.

'He left you when you were broken,' said Kit, hugging her fiercely. Seconds later they were all entangled, a damp, mascara-streaked knot of limbs and snorts.

Beth surfaced first. 'Aren't we meant to be having fun? I'm fairly certain ugly crying isn't on the agenda.'

'Too right,' said Diana, grabbing tissues and passing them round. 'Let's toast something less tragic. To friendship. Because when life throws muck, friends are the best splash guards.'

'To friendship,' echoed the others, raising their glasses.

Beth smiled, but as the glasses clinked, her thoughts betrayed her. Kieran's face flickered across her mind. Kind, curious, cautious. *And cute.*

She groaned inwardly. *No, no, no. Do not go down the cute path.*

The thought was quickly replaced by an image of Gigi's smirking, jewel-toned face. *What's it like to have friends?* he'd asked her.

Oh, Gigi. Human life is messy, exhausting and beautiful. Maybe being trapped in a pinball machine isn't so bad.

'Did you just mumble a name?' Diana eyed her suspiciously.

'What? No. I didn't—'

'I swear you said "gee-gee". Like horses. You betting now?'

The absurdity cracked Beth's composure and she burst out laughing. 'No, absolutely not! Let's move on and pour another round before you sign me up to Gamblers' Anonymous.'

An hour later, the laughter had softened to snores. Diana, Kit, and Nina were draped in an ungainly heap on the big sofa, limbs and onesies forming an avant-garde sculpture of friendship. Beth, still sober, crept into the small guest room, immaculately made up with her favourite bedding. It was cosy and quiet: her little pocket of calm for the coming hours.

She put down her mug of tea, kicked off her slippers and climbed into bed. The duvet was soft as a cloud. The mattress dipped in just the right place. It reminded her of childhood, a bittersweet memory.

'Can you hear me, Gigi?' she whispered into the darkness.

For a moment, nothing. Just the hush of the street outside and the faint creak of the old radiator.

Then: 'Loud and clear, darling.' His voice shimmered through the air like distant chimes. 'Though your internal acoustics could use a little soundproofing. Bit echoey in there.'

Beth groaned into her pillow. 'Don't give me a hard time, Gigi.'

'Excuse *you*. You summoned me. Long-distance metaphysical hotline. Premium rates apply.'

'I didn't summon you! I was just … thinking.'

'Darling, I can hear your breathing. You sound like a punctured bicycle tyre. You're moping.'

'I'm decompressing,' she said.

'Same thing. Just less glamorous.'

Beth rolled onto her side, smiling despite herself. 'Have you been reading self-help books?'

'*Men Are from Mars, Women Are from Venus*. Riveting read. Absolute nonsense, of course. Both men and women are aliens, as far as I'm concerned.'

Beth snorted into the duvet. 'So what now, Gigi? I just move on?'

'Naturally. Preferably with flair. And perhaps, as fate would have it, there's someone out there who could help fill the cracks. Properly, like Polyfilla applied by a professional.'

Beth peeked out from under the covers. Silly, as he wasn't actually in the room. 'You're not matchmaking, are you?'

'Heaven forbid. I'm a genie, not Tinder in a tuxedo. But someone *is* hovering on your horizon. He listens, which is more than most mortals manage. Fate's been giving him a nudge.'

'Fate can wait,' she muttered, half-asleep.

'Fine, fine,' said Gigi, his voice softening to a soothing cadence. 'Rest, darling. But wash your face next time. Romance favours the freshly cleansed and moisturised.'

Beth's laughter dissolved into sleep, a faint warmth blooming in her chest. Fragile, uncertain, but unmistakably hopeful.

Chapter Thirty

'Really? Wow, that's … that's fantastic. Honestly, thank you so much. I'll be in touch.' Kieran hung up, punched the air, and shouted, 'Get in!'

Prom hissed, flicked his tail in disgust, and stalked out.

'Fine! No one likes a sore winner,' Kieran called after him. 'We could be dining on caviar soon, you ungrateful squatter.'

He dropped onto the sofa, grinning like an idiot. Three potential investors. Three! It wasn't a done deal, but Closet-Aura was finally getting noticed, and with Alison recommending him for boutique website builds, there could even be cash flow again. The kind that might pay for plastering, not just tinned beans.

Strolling past the pub earlier, after picking up milk and bread at Janette's, Kieran had spotted a poster for an Open Mic Night.

All welcome! Join in the fun, whether you sing like an angel or crack jokes like Billy Connolly. Tickets £10. All proceeds go to Alzheimer's Research.

'Jeez, not another crazy night in store.' Kieran wondered if Ed and Angela were being a bit OTT with events at the pub. From what he could gather, they wanted to attract more people to dine at The Jekyll and Hyde. He'd dodged the tombola, which, according to Janette, had been 'as successful as a vegan night out at a steakhouse'. Still, he couldn't help wondering what Beth made of it all.

Why don't you ask her?

Kieran froze. The voice was as clear as if someone had spoken beside him.

He glanced around. No one was there. Just Prom, glaring from the doorway.

'Great,' he muttered. 'Now I'm hearing things. Or the cat's psychic.'

Prom blinked, unimpressed.

'You're not fooling me,' Kieran told him. 'I've seen your breakdancing. Well, I did in some weird dream. That's not normal cat behaviour.'

The beginning of another headache crept behind his eyes. He rubbed his temples. Maybe he *did* need to see a doctor. Or a priest.

He distracted himself by checking his phone. A message from Charlie, sent earlier, which he'd somehow missed.

Mate, I am exhausted! Twenty-two hours of labour, contractions you wouldn't believe, and that gas and air is bloody useless. Kidding. I'm a daddy again, ten days later than expected, and Heather is a complete legend. Even when she squeezed my hand so tight I felt bones crack. And I'm sure she didn't mean it when she said we were never, ever having sex again. Anyhoo, baby Ellie is a beauty. Jacob said she looked like a squished pink frog, but he'll grow to love her. Or bung her in the microwave. Sorry for long message. Hyper dad here Lol

Kieran grinned, typed a quick *Congrats!* then opened his laptop. *Right. Baby gift shopping. How hard can it be?*

Very hard, apparently. The internet offered everything from the cute to the unhinged: sleepsuits embroidered with *Future Prime Minister*, mugs reading *I Survived My Parents' Sleepless Nights*, and a crocheted "first moustache".

He finally settled on a buttercup-yellow outfit and paid extra for gift wrap. Then his fingers hovered above the keyboard. He could ask Beth for advice…

'Bad idea,' he muttered. He remembered how she'd frozen when Jinnie had offered her baby Dahlia. Maybe she wasn't a baby person. Or maybe there was a story there. Something darker.

He pushed the thought away. Enough overthinking. He needed lunch, and the cupboard was bare.

'Cost be damned,' he said, grabbing his jacket. He ignored the traitorous flicker of excitement in his chest. Seeing Beth wasn't the *reason* he was going to the pub. Not exactly.

Entering the pub, Kieran spotted a few familiar faces. Wilma and Jinnie, with baby Dahlia sitting on Jinnie's lap. Jo and her husband Harvey, chuckling in a corner as they looked at something on a phone.

'Hi, Kieran.' Angela gave a table a quick wipe and pointed at the menu board. 'Beth's trying out a few new recipes based on customer feedback. Taking everyday ingredients and giving them a unique twist.'

'Hmm. Fiendish fish fingers with linguine and red onion relish. Malevolent meatballs on a bed of buttery mash.' Kieran grinned at Angela. 'Still going for the quirky names?'

Angela shrugged. 'There's no harm in it, and we've had a couple of lovely online reviews praising both the food and the naming thing.'

Kieran ordered the fish fingers and a soda water and

lime. As he waited, Sam Addin came in and joined Jinnie and Wilma. Seconds later, Harvey kissed Jo on the cheek and left – then she joined Jinnie, Wilma and Sam.

Kieran fiddled with a beer mat, suddenly on edge. Was it his imagination, or did they keep giving him furtive glances?

'Here you go.' Angela handed him his drink. 'Beth is doing fiendish things with the fish fingers. Won't be long.'

Kieran watched as a group of people arrived, conspicuous in baseball caps and brightly coloured shorts and T-shirts. They commented loudly on the pub décor in southern American drawls.

'Howdy!' bellowed the tallest of them, a man in his late sixties with close-cropped grey hair, his voice like a foghorn over the quiet clink of glasses. 'Do y'all serve iced tea?'

A moment of silence, then Wilma called out, 'Aye, son, we've got tea. Comes hot, like it should.'

The tourists shuffled in, stamping their hiking boots and grinning as if they'd stumbled onto a film set. A blonde woman, all bounciness and enthusiasm, leaned over the bar. 'This place is *adorable*! What's it called again? Hyde and … how d'you say it?'

'The Jekyll and Hyde,' said Ed, wiping a glass. 'Named after a book. Perhaps you've heard of it?'

'Oh, sure,' drawled one of the men, adjusting his baseball cap. 'That's the one where the guy turns into a werewolf, right?'

A groan rippled around the pub. Kieran coughed into his hand. As he did, Beth appeared with a wry smile on her face.

'Close enough,' said Ed. 'What'll it be?'

'Well, we were hopin' for some good ol' Scotch whisky,' the tall man said, slapping the counter. 'We've been in Edinburgh three days, saw the castle, that big ol' hill – Arthur's something – and this morning the GPS kinda took us, well, off the beaten track.'

Laughter rippled through the locals.

Ed poured them generous drams and slid them across the bar. 'Welcome to Cranley,' he said. 'And if you're hungry, our wonderful chef' – he gestured to Beth – 'makes the finest food in these parts.'

Beth gave a little curtsy, which made the blonde woman squeal with delight. 'This place is simply darling!' she declared, before Angela guided them to a table and dished out menus.

'Enjoying your fiendish fish fingers?' Beth said, sitting down opposite Kieran.

'I can say with all confidence they're a million times better than the budget ones from Janette's shop.' Kieran scooped up another mouthful, having never imagined that the combination of fish fingers and pasta would pass his lips.

'Are you coming to the Open Mic Night?' Beth's nose wrinkled as she spoke.

'Will I be in your bad books if I don't?'

Beth laughed. 'How do you know you're in my good books?'

Kieran adopted a thinker's pose, chin resting on his fist. 'Why wouldn't I be?'

Beth's demeanour changed as her gaze alighted on Jinnie, Wilma and co. A tensing of her jaw, a widening of her eyes. Something seemed to pass between them, but what?

'Beth, are you OK?' Kieran's heart beat a little faster.

The raucous laughter of the American group broke the spell. Beth looked at Kieran. 'I'm fine. It's … nothing.

Ignore me. To repeat my question, are you coming to another fun-filled evening of madness at The Jekyll and Hyde?'

'Only if you promise to sing. Can you sing?'

The Americans were now indulging in some singing themselves – a tuneless rendition of 'Jolene' which no amount of whisky could enhance.

Beth stuck her fingers in her ears, then extracted them. 'Marginally better than the Dolly Parton fan club over there, but I've no intention of warbling unless it's in the privacy of the shower. You?'

Kieran wasn't about to admit he'd been in both the church and school choir as a child. 'I can hold a note, but that's about it. Maybe you can channel your inner comedian, then. Draw on your life experience to have them rolling in the aisles.'

To his dismay, Beth got up to leave. 'Oh, Kieran.' Her face was a mix of sadness and amusement. 'You have no idea how much comic material there is inside me.'

Chapter Thirty-One

'Testing, testing.' Ed tapped the microphone – a new one since quiz night – and the karaoke machine crackled obligingly. He nudged the big telly on the makeshift stage; lyrics scrolled in chunky white type.

'Sing something!' called Rose, replenishing crisps and peanuts.

'Go on, Ed,' Angela chimed in, bouncing a fractious Ruairi on her knee. 'Give us your Lewis Capaldi.'

Beth hovered at the edge of the room. She'd nipped to the basement earlier out of habit, but there'd been no shimmer of butterfly, no glimmer of Gigi. Just the low hum of refrigeration and her own heartbeat in her ears.

The Jekyll and Hyde was rammed. Fairy lights looped round the beams lent a soft glow that made July look like Christmas in denial. Instead of table service, Beth had set out a buffet: salads and cold cuts, herby quiches, then a two-way dessert duel – black-cherry cheesecake versus tiramisu. Rose and Angela stood guard with tongs, stopping the greedy from going full piglet.

'Nice to see y'all again,' Ed said to the returning Americans – Trey, Melinda, Brett and Dana – as they breezed in, sunburnt and delighted with themselves.

'Wouldn't miss it for the world,' Trey declared. 'Found a last-minute Airbnb. We're yours till Thursday.'

'Right then.' Ed cleared his throat. The opening bars of 'Forget Me' pulsed from the speakers, and to everyone's mild astonishment, he nailed it.

'You're a dark horse, laddie,' Wilma told Ed, helping herself to couscous. 'Able to hold a tune, unlike you know who.'

'Sadly true,' Gus admitted. 'Might give it a go later.'

'Pass the earplugs,' Wilma muttered.

Beth ferried platters back and forth. When her phone buzzed, she glanced down. A photo from Luke, showing him whittling on some sun-struck shore, grinning like a man who'd married driftwood. Her thumb hovered over a heart, then retreated to a thumbs-up. Neutral. Harmless.

She clocked Kieran weaving through the crowd – hair damp, wearing shorts and a T-shirt and annoyingly … present. She lifted a hand, but he didn't see.

Ed peered at the sign-up sheet. 'First up, it's Janette and … Alison!'

Thunderous applause. Janette hauled Alison stage-wards like a cheerful kidnapper.

'Poor Alison looks like she'd rather have an enema,' Ed muttered, close to the mic. The room snorted as the intro hit. Janette went full Elton; Alison did her best Kiki Dee. The harmonies were optimistic, the enthusiasm irresistible. Everyone sang along, badly and joyfully.

Elton jolted Beth's memory back to quiz night, to genies, pinball and meddling. She scanned the room, spotted Kieran deep in conversation with Jinnie and ducked towards the rear door, pulse speeding.

'Gigi?' she whispered, as she entered the basement. 'Are you there?'

Zip. Nada. Silence.

She fished a pound coin from her pocket and pressed it uselessly against the Wish Master's coin slot. No click. No glow. She thumped the cabinet, winced, then—

'Beth?' Angela stood in the doorway, brow furrowed. 'Everything OK?'

Beth pasted on a soothing smile. 'Just catching my breath. It's … therapeutic down here.'

'If this is your safe space, I'm all for it,' Angela said. Somewhere above, 'Achy Breaky Heart' started up with a twang. 'The Americans have gone full Billy Ray Cyrus. Sorry, maybe that song's too close to the bone.'

'It's fine,' Beth said evenly. 'Honestly, my heart is healing. Come on, let's add some comedy to the mix before Gus murders "My Way".'

Back in the glow and clamour, Ed tapped the mic. 'Next up, it's the one, the only, Mr Sam Addin. Wizard of words and former purveyor of antiques.'

Sam shuffled up, pushed his glasses up his nose, glanced at notes. Jinnie whooped. Sam cleared his throat.

'Good evening. I'm Sam. I used to run an antiques shop. Now I write thrillers. Same job, really – fewer sideboards, more bodies. For the record, I've never killed a customer, though I've been tempted.'

A polite laugh. He ploughed gamely on. When the final pun limped home, the applause was generous.

Kieran appeared at Beth's elbow, mouth tilted. 'He shouldn't quit the day job.'

'He already did,' Beth murmured, lips twitching.

Then timid Peggy took the stage and slid into a silken 'My Baby Just Cares for Me' that turned heads and raised eyebrows.

'That wisnae on my bingo card,' Wilma told Beth as Ed called a short break. 'Gus, you can do Shirley Bassey next.'

Gus guffawed. 'Come on, grub's up.'

Kieran nudged Beth. 'You're not tempted? Chef by day, stand-up sensation by night?'

'Cranley does not need a set about bin bags and bain-maries,' Beth said. 'Trust me.'

'But you said you had material for days.' He widened his eyes, his expression mock-pleading. 'Let it out.'

'Some things are better left unsaid,' Beth replied, softening. 'And I need to check on Rose.'

Ed introduced a ruddy-cheeked stranger in tartan trews. 'This is Kenny, visiting from his usual hostelry, with some poetry.'

Kenny recited 'Love Is a Loch Ness Monster', which went downhill at *Aberdeen* and bottomed out at *duvet*.

Janette cupped her hands. 'Kenny, that was crap, but at least it rhymed!'

The Texans whooped like he'd won a Grammy. Melinda announced, 'We hope to see the Loch Ness monster!'

Wilma muttered, 'You willnae find him in Aberdeen, hen.'

Beth escaped to the loo, splashed her face, reached for paper towels – and froze as a voice slid silkily through her thoughts.

It's your turn, darling.

'Go away,' she hissed at the mirror. 'I'm not getting on that stage.'

Party pooper. Ooh, look who's up next.

Beth burst back into the bar. Kieran stood at the mic,

dazed, as the intro to 'Can't Take My Eyes Off You' swelled. The house lights dipped, a soft spotlight bloomed, and Kieran caught Beth's eye and gestured for her to join him. Within seconds she was beside him, bathed in its glow, like a coin drawn to a magnet.

He sang – nervous, true, a shade off-key but with feeling – and the crowd melted. Beth felt a spark as their eyes met and lingered, making the world fade away for a moment.

When the last 'I love you, baby' died, the pub erupted. Wolf-whistles, whoops, someone bellowing, 'Get a room!'

Kieran angled the mic away, looking at her. 'Maybe the universe is trying to tell us something.'

'Or maybe the universe needs to mind its own business,' Beth said, but her mouth wouldn't behave and kept trying to smile.

Kieran lifted the mic again. 'OK, hear me out, folks. I think the chef should get up and do a turn. For me.'

Terror fizzed. So did something that wasn't terror.

From somewhere near the back stairs, a whisper curled like smoke. *Do it, darling. I'll make sure you shine brighter than a fireworks display at Hogmanay.*

Beth exhaled. 'Fine. But if I die of embarrassment, you're paying for the funeral buffet.'

Kieran spun to face the room. 'Ladies and gents, the chef herself. Beth Calder!'

Foot-stamps. Cheers.

Beth wrapped her fingers round the mic like a weapon and cleared her throat. 'Evening, I'm Beth. I cook for most of you, so if this goes badly, I can always spit in your soup later.'

A ripple of laughter. Real laughter. She pressed on.

'People say cooking's like love: it needs a lot of patience and a bit of heat. That's a lie. Love burns quicker, costs more, and leaves a bigger mess. At least with a steak pie you know where you stand.'

A bigger laugh. Her shoulders relaxed a fraction. She talked about deep-fried Mars Bars and defibrillators, then customers who say 'I don't really *do* gluten' then ask for extra sticky toffee pudding. How dishwashers sound like mournful cows and soufflés should only be attempted by the very brave or incredibly stupid.

It was glorious. For five pulse-racing minutes she forgot about Luke and his driftwood. And Gigi. She forgot to be afraid.

She looked across and saw Kieran, grinning from ear to ear, and it warmed her from the inside out.

And then, predictably, a certain genie couldn't keep his hands in his pockets. A soft *pfft* sighed through the ceiling vents and a smattering of gold glitter drifted down, settling on hair and shoulders, beer and cheesecake, turning the pub into a snow globe of sparkle.

'Oh, for heaven's sake,' Beth muttered, as Ed and Angela looked up, baffled.

Kieran reached out and brushed a flake of glitter from her fringe, his eyes locked on hers. 'Best open mic ever.'

'Glad you think so,' she said, trying not to lean into the touch. Her pulse ricocheted like a silver ball in a maze.

Always trust your genie friend, purred the voice in her head. *A touch of pizzazz never hurt anyone.*

Beth rolled her eyes at no one. 'Sure,' she thought to herself. 'But it might just turn my life upside down.'

Chapter Thirty-Two

'Oh, Beth.'

Kieran stroked her skin. It felt incredible, as if she'd bathed in every unctuous lotion and potion known to womankind. Like silk spun by the crème de la crème of silk-worms, its softness both breathtaking and arousing.

'Oh, Kieran.'

He stroked her skin again. So incredible, so, so … hairy? Hang on a minute, Beth didn't strike him as the hirsute type. What the—

'Miaow.'

Kieran squeezed his eyes shut. If he kept them like that, reality wouldn't swipe him in the face. Unlike Prom, who swiped his cheek with a paw.

'Get off me!' Kieran sat up and inadvertently knocked Prom off the bed. Prom gave a disgruntled yowl of disapproval.

Now fully awake, Kieran felt guilty about his violence. Not that he'd *been* violent, but fantasising about Beth whilst petting Prom was all shades of wrong.

'Sorry, mate.'

Prom arched his back, stuck his tail in the air and swanned out of the bedroom.

'You're an idiot.' Did he mean Prom, or himself?

Whatever.

After a quick breakfast, Kieran considered a trip to Edinburgh. For all its charm, a little Cranley went a long way.

'Behave yourself, Prom,' he said, checking windows and doors as if he lived with a furry Houdini.

At the station, Kieran clocked Jinnie and Sam wheeling Dahlia in her buggy.

'Hi, Kieran, how are you?' Jinnie adjusted the visor on Dahlia's buggy, shading her from the July sun.

'Good, thanks. Just fancied a change of scenery.'

'Same here,' said Sam. 'I just finished the third draft of my latest book, so we're treating ourselves to lunch at The Crooked Cauldron.'

'That's a new one to me.' Kieran had eaten at his fair share of Edinburgh restaurants, but not that one.

'It's really nice,' added Jinnie. 'A favourite of Jo and Harvey's. In fact, they got engaged there!'

'Lovely,' said Kieran, not remotely interested in where Jo and Harvey had got engaged. Despite Jinnie and Sam's friendliness, he couldn't shake off the feeling that something was *weird.* They had given off a peculiar vibe while huddled in the pub with Wilma and the others.

'Ooh, the choo-choo is coming!' Jinnie went into full mum mode, whisking Dahlia out of her buggy and flapping her little hand at the incoming train.

'Right. Well, congratulations on finishing the book, Sam.'

Sam sighed heavily. 'If only. I might get it right by the tenth draft if I'm lucky.'

'Sounds about as painful as my app. Which I won't bore you with. Enjoy your lunch.'

Kieran deliberately picked another carriage. That was more difficult than it sounded, as there were only two. Rude? He didn't care. He didn't want to analyse what, if anything, was going on.

At Waverley station, he deliberately sprinted up the stairs to Princes Street. With a baby and buggy, Jinnie and Sam would take longer to disembark.

Kieran headed to George Street, where high-end shops peddled their wares. Well-known brands, but did they tick the sustainability box? And did the public give a shit? ClosetAura could be a compass: cut through the sludge, show people what to buy, what to skip, and why.

'I need that outfit.' A woman halted in front of him so abruptly that Kieran slammed into her back. *Damn.* Stammering an apology, he moved on.

The next shop brought him up short. Fitness, Witness. He gazed at a window full of stretchy, impossibly sleek and hideously pricey gym and yoga wear. The mannequins had inflated breasts, waists that suggested they lacked an internal organ or two, and legs that went on forever.

'Yep,' Kieran said. 'Completely realistic.'

'Kieran.'

Kieran dragged himself away from the window display. That voice. Husky, with an undertone of 'shall we have sex now, or later?'

'Lisa.'

Looking drop-dead gorgeous, as always. Kieran's nether regions did an involuntary memory surge. He thanked the gods of small mercies for wearing baggy shorts.

'Well, this is a surprise.' Lisa said and pasted on a smile. Because she couldn't genuinely be pleased to see him, could she?

'It is. I was considering some skintight Lycra shorts, but you always said I looked like I was smuggling walnuts in my underwear.'

Lisa emitted a tinny laugh. 'I never said that. Oh, shit, did I really say that?'

'Yes, you did.' Kieran adopted a wounded expression. Lisa pouted, and Kieran noticed her lips seemed bigger than before. As did her breasts. Surely health-obsessed Lisa, who balked at taking antibiotics and swore she'd never have plastic surgery, hadn't gone down that route?

'You're staring, Kieran.' She flicked her glossy ponytail.

'Am I? Sorry, you just look a little … different.'

'I've lost a few pounds.'

And gained a few elsewhere, he didn't say.

'How's Sven?' That name had given Kieran nightmares. And dreams in which he'd crushed his yoga-pants-clad balls in a vice, cracking them like nuts. Bigger than walnuts, but…

'He's great. Totally great. He's in Thailand, leading an ashram. Giving people a space to immerse themselves in spiritual practices, personal growth, and self-discovery.'

Lisa sounded as if she was reciting from a brochure. And wasn't that a glimmer of a tear in her eye?

'Right up his street. OK, I think I'll head off. No need for Lycra, just strong coffee and a bite to eat.'

'Can I join you?'

Every molecule in Kieran's yoga-averse body screamed no. *Make up an excuse.* But a tiny part of him wanted to suss out the situation. 'Sure. But aren't you planning on buying something?'

Lisa shook her head. 'Nah, you know I could kit out this shop twice over with my fitness wear. Come on, there's a fab coffee shop on Hanover Street that does the best gluten-free vegan cakes.'

As Lisa bounced off, Kieran wondered if he should sprint in the opposite direction. No, that would be mean. Besides, he'd already established his running skills left a lot to be desired.

Oat Couture gave off a healthy and holistic vibe. Everyone in the café looked as if they worked out daily and bleached their eyeballs regularly.

'Sylvie!' Lisa launched herself at a petite brunette slicing a cake that resembled a cowpat. If cows pooped in neat rectangles.

'Lisa!' The young woman put down her knife and hugged Lisa. 'So good to see you. And is this your new boyfriend? Registering high on the cute-ometer!'

Eh, what? Kieran didn't mind the 'cute' rating, but why would Sylvie say that, unless…

Lisa emitted a forced laugh. 'No, absolutely not. I'm still with Sven. Loved up as ever. This is an old … friend.'

Kieran didn't know how to feel. Demoted from ex-boyfriend to old friend, and the 'absolutely not' stung.

'Oh, sorry.' Sylvie picked up the knife and continued slicing the cowpat. The label said *Chocolate Avocado Fudge Cake*. 'I thought I heard… Never mind. What can I get you guys?'

Kieran and Lisa ordered. Oat-milk cappuccinos and a slice of the fudge (sludge) cake for Lisa, Kieran opting for lemon and blueberry polenta cake.

Dispersing the fern design in her coffee froth, Lisa pursed her inflated lips. 'So, are you seeing anyone?' she asked. 'As in a woman?'

Kieran snorted. 'I knew what you meant, Lisa, unless you think I need a shrink or I've started hallucinating.'

'The same old Kieran. Always quick with the sharp retorts, usually as a way of avoiding an answer.'

Kieran took a bite of his cake and chewed it slowly, knowing this would wind Lisa up further.

'By the way, everything's fine with Sven. I don't know what Sylvie's talking about.' As she spoke, Lisa tore apart three sugar sachets and stirred them violently into her coffee.

'That's great to hear. And no, I'm not seeing anyone.' Kieran batted away an image of Beth, and his embarrassing snuggle with Prom.

'And how's the app thing going?'

Lisa had never shown an interest in what she described as 'boring techie stuff'. To be fair, Kieran hadn't exactly embraced Lisa's super-zen lifestyle. He'd boggled at her ability to subsist on kale and beetroot shots, dedicate a whole cupboard to reusable water bottles, and bend into shapes that made him question basic human anatomy.

'It's going. There's some interest from investors, but a lot of work still to be done. I could show you the rough design if you're—'

'I lied!' Lisa wailed, and a solitary tear trickled down her perfectly made-up face.

Kieran had never seen Lisa ugly cry. Even when her beloved dog Wolfie died, she'd wept prettily. 'I lied about Sven. He's not in Thailand. He's in Twickenham with bloody Tania!'

Nice alliteration. Not massively relevant, though, and Kieran's knowledge of Twickenham extended no further than rugby. As for Tania…

'She's been sniffing around him for ages. Thrusting her

tits in his face and whimpering about how *connected* they are, and could she have one-on-one sessions with him?'

'Maybe she completes him.' *Ah, cheap shot, Kieran.* One which sailed over Lisa's head.

'We were good together, right?'

Kieran looked at the face he'd once adored. Inflated lips and boobs aside, she was still Lisa. A bit loopy, very bendy, and … did she want to try again?

'Kieran, can we try again?'

Oh, help.

Chapter Thirty-Three

'Of course you can have another go on the swing! Wait a second, I'll be right there.'

Beth wrapped up the leftover sandwich – Poppy's favourite tuna on wholemeal bread – and scanned the park for Poppy's older brother, Will. He was safely digging in the sandpit, a fierce look of concentration on his face.

They looked so much like Luke. The same hair colour, the way they crinkled their noses when puzzled or annoyed. But they had Beth's tenacity. Whatever the task, they stuck with it. They never, ever quit.

'Will!' Beth called to her son. He didn't hear her. 'Will!'

This time he looked up, but his features were blurred. He didn't look like Luke anymore. And Poppy, sitting on the swing, didn't look like her daughter.

'Where are my children?' Beth screamed, racing towards them. The faster she ran, the more they faded. Shadows with familiar faces, much younger faces, babies—

Beth, wake up.

Beth wanted the voice to go away. To seek refuge in the

moment when she'd had a family. Two perfect children, a future to look forward to. But the voice persisted. 'Beth?'

Dragging her head off the pillow, Beth squinted at the doorway.

'Hey, it's only me.' Angela stood awkwardly, body behind the door, head poking in.

'Oh, hi, Angela.' Beth brushed a sweaty strand of hair from her face. She felt exhausted and sure she looked a wreck.

'Sorry, I heard you cry out. Bad dream?'

Beth nodded. Except it had been a lovely dream. Beth, with two children. Normal life. Ordinary magic.

'Listen, stay in bed if you want, but Jinnie's here with Dahlia. We thought we'd stroll into the village with the little ones and grab a coffee at Jo's. Do you want to join us?'

Beth's first thought was an emphatic no. Then she pictured two sleeping faces, the scent of warm milk, a life she'd banished to the land of if-only.

'OK, no worries.' Angela moved to close the door.

'Wait. Fresh air would be good. Give me half an hour.'

Angela smiled. 'No rush. Getting the monsters kitted out takes forever.'

A fast shower, mascara, the faintest bloom of blusher. Leggings, T-shirt, denim jacket. Trainers. Backpack. 'You can handle this,' she told the mirror. 'They're just babies.'

Beth made her way to Angela and Ed's quarters. Jinnie and Angela sat at the scrubbed pine table, nursing cups of coffee.

'Hi, Beth. Glad you can join us.' Jinnie waggled a rattle in front of Dahlia, already strapped into the double buggy. Ruairi, seated in a highchair, eyed a bowl of mashed banana with disdain.

'We're trying to introduce them to solids,' said Angela,

with a sigh. 'Which makes mealtimes a tad more interesting.'

'But nappies a lot less appealing!' said Jinnie, with a wry grin.

On the way to A Bit of Crumpet, Jinnie's curiosity went into overdrive.

'How come we know so little about you?'

'Do you have a big family?'

'Why choose Cranley when there are far more exciting places to live?'

Beth wished – which immediately brought Gigi to mind – that she had Diana's backbone. Her ability to plough through crap and come out smelling of roses. She imagined Diana's response: 'No comment, meaning none of your fucking business.'

But Beth liked Angela and Jinnie. Being direct – rude – wasn't in her DNA. So she settled for vague responses.

'Nothing much to tell, sorry.'

'Parents gone, no siblings.'

'I wanted a fresh start. Cranley is just what I needed.'

Angela halted. 'Jinnie, give the poor woman some air. We'll catch you up.'

Beth looked down at the buggy. In the time it had taken them to reach the café, both babies had drifted off. Ruairi twitched slightly; Dahlia blew a tiny milk bubble.

'Beth, Jinnie doesn't know all about Luke,' Angela said softly. 'It's not my place to share that stuff.'

Beth nodded. 'Thanks, Angela. I appreciate that.' She gave Angela a hug before they followed Jinnie inside.

'Ladies, have I got news for you!' Janette pushed aside her half-eaten steak bake and clapped her hands with glee.

'Janette, you promised to keep this under your hat.' Jo mimed zipping her mouth.

'Ach, it'll be all over the showbiz news soon enough. Harvey's just landed himself a part in a Hollywood blockbuster!'

Beth, Angela and Jinnie gasped in unison. Jo, however, made a 'calm down' gesture. 'That's stretching it a bit, ladies. He's got a minor role as a sidekick to that actor who seems to be in everything these days. Damn it, what's his name?' Jo scrolled through her phone, turning it to face her captive audience.

'Bloody hell,' declared Jinnie. 'That's Pedro Pascal! Ooh, I loved him in *The Last of Us.* Even if I sobbed when he—'

'Stop!' said Beth. 'I haven't seen it yet.' Not entirely true. She'd watched an episode with Diana and ended up switching to a cute romcom. Too gruesome. Although Beth and Diana had agreed Pedro was very easy on the eye.

After a few minutes of excited chatter about Harvey's step up the acting ladder, they placed their orders and sat down.

Beth looked at her two newish friends. Nice people, leading happy lives. Well, she assumed they were. People hid things all the time. Like the small matter of a genie in the basement: not something you casually brought up over coffee and cake. But she could tell Jinnie about Luke.

'I'm married, Jinnie.' She looked at Angela, who gave a barely perceptible nod. 'Angela already knows. We're not together, which is probably stating the obvious. The reason we're not together is difficult to talk about.'

Jinnie reached out and squeezed Beth's hand. 'Then don't talk about it. Sorry about the grilling earlier. Sam tells me I'm too nosy for my own good.'

'Nosy is just another word for curious.' Beth smiled just

as Dahlia woke. Her serene features transformed into a full-blown scowl of anguish.

'Oh, so sorry.' Jinnie rummaged in her bag, located a scarf and draped it around her. 'She needs feeding, but my milk supply's been rubbish. And she won't latch on, then when she does, it hurts.'

To prove the point, Jinnie winced as Dahlia engaged and then squirmed away. 'Oh, help. Now I'm leaking. How embarrassing. Excuse me.' Jinnie plonked a now-apoplectic Dahlia back in the buggy and ran to the toilets. Roused from his slumber, Ruairi joined in.

'Bet you wish you'd stayed in bed,' sighed Angela, unstrapping her son. 'This one's bottle-fed, so I'll get Jo to warm it up if you could maybe hold Dahlia for a second.'

Beth looked at Angela in horror. *Surely she doesn't expect me to take charge.*

Dahlia's cries grew louder. A couple in the corner tut-tutted, and Jo made her way over.

You can do this, Beth.

Gigi. The voice in her head. Often irritating and unwanted, but now it soothed her. She *could* do this.

'Come on, little one.' Beth eased Dahlia free and pulled her close to her chest. The warmth, the smell, the sheer fragility of her cracked something in Beth's heart. A tiny person, trusting in her to provide comfort. 'There, there. No more tears. You're safe.'

Dahlia's sniffles subsided. Beth hugged her closer. Everything around her faded away. She'd woken this morning broken by a dream. But this was reality, and it hadn't broken her.

'Beth, thank you!' Jinnie reappeared, gratitude etched on her face. 'Look at her. You have the magic touch.'

Beth passed Dahlia back to her mum. 'There's no magic

involved. You have a beautiful daughter, and that's something…'

It felt as if the entire café paused. A freeze-frame moment. 'That's something to treasure. And if you ever need a babysitter, call me.'

Bravo, purred Gigi. *Baby steps, darling, if you can excuse the appalling phraseology.*

Oh, you're forgiven, Gigi.

They wandered home the long way, past the cottage with no name. The stonework looked less battered than it had. Someone was trying.

'I think you and Kieran would make a nice couple,' Jinnie said, as if remarking on the weather.

'Do you?'

Angela's eyes were kind. 'We've seen you together.'

'At open mic.'

'And other times.'

Beth opened her mouth to protest and then closed it again. *Couple.* The word ricocheted somewhere dangerous.

Up ahead, Kieran appeared, framed by sunshine and midges. The part of Beth that ran on impulse wanted to sprint towards him and blurt; *I held a baby.* Ridiculous. Not his business. But…

A sleek 4x4 swung to the kerb. An attractive woman climbed out and wrapped Kieran in a hug. It lasted a beat too long. From this distance, the kiss looked like lips.

'Beth?' Jinnie's voice tugged her back. 'Who's that with Kieran?'

The pair got into the car. The 4x4 slid away.

Beth swallowed. 'How should I know?' She turned away from where the car had been. 'Come on,' she said briskly. 'Let's get out of here.'

Chapter Thirty-Four

'I'm not planning on moving in,' said Lisa, nudging aside Kieran's toothpaste and parking a small army of skincare bottles on the shelf.

'Mm. Could've fooled me.'

In forty-eight hours, she'd annexed a hanger-rail, commandeered a drawer, and was now giving his bathroom a facial. Every fibre in Kieran's body had yelled *don't do this* when she'd suggested they 'see how it feels'. But here she was, snuffling through his cottage like a truffle pig in Lululemon.

'This place could be so much homelier.' She misted the air with something botanical. 'Those towels are an affront to skin. And your bed… Is that an actual dip in the mattress? Are the sheets Egyptian cotton? Thread count matters.'

Thread count, in Kieran's world, was somewhere below 'remember wheelie-bin day'. He was grateful to have a bed at all. Sharing it, however, was a different matter.

'I'm fine with us hanging out and seeing how things go.'

Kieran didn't particularly feel fine about it, but Lisa had a talent for making herself impossible to ignore.

'Are you really going to sleep on that cat-hair-covered sofa?' Lisa's nose twitched in revulsion. 'It's probably full of fleas.'

Prom padded in and twined round Lisa's ankles. She shuddered, then stroked him with two fingers as if he might detonate. 'I never pictured you with a cat,' she said. 'He's … sweet. In a rescue sort of way.'

Prom purred without commitment. Lisa side-stepped him and whipped out her phone. 'Lucy's got a Sphynx, Cleo. Isn't she adorable?'

Kieran studied the photo. 'If ears, wrinkles and nakedness are your thing.' He refrained from commenting that the cat reminded him of Sven.

Lisa huffed. 'OK, I know I'm rushing things, but let's see if we can recapture what we had.' She gave him that bewitching lopsided smile. Kieran's insides churned like a storm-tossed fishing boat. *Damn it.*

'Why don't we go to the wine bar and share a glass or two? Sven was *so* controlling about alcohol, but I'd like to get a little tipsy.'

'Erm, what wine bar?'

'Kieran,' she said sadly, as if discovering Santa wasn't real. 'Doesn't every place have a wine bar? You know, that serves wine – duh – and maybe tapas-style nibbles.'

Kieran followed Lisa as she headed downstairs. Prom sat on the bottom step, eyeing Lisa with disdain.

'Get out of the way, you silly cat!' Lisa skirted around him.

'Cranley has a corner shop, a hairdresser, a café, a boutique and a pub.' Kieran tried and failed to expand further on the village's amenities.

Lisa halted. 'When you said this place was sleepy, I didn't know you meant halfway to a coma! I'd go bat-shit crazy living here. Sorry, that was rude. Obviously, when I left, you needed complete peace. I get it.'

'The pub's nice.'

'Does it serve food and drink?'

'That's the general definition of a pub. The food's amazing. There's a newish chef, Beth, who's really shaken things up, and—'

'You had me at drink.' Lisa grabbed Kieran's hand and hauled him towards the door.

Inside The Jekyll and Hyde, heads turned. Not at Kieran. At Lisa – yoga-honed, Lycra-bright – moving through the room like an exotic bird that had escaped from an aviary.

'Wow.' Lisa inhaled and blew out through her nose. 'This is … interesting.'

Interesting being code for so far out of Lisa's comfort zone, she might need to apply some essential oils and chant a mantra or two.

'Kieran!' Ed clapped him on the back. 'Good to see you, mate.'

Lisa smiled coquettishly, waiting for an introduction.

'This is Lisa. Lisa, this is the pub's landlord, Ed.'

Ed shook her hand. Kieran noted she looked distinctly miffed at the lack of the preface 'my girlfriend'.

'Welcome, Lisa. Good to see a new face here.'

'Aye, and a bonny one at that,' croaked Jimmy, clutching a double shot of whisky.

'Eyes on the glass, not the—' hissed Ed, as Jimmy tottered behind Lisa, staring appreciatively at her rear. 'What can I get you, Lisa?'

'Ooh, I would love a glass of rosé,' said Lisa. 'Or maybe a bottle? To share, of course. Do you have organic wines?'

Ed pursed his lips. 'All our wines are ethically produced in a Highland commune where pesticides are banned, and the peasants crush the grapes with their bare feet.'

'Really?' Lisa clapped her hands in glee – until Ed and Kieran guffawed with laughter.

'Oh, hilarious. Fine, we'll have whatever you've got.'

A tray swept past with Beth behind it. Steam curled above the plates. Her apron strings were crossed neatly on her back. All as usual, except she didn't look at him. Kieran felt the miss like a draught.

'Are you hungry?' he asked Lisa, grabbing menus.

'Do you know her?' Lisa asked, watching Beth's retreating shoulders.

'That's Beth, the chef.' *Friend? More? Stop it.*

'Let's hope her food's nicer than her miserable face,' Lisa murmured, scanning the board. 'Cute names, heavy on meat. "Killer Kedgeree" … promising.'

'It's great,' Kieran said, and pushed down a memory: Beth on a stool, her voice low, speaking of otherworldly things. A conversation she'd shut down.

'Don't you get bored here?' Lisa asked, tilting her head.

'Boredom's a mindset,' he said. 'I've got the app, the cottage, Prom. It's enough.'

Lisa laughed. The sound, bright and jangling, bounced off the old wooden panels of The Jekyll and Hyde. 'But you're *so* talented. This place is for codgers and people who gave up. Look around, Kieran. Is this where you want to be?'

He looked. Ed and Angela were shoulder to shoulder in the slipstream, sneaking a quick cuddle. Rose was blethering to a couple in their eighties. Jimmy cradled his dram like a fragile artefact.

Warmth. Normality. Everyday life.

'Right now, yes.'

Food arrived. Lisa dissected her fish, stole a forkful of his mac and cheese, declared the wine acceptable. She talked thread count, organic vineyards, hygge. He nodded, half-present, watching Beth glide from table to table, a quiet sun the room orbited. When her path brought her near, he tried to catch her eye. She glanced away.

'Sven was a mistake,' Lisa said suddenly, snapping Kieran out of his reverie.

'And you realised that when he cheated?'

A flicker of emotion crossed Lisa's face. Whether it was hurt or anger he couldn't tell. 'I already knew. He doesn't laugh. We used to, right? You and me.'

Did they? Lisa had tolerated his favourite comedy shows, not loved them. Maybe they'd laughed more at the start, before kale and mantras and everything else.

'Listen, I'm only here two more days,' she said, topping up their glasses. 'Let's see how this feels.'

Kieran looked at Beth again. She was smiling at a table of Americans, the smile reaching her eyes. When she finally met his gaze, something like sadness crossed her face, quick as a cloud. Then she turned away.

'Let's settle up,' Lisa chirped, gathering her bag. 'We can talk about ways to spruce up the cottage. Make it more homely and welcoming. It just needs a woman's touch.'

They stepped into the evening light. Cranley wasn't a wine bar and tapas place. It was something else. Maybe he'd been OK with *something else*, right up until he complicated it.

Have I just messed that up? he thought but didn't say.

Prom would have answered. Prom always did.

Chapter Thirty-Five

It had started as a teenage sulk of a sky – low, moody, and oppressive. By mid-afternoon, the first fat drops of rain splashed on the cobbles of Cranley's main street, leaving dark freckles that quickly bled together.

Beth stepped out of the back door of The Jekyll and Hyde, kitchen heat colliding with the sudden chill outside. A strong gust of wind tugged at her apron and she shivered.

'Oh, brilliant,' she muttered, watching the rain bounce off the bins. 'Exactly what we need.'

Inside, the old pub groaned as if in harmony with the change in pressure. Bottles rattled faintly on the shelves. Down in the basement, something gave a hiccup – a bright metallic *ping!* – followed by a faint, petulant voice only Beth could hear. 'That's not thunder, is it?'

Beth froze.

'Gigi, don't start,' she hissed, glancing towards the handful of sodden customers who'd braved the downpour.

'It's *atmospheric*, darling. Storms make me feel positively giddy. I love, love, love a good old hooley. Wind howling and things flying around. Makes me want to—'

'No.'

'But—'

'You're not doing anything. It's just weather. It'll pass.'

There was a wounded hiss, like a kettle on the brink of boiling. 'Fine. But if you need a little magic to keep the water out, I'm your genie.'

'I need a mop, not a miracle,' she muttered, retreating to her chopping board.

By five o'clock, the rain was biblical. Sheets of it slanted sideways, drains gurgling in protest. Out front, the street shimmered like a river, the flower tubs outside the bakery floating away like little lifeboats.

The door burst open and Kieran stumbled in, drenched, hair plastered to his forehead. 'Got an ark out back?' he asked, shaking water from his sleeves.

Beth tossed him a towel. Tried to keep her tone even. 'Just the mop and bucket. Are you all right?'

'The power's gone at the cottage: the road's half-flooded already. Lisa's doing her best to stay positive, which mostly involves lighting scented candles and asking when the Wi-Fi will come back on.'

Beth gave a small, tight smile. 'She sounds helpful.' She didn't particularly want to know about Lisa and what her appearance in Cranley meant.

Kieran laughed, rubbing his face dry. 'That's one word for it.'

Moments later half the village arrived, in a wave of dripping coats and loud complaints.

'Jeez Louise!' shouted Janette, dragging Alison and Hector behind her. 'The forecast said rain, no' Armageddon!'

Beth snapped into action, making toasted sandwiches and heating up soup, while Kieran helped Ed fetch towels from upstairs. The wind howled and the lights flickered on and off.

As Beth worked, she heard a familiar voice whisper in her ear.

'You said no miracles,' Gigi purred, 'but someone needs a hero. A small nudge of fate, perhaps. Something impressive. Something—'Beth burst into the basement just as he started to hum. 'Don't even *think* about it!' she snapped, wiping her hands on her apron. 'You'll make it worse.'

Gigi pouted, his eyes glowing like twin marbles. 'You underestimate my prowess.'

'No magic, Gigi. Promise me.' Beth felt scared – by the storm, and also the inner tempest created by Kieran's presence.

Gigi sighed. 'Fine. But you'll regret it when you think about how much fun I could add to the mix.'

Beth gave him a warning look and went back upstairs.

The pub had become a storm shelter. Locals huddled as Ed and Angela placed candles as a precaution on the tables and Rose scurried around with toasties and soup.

'Beth, we're out of clean bowls! Can you—'

'On it,' she said, rolling up her sleeves.

Through the front windows, the world was a blur of silver rain and floating debris. She tried not to think about Kieran, who was helping a group of villagers move furniture away from the door, his soaked shirt clinging to his back. Every time she looked at him, something in her chest tightened.

And then Lisa swept in, wearing pastel leggings and an enormous hessian poncho, holding a yoga mat above her head like a useless umbrella. 'Kieran!' she wailed. 'The cottage smells *damp*!'

'That's because it is,' he said, laughing.

'I can't *breathe* in there, it's so … moist! Do you know what humidity does to my skin?'

Beth bit the inside of her cheek to keep from smiling.

Lisa spotted her. 'Oh, hello,' she said with the fake friendliness of someone remembering a name from the wrong conversation. 'Still cooking, I see.'

'Still raining,' Beth said evenly.

Kieran looked as if he wanted to sink through the floor.

Beth went back to the kitchen, pretending not to care. She ladled soup into bowls and told herself she was absolutely, definitely not listening for the sound of Lisa's laugh. That the storm didn't reflect her inner turmoil. That her emotions bore no resemblance to the tempest raging outside.

But Gigi, of course, *was* listening.

In the basement, the genie flicked through the noise of the pub like someone tuning an old radio. He heard Lisa's voice and scowled.

'This one's trouble,' he said to himself. 'My Beth deserves better. Time to have a little fun.'

He snapped his fingers. A faint shimmer of light rippled up the stairs.

In the main room, Lisa shrieked. 'My *hair*! It's gone frizzy!'

The villagers turned. Her sleek ponytail had exploded into a bouffant halo of manic curls.

'Must be the storm,' said Kieran, valiantly suppressing a smile.

Beth froze in the doorway, horrified. She looked down at the basement. 'Gigi!' she hissed.

'I didn't do anything!' came a distant, innocent voice.

'Undo it!'

A reluctant *poof*, and Lisa's hair returned to its usual perfection.

Beth exhaled and returned to the bar, heart hammering. She caught Kieran's eye. He gave her a questioning look, but she shook her head.

Outside, the rain intensified. The pub lights flickered. Then, with a sigh, the power went out.

Gasps filled the room.

'Everyone keep calm!' Beth said quickly, snatching up a box of matches. 'Ed, let's light the candles.'

'I'll help.' Kieran took a proffered lighter from a customer clutching a packet of cigarettes and grumbling about being unable to smoke.

They moved around the bar together, striking matches and setting small circles of light on the tables. The glow softened the faces around them: tired, wet, but grateful.

'You're good in a crisis,' Kieran said quietly.

Beth smiled without looking at him. 'I work in a kitchen. Everything's a crisis.'

He laughed, and for a moment the tension between them felt almost warm.

Lisa appeared beside them, holding a candle as if it might explode. 'I can't *possibly* stay here all night!'

'You can go outside if you prefer,' Ed said. 'Isn't rain-water good for the skin?'

The villagers chuckled. Lisa glared and flounced off to a corner table, where she began scrolling uselessly on her dead phone.

Beth caught Kieran's eye, and for a heartbeat, the storm outside seemed very far away.

Before she could speak, a faint rumble came from below.

Not thunder this time, but something suspiciously like laughter.

'No,' she breathed. 'Not now.'

'What?' Kieran asked.

'Nothing! Just … the boiler. It's temperamental.'

A moment later, bubbles of golden light drifted up through the floorboards, swirling around Lisa's table like fireflies. The villagers gasped.

'Oooh, look at that!' cried Peggy. 'It's like fairy lights!'

Lisa blinked. 'Finally, some ambience.'

Beth bolted for the basement. 'Gigi, stop it right now!' she whispered furiously.

'It's just a bit of mood lighting,' he said sulkily. 'It's dark up there.'

'People can *see* it!'

'Oh, right. Sorry.' The lights vanished, leaving only the candles.

When Beth emerged again, everyone was talking about the strange glow.

'Must be swamp gas,' said Jimmy.

'Or maybe the whisky fumes have reached critical mass,' someone else joked.

Kieran grinned at Beth. 'You really have got a magic touch tonight.'

She laughed weakly, wiping her hands on her apron. *You have no idea.*

The hours dragged on. Rain hammered the roof like applause. The old men swapped stories about the last great flood of whatever year sprang to mind.

Beth moved quietly among them, topping up bowls, checking blankets, her presence calm and practical. She sensed Kieran watching her and her earlier frostiness melted.

Lisa eventually dozed off, her head tipped back, snoring faintly through a flimsy chiffon scarf.

'She'll catch cold,' Beth murmured, covering her with a spare blanket.

'You're too kind,' Kieran said.

'I'm just keeping the peace.'

'Still kind.'

Their eyes met. For a second, the noise of the pub faded. All that existed was the candlelight between them and the steady drumming of rain.

Then Gigi, ever impatient, decided to help things along.

A gentle nudge of magic, a flicker of power – and every candle in the room suddenly flared, golden and romantic. The villagers cheered.

Beth screwed up her eyes. 'I'm going to strangle him.'

'Who?' Kieran asked, bewildered.

'The – boiler. Still temperamental.'

He chuckled. 'You're full of surprises, Beth.'

'That's me,' she said softly.

By dawn, the storm had spent itself. Cranley was drenched but standing. The Jekyll and Hyde had held fast, mostly thanks to Beth.

As villagers drifted into the washed-out morning, Kieran lingered at the door. 'You were incredible last night,' he murmured.

'I only made soup.'

'You kept everyone calm. Including me.'

Beth smiled. 'Then I did my job.'

Lisa's voice floated up the street. 'Kieran! The cottage is still *damp*!'

Beth sighed, half-amused, as Kieran walked after her.

From the basement came a smug whisper: 'You're welcome.'

Beth smiled to herself. 'You're grounded,' she muttered, though she couldn't hide the warmth in her voice.

Chapter Thirty-Six

'The woman is a legend.'

'Lisa?'

'No! I'm talking about Beth.'

Kieran stuck his tongue out at his friend. They'd arranged to FaceTime whilst Heather was out with Jacob. Lisa was in the bedroom, plugged into a meditation app for the next hour.

'Ah,' said Charlie, waggling his eyebrows. 'Would that be pub chef Beth, who you dismissed as a possible love interest?'

'I didn't dismiss her. I just didn't—'

'You said there was nothing to tell. Now she's a "legend"' – Charlie did annoying air quotes – 'so please, expand.'

Kieran rubbed his forehead. He'd told Charlie about Lisa's unexpected reappearance earlier in the call. To Charlie's credit, he hadn't mocked him. Yet.

'The village flooded last night. People took shelter in the

pub. Beth kept everyone fed, calm, organised – like she'd trained for crisis management.'

Charlie nodded gravely. 'Very wise. If I were up to my neck in water, I'd head straight to the pub too. I'd head there right now, if I weren't trapped with this one.' He tilted the camera towards Ellie, sleeping angelically in her crib.

'She's cute,' said Kieran.

'She's an energy vampire,' said Charlie. 'Love her, but she feeds on my will to live.'

'Are you breastfeeding her personally?'

'With my hairy chest? I don't think so. Now stop deflecting and tell me exactly how Beth earned "legend" status.'

Kieran told him. The blackout, the candles, the calm. The way Beth had joked with drenched villagers while handing out mugs of soup. 'She's got this presence. It's hard to explain. Just … something magical.'

Charlie grinned. 'She's *bewitched* you, mate. And Lisa?'

'Complained a lot, then fell asleep.'

Back at the cottage, Lisa had moaned nonstop about her ordeal and demanded he order a dehumidifier *immediately*. She'd then spent an hour straightening her hair and another gossiping on the phone. Kieran had caught snippets: *"nightmare", "yokels", "cheap plonk."*

'I don't get it,' said Charlie. 'She dumped you for Yoga Ken, and the moment he cheats, she's back like a rash.'

Kieran fiddled with the strap of his watch, which his parents had given him on his twenty-first. 'Yeah, well. She's not a bad person, just a bit…'

'Flaky? Self-absorbed? Full of shit?'

'Don't hold back, Charlie.' Kieran felt he should defend Lisa – she had been his girlfriend for three years – but the words didn't come.

'I won't. You're too polite. Be honest with yourself.'

Ellie stirred. Charlie grimaced. 'Speak of the devil – and she's filled her nappy. Seriously, mate, be careful. Lisa'll suck the joy right out of you. Clear your head and think about what *you* want, not the tantric crap she sold you last time.'

'Just because she likes to shower before *and* after sex, that doesn't make her evil.'

'It makes her *weird*. Anyway, I've got a code brown to deal with. Keep me posted, especially about Beth. Something's cooking there.'

Grimacing at Charlie's cooking pun, Kieran returned to his app. Little by little, it was looking more functional. Like something people might pay for. Use, in fact. Which was the whole point. Why create something that floated quietly in an ocean of apps when it needed to stand out?

Beth stands out.

Kieran froze. Then he looked round the room for the source of the voice. As before, there was nothing.

'Go away,' he muttered.

Prom paused mid-groom, tail twitching.

'Embrace the present,' said the same silky voice, 'and stop dwelling on the past.'

Kieran blinked and stared at the cat. 'Did you just…?'

Prom stared back, unblinking.

He remembered that night at the pub: the voice whispering in his mind.

'This is not real. I need air,' he said, grabbing his trainers.

Outside, Cranley glistened. The storm had scrubbed everything clean. Branches littered the pavements, flower tubs sat askew, but the air tasted fresh, sharp with petrichor.

He ran past Jo's café and she waved at him, scarf flapping. Past cottages drying out, the villagers sweeping debris.

Each stride loosened something. The memory of Beth's calm during the chaos replayed in his head: her laugh, her steady hands, her refusal to panic. *She's different*, he thought. *She makes the noise in my head quiet.*

The stream beside the road had swollen into a fast, muddy ribbon. He paused to catch his breath, staring into its restless churn. Maybe he was running from Lisa. Maybe from himself.

'You think too much,' came the voice again – amused, musical.

Kieran stiffened.

'You really ought to relax. All that brooding's bad for the complexion.'

'You're not real,' he whispered.

'If that helps you sleep,' said the voice, fading like the last pluck of a harp string.

He blew out a shaky laugh and started running again. *Maybe I need to see a doctor*, he thought again, but there was something oddly comforting in that unseen presence. Mischievous, but not unkind.

By the time he reached the ridge, the clouds had broken. Sunlight spilled over Cranley, turning the wet rooftops to gold. The Jekyll and Hyde stood proud at its heart, white walls gleaming. A tug in his chest pulled him towards the pub. Towards *her*.

He hesitated, then ran downhill.

Beth was back in the kitchen, sleeves rolled up, laughter rising above the clatter of plates. The lunchtime rush was ebbing. She'd been up since dawn, helping organise meals for families hit by flooding. Her hair was in a messy bun; flour streaked her cheek.

She heard a knock at the back door and opened it to the welcome sight of Kieran.

'You going to lurk there all day or come in and eat something?' she said with a smile.

He grinned. 'That's an offer I can't refuse.'

Beth ushered him in. 'Come on, I've got a ton of left-overs. Be my taste tester.'

'Best offer I've had all week.'

He stepped into the warmth. The kitchen smelt of pastry and rosemary. They sat at the prep table, sharing pie and chips. The silence between them was comfortable, companionable.

'So,' Beth said eventually, 'how's the cottage? Still got your guest?'

'Yup,' he said, grimacing. 'Lisa's fine. Just … not really fitting in. Or maybe I'm not.'

'She didn't strike me as the Cranley type. Or the *you* type.'

'Understatement of the year.'

Beth smiled. 'Are you getting back together?'

He shook his head. 'She wants to. But she wants the version of me that doesn't exist anymore.'

'Good,' Beth said softly. 'You deserve to be happy as you are.'

Something flickered between them – a pause, heavy and fragile. Kieran wanted to reach for her hand, but before he could, Angela burst in. 'Oops, sorry! Didn't mean to interrupt anything.'

'You're not,' Beth said quickly. 'What's up?'

'Jinnie's poorly, Ed's out, and I've got a dental appointment. Can you look after Ruairi for an hour?'

Beth looked at Kieran, a spark of panic in her eyes. Then it vanished, replaced by an expression of resolve. 'Of course. Bring him here.'

A few minutes later, Ruairi was snoozing in his car seat

in the corner. Angela blew kisses, promised chocolate as thanks, and dashed off.

'He's a cutie,' said Kieran, watching the baby wriggle in his sleep.

'They all are,' said Beth, stacking plates.

'My mate Charlie's just had another one. Ellie. He's exhausted but happy.'

Ruairi whimpered. Beth unbuckled him, pressing him gently to her chest. 'There, there,' she murmured, swaying instinctively.

'You're a natural,' Kieran said quietly.

Beth gave a small, shy laugh. 'Hardly.'

'How's Charlie coping with a newborn?'

'Fine. Ellie was two weeks late, but healthy.'

'Some babies never arrive at all,' Beth whispered.

The words hung in the air like smoke. She turned away sharply, her chin on Ruairi's soft hair.

'I should go,' Kieran said, his voice low. He didn't want to leave, but something in her tone told him this was dangerous territory.

'Sure,' said Beth, managing a faint smile. 'Good to see you, Kieran.'

Outside, the air was warm again, the world deceptively calm. He jogged home slowly, thoughts tangled. Lisa. The voice in his head. Beth.

It's just the aftermath of the storm, he told himself. *That's all.*

But as he ran, the quiet inside him felt fragile. As if the storm hadn't ended but gone underground, waiting to rise again.

Chapter Thirty-Seven

'You've been ignoring me.'

'No I haven't. I've been busy, that's all.'

'Pah.'

A sulky ripple of light skittered across the pinball glass. Gigi materialised in ruffled cuffs and a velvet waistcoat the colour of a bruised plum.

'You've not so much as looked at me in three days. Three! Do you know what that's like in genie years?'

Beth folded her arms. 'No, and I don't care. I've enough on my plate without pandering to a supernatural ego trapped in a seventies arcade relic.'

'You wound me, Beth.' His voice deepened theatrically and he clasped his hands together, protruding from the Austin Powers-worthy frilly sleeves. 'Do you remember when you used to confide in me? All those nights when you'd come down here with a cup of tea and tell me about your tragic little marriage.'

'I did not!'

'And now you've replaced me with Kieran.'

Beth's cheeks burned. 'I haven't replaced you with anyone. Kieran's just…'

'Handsome?' Gigi supplied. 'Brooding? With a voice that makes you go all squidgy around the edges?'

She glared at him. 'Kieran is my friend.'

'He's your *crush,*' Gigi corrected, smugly. 'And I may have, you know, helped him along a bit.'

Beth's stomach churned. 'Helped him how?'

The lights flickered. Gigi lowered his voice. 'I've been talking to him, in his head. Little nudges: a whisper here, a thought there. "Beth looks nice today," that sort of thing. Nothing harmful.'

'*What?!*' Beth's voice shot up an octave. 'You've been *in his head*? Gigi, that's – that's—Oh my God, that's *violating*!'

'Oh, don't be such a drama llama. It's not like I've been rummaging around in his memories. I'm just … curating the atmosphere. Encouraging positive feelings.'

'You're manipulating him!'

'Manipulating is such an ugly word. Think of it as … matchmaking.'

Gigi sighed, the glitter dimming slightly. 'Relax, Beth. I can't make anyone love anyone. I can only amplify what's already there.'

Beth covered her face. 'Gigi, you can't just go around playing Cupid with real people. Kieran's been through enough without you mucking about in his brain.'

'You're welcome,' Gigi said brightly.

'You're unbelievable.'

'Thank you.'

Beth was still fuming when she bumped into Ed, cheeks slightly flushed, a towel slung over his shoulder.

'Everything all right?' he asked, glancing past her to the

pinball machine. 'You look like you're about to throttle something.'

'Just … having a word with the electrics,' said Beth, shooting the pinball machine a murderous look.

'Want me to take a peek?'

'No!' She checked herself. 'I mean, it's fine. Honestly. How's the beer line?' They'd had problems earlier, with punters complaining about having to drink from poncy bottles.

'Flowing like a dream.' He grinned. 'I still think we should get that beauty upstairs. Maybe a jukebox, too.'

Beth bit her lip to avoid screaming.

'They're here!' Angela called, from above.

Ed pulled a wry face. 'Sorry, I meant to say that my folks are visiting for a couple of days. Dad's grand, Mum is too, but…'

'She has dementia,' Beth said softly. 'I'm so sorry.' She patted Ed's shoulder.

He gave a small, tired shrug. 'It is what it is.'

They climbed to the bar. Ken – an older, handsomer version of Ed – folded his son into a hug, then Angela. As he stepped back Mags clung to his arm, eyes skittering around the room.

'Well, this is lovely,' Ken said. 'Isn't it, love? You remember The Jekyll and Hyde, don't you?'

Mags smiled vaguely. 'It's very nice. Oh, is that your friend? The one from the caravan park?'

Ed blinked. 'No, Mum, that's Angela. My partner. You've met her before, remember?'

'Have I? Oh, that's nice. Hello, Alice.'

'Close enough,' Ed said gently.

Beth's chest tightened. She had grieved for babies that

never were; this was grief for a person dissolving in front of you. Different pains, both sharp.

'Come and sit down,' she said, guiding Mags to a table. 'I'll get you a cuppa.'

'She's worse,' Ed murmured as Beth passed him. 'Dad says she's started wandering at night. Keeps packing to go "home".'

Beth squeezed his shoulder. 'I'm sorry.'

When she brought the tea, Mags brightened at the biscuits. 'Ooh, shortbread! I used to make these, didn't I, Ken?'

'You did, love,' Ken said, smiling. 'Best in the village. Jo always said she didn't know how you got them so buttery.'

Mags beamed, then frowned. 'Who's Jo? Is he the awful plumber who never cleaned up? I don't remember.'

Ken took her hand. 'That's all right. I remember enough for both of us.'

Beth blinked hard and turned away to polish a glass that didn't need polishing.

Later, after Ken had coaxed Mags upstairs for a lie-down, Ed slumped at the bar with a whisky.

'She didn't even recognise the pub at first,' he said. 'They ran this place for years. She used to belt out karaoke on Fridays. Now she doesn't know what "Dancing Queen" is.'

Beth poured herself a splash of wine and sat beside him. 'She knows she's safe with you. That's what matters.'

He smiled, faint and grateful. 'You're kind, Beth.'

'Remind me to have that engraved on my headstone.'

They both huffed a laugh.

Her phone pinged. She glanced down, expecting Diana's meme of the day. Instead, a message from Luke:

I can't stop thinking about you.

Beth's heart stuttered. Weeks of silence, then that. She shoved the phone into her pocket.

'All right?' Ed asked.

'Yeah,' she lied.

'If you need to talk—'

'I don't.' It came too fast. She softened. 'Thank you. Not tonight.'

He nodded and drifted to the snug, where Ken was swapping stories with Jimmy.

Beth retreated to the kitchen, stacked plates, wiped a clean surface. Eventually, inevitably, she went downstairs.

Gigi hovered above the playfield, his lights dim. The machine gave a small, mournful ping.

'You're quiet,' she said. 'Or are you busy meddling in someone else's skull?'

'Even I know when to keep schtum,' he replied, surprisingly gentle. 'That message rattled you.'

'It didn't.' She frowned. 'It was nothing.'

'Luke,' he said, as if tasting the name. 'He wants back in your head.'

'You stay out of mine.'

'No need. You're radiating "conflicted woman seeks closure" in pink and gold neon lights.'

Beth let out a long breath. 'He says he can't stop thinking about me. Which is funny, because he had no trouble not thinking about me when he left.'

'People are idiots,' Gigi said. 'Present company excepted.'

'Thanks.'

'Maybe he's genuine,' he added softly. 'Maybe he's realised what he's lost.'

'And maybe I've realised I'm better off without him.' Her voice went for resolute; her heart refused to cooperate.

Gigi drifted closer. 'You deserve happiness, Beth. Whether that's with Kieran, alone, or … elsewhere.'

She half-smiled. 'That's oddly kind. I thought genies just granted wishes. Not that we've been stellar on that front.'

'I am a delectable law unto myself.'

She laughed, despite herself. For a moment, the basement felt still. A bit like the quiet before stormy weather rolled in.

Her phone buzzed again. She hesitated, then looked.

Please, can we talk? I'm outside.

Beth's breath snagged. She stepped to the tiny window, peered up at the wet street.

He was there. Hands shoved in pockets, looking up.

'Well,' Gigi murmured. 'Things just got interesting.'

Beth didn't move. Her heart thudded in her chest, torn between a past that had just reappeared and a future she didn't know how to navigate.

Luke gave a tentative wave and entered the pub.

Chapter Thirty-Eight

Kieran had begun to think the voice had gone for good.

Two whole days had passed without it – no strange murmurs just as he was falling asleep, no sardonic asides pin-pricking his thoughts. Bliss. Maybe the long hours at his laptop had scrambled his grey matter. Or perhaps this was simply what village life did to people.

He was sitting at the kitchen table, wrestling a clothing website into something presentable for one of Alison's friends, when the cursor froze. Faint as breath, the voice was there again.

You've been sulking.

Kieran's shoulders tightened. He looked around the empty kitchen. Only Prom, sprawled on the windowsill, twitched an ear.

'Right,' Kieran muttered. 'That's enough. Either I need more sleep or less coffee.'

Prom opened one eye, as if unimpressed by either suggestion.

The voice said no more, but the air felt different. Faintly

humming, as though something unseen had leaned in to listen. Kieran rubbed the back of his neck, trying to shake it off.

Lisa appeared in the doorway a few minutes later, wearing his favourite sweatshirt. The one she'd 'borrowed' because she was cold last night. 'Morning,' she chirped, far too cheerfully for Kieran's current mood.

'Morning,' he said, staring at the screen as though fonts and layout options might rescue him.

She opened the fridge. 'You're out of oat milk,' she said.

'Then use normal milk.'

'You know it upsets my stomach.'

'Then maybe go buy some,' he said evenly, knowing full well that oat milk didn't feature on the shelves of Janette's shop.

Her head snapped up. 'You're in a mood.'

'I'm working.'

'You're always working. It's boring.'

Kieran closed the laptop with a quiet click. 'Lisa, we agreed you'd stay a few nights. Don't you need to get back to work?' As far as he knew, Lisa still worked as a freelance personal trainer/yoga coach/lifestyle guru.

'I cancelled my bookings for a month to rediscover our connection, but you're on another planet most of the time,' Lisa pouted.

Kieran refrained from pointing out that Lisa inhabited her own planet, where oat milk was a basic human right and everyone else an inconvenient asteroid.

'You don't want me here,' she said flatly, tugging the sleeves of his sweatshirt over her hands.

He hesitated. 'It's not that. It's just—'

'You've met someone,' she cut in.

'What? No.'

'You have.' Her eyes narrowed. 'The woman from the pub. Beth.'

His stomach tightened at the sound of her name. 'Lisa, please don't start.'

'You've always had a type,' she said bitterly. 'Quiet, complicated ones who need fixing. You love a project.'

'That's not fair.'

'Neither is you kicking me out because you've found someone else to moon over.'

'Lisa,' he said again, softer this time. 'It's not like that.'

She turned sharply, grabbed her coat from the chair and stormed out. The door slammed hard enough to make Prom jump.

Silence fell, heavy and accusing.

Prom padded across the table and brushed Kieran's arm with his tail.

'Don't you start,' Kieran said, scratching the cat's head anyway. Prom purred, low and oddly knowing.

By lunchtime, Kieran had given up pretending to work. The light rain had eased off, and the cottage walls were closing in. He pulled on his jacket and headed out. He had no idea where Lisa was – perhaps browsing in Alison's boutique or sipping coffee at A Bit of Crumpet, where Jo provided a variety of non-dairy milk options.

Cranley village smelled fresh. Kieran inhaled lungfuls of air, keen to eliminate the dampness that still pervaded the cottage. He waved at Peggy, welcoming an elderly customer at her salon. Further along, Sam was unloading something from his car, but Kieran scuttled past. He didn't want conversation: just some headspace free of Lisa's chatter and the voice that niggled at him.

He passed the boutique and nodded to Alison, who was rearranging a window display of colourful scarves and shiny sandals. She waved, cheerful as ever, but his attention had already shifted.

Beth was walking on the other side of the street. And she wasn't alone.

A tall man with messy hair and the kind of easy confidence Kieran instantly distrusted was beside her. He was talking animatedly. She was listening, expression guarded, arms folded tight across her chest.

Luke. It had to be.

Kieran had never met him, but he'd heard enough from Beth and others – the estranged husband who'd done a runner to some island on a vague quest of self-discovery. Seeing him now was oddly jarring, as if a character from a story had stepped into the real world.

Beth laughed at something Luke said, though it sounded forced even from across the street.

Kieran's chest tightened in a way he didn't want to examine. He told himself to keep walking. He managed a few steps.

Beth reached up to tuck her hair behind her ear. Luke leaned closer: too close.

Something – jealousy, protectiveness, sheer stupidity – flared hot under Kieran's ribs.

Go on, the voice whispered faintly. *Say something.*

He froze, looking around, heart thudding. No one was near. Just the sound of a car passing and the giggles of two young women walking in front of him.

'No,' he muttered under his breath. 'Not this time.'

He shoved his hands in his pockets and strode off down the lane, ignoring the faint laughter that might have been Luke's, the voice's, or both.

The rest of the afternoon passed in a blur. Kieran went home, made tea, stared at his laptop until the words on the screen stopped making sense. The voice didn't return and neither did Lisa, though every now and then Prom would look up sharply, as if hearing something Kieran couldn't.

He gave up at six, having texted Lisa and received no reply, and wandered into the village. The Jekyll and Hyde glowed warmly through another downpour, golden light spilling onto the wet pavement. He hadn't planned to go in, but his feet seemed to decide for him.

Inside, the air was thick with the smell of beer and chips and the low hum of conversation. Ed was behind the bar, chatting with a customer, but there was tension beneath his smile. Kieran caught a few words about Ed's mum not recognising the pub and felt a pang of sympathy.

'All right, mate?' Ed asked, pouring a pint.

'Yeah,' Kieran said, though he wasn't sure it was true. 'Is Beth about?'

'Downstairs, maybe. Or she might have popped out. Sorry: Mum had an episode earlier, so it's been a bit stressful.'

Kieran nodded, hesitated, then pushed through the side door that led to the basement.

The air down there was cooler, tinged with the faint metallic tang of old machinery. There was no sign of Beth. A pinball machine sat in the corner, its lights blinking lazily like a half-asleep eye.

He stared at it for a moment. Something about it made his skin prickle – not with fear, exactly, but awareness. As if there was a connection between it and the voice he kept hearing.

'You're losing it, mate,' he murmured.

The machine gave a faint *ping*.

Kieran jumped. 'Bloody hell!' He stepped back, heart

hammering, and half-laughed at himself. 'Right, enough of that.'

When he returned upstairs, Beth wasn't around. The place had quietened: a few locals lingering over pints, Angela chatting softly with Ed.

Then he heard raised voices from the doorway. Beth's, and a man's.

'Luke, don't—'

The door slammed. The sound cut through the pub like a gunshot.

Beth came in and stood just inside, pale and breathing hard, her phone clutched tight. Rain glittered on her hair. For a moment, she looked as if she might faint.

Kieran crossed to her without thinking. 'You all right?' he asked quietly.

She looked up, startled, as though she hadn't realised anyone was watching. 'I'm fine,' she said, though her voice trembled.

'You don't look fine.'

Beth gave a shaky laugh. 'That obvious?'

'Only to the observant,' he said.

Something in her expression softened. The tension in her shoulders eased a fraction.

'Come on,' he said gently. 'Let's sit down.'

She hesitated, then nodded. He guided her to the corner table furthest from the door and fetched drinks – white wine for her, whisky for him.

'Thanks,' she murmured, fingers curling round the glass.

'You don't have to talk about it,' he said, 'but... If you want to, I'm listening.'

Beth stared into the wine. 'He says he wants to talk. That he can't stop thinking about me.'

Kieran's jaw tightened. 'Right.'

'He turned up outside the pub tonight. I thought I was imagining it.' She gave a helpless little shrug. 'I don't know what I'm meant to do.'

'You don't owe him anything,' Kieran said quietly.

'Maybe not. But it's hard to unlove someone when you once did.'

He understood that far too well.

They sat in silence for a while, the low murmur of the pub wrapping around them. Rain streaked the windows, and a gust of wind rattled the door.

Beth took a sip of wine, her hand still trembling slightly. 'Sorry. You probably didn't come here to play counsellor.'

'Don't worry about it,' he said. 'I've had worse evenings.'

'Really?'

'Well, there was that time Prom brought in a dead mouse and dropped it on my keyboard mid-Zoom chat.'

She laughed – properly this time – and some of the colour returned to her face. 'Thanks,' she said softly.

Kieran met her eyes and managed a small smile. 'Anytime.'

He wanted to ask Beth about the pinball machine, but that didn't seem appropriate right now. And whatever happened with Luke … that was Beth's decision. Even if the thought of them getting back together hurt.

Chapter Thirty-Nine

'Come on, it'll be fun!'

Beth pulled a 'your idea of fun is different to mine' face. Diana retaliated with a passable impression of someone with severe constipation.

'I shouldn't take time off,' Beth said, even though Ed and Angela had already given the thumbs up.

'Hon, all work and no play makes Beth a very dull girl. And we need to talk about Luke. Which admittedly doesn't come under the fun umbrella, but needs must.'

Beth glanced at the week's chalked-up specials. They'd scaled back from her early, ambitious menus. Ken – steady, sensible Ken – had nudged them that way during a group chat a couple of nights back.

'Maybe save the fancy stuff for Easter, Halloween and Christmas,' he'd suggested, while Mags blinked and asked if someone might take her to the toilet. Beth's heart had ached for all of them.

'But a spooky escape room! I mean, what's that all about?'

'OK, hear me out,' Diana said. 'It's not just an escape room – it's an *experience*. It's called Shadows of Auld Reekie and it's set under Edinburgh, in old vaults that are supposedly haunted by Burke and Hare. You know, the body-snatching guys? Charming, really. There's fog, flickering lanterns, and apparently a ghostly piper who leads you into the tunnels if you listen closely enough. Total goosebumps.'

'Couldn't we go to a spa and have massages and pedicures instead?' For a moment, Beth imagined herself swaddled in a white robe, toenails painted hot pink, aching muscles eased by a hunky masseur.

Diana ignored her. 'You and I will solve puzzles from Dr Jekyll's lab, decoding his notes before Hyde takes over, and try not to let the Mackenzie Poltergeist blow out the lights. There's even a bit where you have to chant in Gaelic to seal a curse.'

Beth wouldn't have known a word of Gaelic if it had come up and bitten her. Apart from the name of Luke's island, which he might or might not have returned to. Their parting had been bitter, to say the least.

'Beth, come on! You've been moping about Luke, dithering over Kieran and digging yourself into a hole. A grave, so to speak. Trust me, this experience is just what you need.'

Diana's enthusiasm worked its slow magic.

'OK, let's do it. But if I get the willies, there'd better be an easy exit door.'

When the call ended, she looked around her quarters. She'd tried to make them homely, but currently they looked spartan and unloved. She wondered what Kieran's cottage looked like. If he'd ever invite her there.

'Not with Lisa still in residence,' she muttered.

That won't be for very much longer.

'Oh, for—' Beth turned. 'Gigi!'

He materialised as if he'd stepped through a velvet curtain, all opaline shimmer and wide, knowing eyes.

'Why the long face?' he asked, though his expression said he already knew. He always knew. He'd pawed at Kieran's thoughts without permission. Someday, she'd have to yank the whole Cranley genie mess into the light. Just not today.

'I want a quiet life, Gigi.'

Gigi flapped his hands in a 'carry on' gesture.

'I feel trapped. Can't go forward, can't go back. If I let go of Luke, I'm letting go of the family I wanted. And I don't want to drag Kieran into my mess. He's got his own.'

Tears coursed down Beth's cheeks. Gigi produced a box of tissues – glittery ones, of course – and she wiped them away.

'Sweetie, having a family doesn't depend on Luke. I mean, maybe your eggs and his thingummy didn't work. Well, they did, but not … you know.' He winced. 'I'm trying for sensitivity.'

'Do you know how many pregnancies end in miscarriage?' Beth's snot levels reached epic proportions. 'One in eight. Maybe one in four. And then there are women who don't want babies who— It's not fair.'

'No one promised fair.' Gigi nodded sagely. 'I'm still stuck down here when I should be enthralling the punters. Life does what it wants.'

Beth laughed soggily. 'Stirring up trouble, more like.'

Gigi's eyes glittered. 'Fancy a game?'

Reluctantly, Beth headed to the basement, Gigi materialising in front of her.

He gestured and the butterfly shimmered into being, its wings a rapid blur. A hiss of brightness, then a clatter of gold coins spilled across the floor, skittering like raindrops on tin.

'Bit heavy-handed,' Beth muttered, dragging an old flour sack from a crate and shovelling them in. 'If I play, do I get a wish?'

'Do you have one in mind?' Gigi arched an elegant brow, the gold shimmer of his eyes reflecting off the pinball machine's glass.

Beth hesitated. The words had been forming for days, twisting themselves into a tight knot inside her chest.

'I want to forget,' she said. 'The miscarriages, all of it. The hospital, the blood, the emptiness. I want it gone. Like it never happened.'

For a moment, Gigi said nothing. He folded his hands and the noise of the world seemed to mute itself: no hum of lights, no faint creak of floorboards. Just the two of them, surrounded by a bubble of stillness.

'Oh, sweet cheeks,' he said softly. 'You don't want that.'

'I do,' Beth insisted. 'I'm tired of crying over what I can't change. Every time I see a pram, or hear someone moaning about sleepless nights, I feel … hollow. I want peace.'

Gigi tilted his head, and for once there was no teasing lightness about him. 'If I erased those memories, Beth, I wouldn't just take away the pain. I'd take the version of you who learned to stand up again. The tenderness, the grit, the wisdom. Pain shapes, even when it cuts.'

'But it hurts too much,' she whispered. 'I thought spending time with Jinnie and Angela's babies meant I'd healed, but the pain is still there.'

'Then let it hurt for now,' he replied. 'You'll heal, in time. Scars aren't pretty, but they're honest. If you wish it away, the ache will find another corner. You'd still feel hollow, and you wouldn't know why.'

Beth studied him, blinking through a film of tears. 'You sound as if you know what that's like.'

Gigi smiled faintly. For a fleeting instant, she thought she glimpsed something ancient and broken in his gaze. Centuries of being trapped, perhaps, of having his own regrets worn down by time.

'Let's just say I've seen what forgetting does,' he said lightly. 'Play with me instead. Give me a frenzy worth writing to the Federation about.'

Beth wiped her cheeks and stepped closer to the machine. The butterfly shimmered above her, its wings flexing at lightning speed. She placed her fingers on the buttons, feeling a faint vibration beneath them – the hum of Gigi's world. 'Same rules?'

'Always,' said Gigi, with a mock bow. 'Score high, and a wish might wobble loose. Score low, and you buy me a metaphorical drink.'

'You don't drink. Do you?'

'Details,' he said, winking.

She launched the ball. A bright ping, and the world narrowed to flippers and rollovers, lights that chased and chimed. Gigi whooped as if he were every crowd she'd ever needed.

'Woohoo, she's got the touch!' Gigi cried, his voice echoing around the pub basement. 'You're in the multiball zone!'

Beth laughed despite herself, the sound bubbling up like a forgotten melody. She'd always been good at pinball, but tonight something clicked. Her reflexes sharpened, her focus narrowed, and her sadness ebbed away.

The score climbed; Gigi's face turned from amused to

mildly alarmed. 'Have you been unfaithful? Been playing behind my back?'

'Shush,' she said, her eyes locked on the flashing lights.

The last ball bounced wildly, defying gravity, before slipping between the flippers. The machine flared gold and emitted a triumphant trill.

'New high score,' Gigi announced, clapping his glittering hands. 'Well, butter my baps and call me Bertrand.'

Beth leaned back, panting lightly, and grinned. 'What do I win?'

'You win,' Gigi said, serious again, 'the reminder that you're still here. Still alive. Still capable of joy. That's worth more than any wish.'

She smiled, a tear sneaking down her cheek. Not the old kind of tear, the heavy, despairing sort, but something gentler. 'You're not a bad therapist, for a magical entity.'

'Oh, I charge by the minute,' he quipped, twirling an invisible moustache. Then, more quietly: 'You've got wishes left, Beth. Use them wisely. Wishing is easy. Living with the consequences isn't.'

The lights dimmed as he spoke, the golden sheen of his form dissolving into the machine. It made a noise like a hiccup before settling into silence.

Beth stood there for a moment, the smell of old wood and dust grounding her. Her heart was steady now, her breath calm. She knew the grief hadn't vanished, but something had shifted inside her. A tiny, crucial sliver of acceptance.

'Two wishes,' she murmured to herself, tracing a fingertip along the glass. 'No pressure, then.'

Somewhere inside the machine, a faint, mischievous chuckle echoed back.

Beth smiled. She pulled out her phone and texted Diana.

I'm in. Bring spare pants in case of spooky accidents.

Upstairs, rain ticked at the window and the pub creaked contentedly in its old bones. Down here, in the dim glow of score reels and stubborn hope, Beth stood with wishes she didn't quite trust and a steadier breath than she'd had in months.

She picked up the flour sack of coins, knotted it tight, and laughed as the butterfly fluttered past her nose.

'All right,' she said to the room, to herself, to the stubborn ache that was beginning to abate. 'Let's live with it.'

Chapter Forty

'Peace, perfect peace.'

Kieran relished the silence. After a full-blown bout of histrionics from Lisa, he needed the tranquility of a quiet cottage. Even a damp, slightly whiffy one.

'I did the right thing,' he said to Prom, curled up at his feet in a semi-conscious coil. 'We were never a good match, apart from in the bedroom.'

Prom stretched and gave him a look of mild distaste.

'Sorry, bud. Too much information.'

Despite her teary objections, Kieran knew Lisa wouldn't be single for long. Another Sven, perhaps. Or not.

'Not my problem,' he murmured, stroking Prom's head.

To get things moving with his app, Kieran had booked a small function room at The Jekyll and Hyde for that evening. Baby steps, but he needed feedback. Ed had happily agreed for a nominal fee, and with Jinnie, Angela and Alison's help, he hoped for a decent turnout of fashion-savvy, eco-minded guinea pigs. Just not too many, as the room wasn't large.

The room, which wasn't used much, had been kitted out for the event. Ed and Angela had dragged in a few mismatched tables, set out borrowed chairs from the beer garden, and scrawled *ClosetAura Meetup – Free Tea & Coffee!* on the chalkboard usually reserved for the day's specials.

The faint hum of music next door filled the gaps between chatter. Angela had strung up fairy lights, which flickered against the ancient red and gold flocked wallpaper. It wasn't glamorous, but it could be the kind of place where small ideas took flight.

Kieran stood near an ancient dartboard, laptop at the ready, pulse hammering. Slides good to go, palms sweaty, regretting the pint of Dutch courage he'd thought would help. Ed gave an encouraging nod from behind the tea urn.

Kieran cleared his throat. 'All right, everyone, thanks for coming. I'm Kieran, and I've been building an app called ClosetAura.'

A few polite murmurs. Someone stirred their coffee noisily.

'So … it's like if your wardrobe had a conscience,' he said, feeling heat rise up his neck. 'It helps you see what you actually wear, what's gathering dust, and what deserves a second life. And instead of doom-scrolling fast-fashion tat, it connects you with UK brands that are genuinely sustainable and match your style.'

He tapped the spacebar. The projector, perched precariously on a bar stool, flickered to reveal the temporary logo: a heart wrapped around a hanger.

'I know I'm not some big tech guru in a black turtleneck,' he added, scratching the back of his neck. 'I'm just trying to make fashion feel good again, for us and the planet.'

There was a low chuckle from somewhere near the biscuit plate.

'I'm looking for a handful of testers,' he went on. 'Tell me what's great, what's rubbish, what needs fixing. Be brutally honest. I promise I won't cry. Much.'

Smiles; a couple of nods. His shoulders loosened.

'So yeah,' he said, gesturing towards a sign-up sheet on the bar. 'If you fancy being part of the first wave of closet revolutionaries, write down your name and email address. You'll get early access, a say in shaping the app, and possibly a free coffee. Courtesy of Ed's generosity, not mine.'

'Oi!' Ed called, laughing. 'You're paying for the biscuits, mate.'

Beth appeared in her chef's jacket, hair loosely tied, a smudge of flour across one cheek. She must have come straight from the kitchen. For a second, he forgot what he was saying.

'Cat got your tongue, lad?' Wilma heckled, which earned some laughter.

Beth slipped into a chair and the room settled. Kieran wrapped up, relieved no one had fled or fallen asleep.

'Thanks, Ed,' he said, gathering his laptop and notes as people dispersed.

'No worries, Kieran. It looks like a lot of people signed up. I did, and so did Angela. She's forever moaning that I own forty shirts and wear the same three things on a loop.'

As the last people filed out, Beth wandered over. 'Closet-Aura, hmm?' she said. 'It sounds intriguing.'

'I'm aiming for mega-successful, but I'll take intriguing.'

They walked together into the pub's low buzz. Alison, sitting with Janette, gave him a thumbs up.

'You're a dark horse,' Beth said, nodding when Kieran

offered to buy her a drink. 'How come you never mentioned before that you're starting a fashion revolution?'

Kieran shrugged. 'Hey, it's early days. More like a fashion … minor uprising.'

Beth laughed, the sound soft and warm against the buzz of the pub. 'Well, consider me on board. Sign me up for your beta thingy. I want to see if it tells me to bin half my manky aprons.'

'Deal. But please don't roast me in the feedback form.'

'No promises,' she said, eyes glinting. 'Depends how good your app is.'

They sat together quietly and sipped their drinks. Kieran felt he should mention Lisa – or rather, her overdue departure – but the time wasn't right. Instead, he soaked up the pub atmosphere. And the feeling of *rightness* with Beth.

As if she sensed his thought, Beth stiffened. She gulped back the remains of her drink and stood up.

'Do you have to go now?' Kieran wanted her to stay. He wanted to spend hours with her, unravelling what made her tick. What made her happy or sad.

'Sorry, the kitchen awaits. Night, Kieran. And for what it's worth, you looked in your element there.'

'I did?'

She smiled. 'It suits you, if you'll pardon the clothing pun.' And she was gone.

Kieran finished his drink and wandered into the now-empty room. He looked around at the higgledy-piggledy chairs, the flickering fairy lights and the sign-up sheet, with Beth's name scribbled halfway down.

He stood there, hands in his pockets, heart doing that annoying hopeful flutter. For the first time in a while, he didn't just believe in the app.

He believed he might make this work, all of it. Closet-Aura, Cranley, and whatever this was with Beth. Maybe, just maybe, his new beginning had materialised in a scruffy back room strung with fairy lights.

Chapter Forty-One

Beth had agreed to the Shadows of Auld Reekie escape room mostly because Diana had insisted it would be a laugh. Standing at the entrance to the vaults, though, with fog curling around her ankles and a faint wail of bagpipes echoing below, she was already questioning her life choices.

'It's all theatre,' Diana said cheerfully, striding ahead with her torch like an intrepid explorer. 'Burke and Hare, ghostly pipers, jump scares. It's all part of the fun!'

Beth caught up and clung to her arm. 'If it's just theatre, why does it smell like something actually died down here?'

The narrow tunnel walls wept with damp; the lanterns flickered in a distinctly malevolent way. When a cold gust of air brushed her ear, Beth gave an undignified squeak and nearly bolted up the steps. Encountering a genie was one thing; this was something else entirely.

Diana, naturally, was having the time of her life. She solved the first puzzle in record time, pressed every suspicious-looking brick in the wall, and even flirted with the projected 'ghost guide'. When a hidden door hissed open and a skeletal hand dropped from the ceiling, Diana howled with laughter. Beth screamed so loudly that the next group applauded.

'Never again!' Back at Diana's, Beth accepted a large glass of wine as they waited for a Chinese takeaway delivery.

'Wuss,' Diana teased, tipping prawn crackers into a bowl. 'You choose next time, and you can pick something with fewer corpses. Maybe a trip to the cinema, to see a romcom with a torrid love triangle. Speaking of which…'

'I'm not in a love triangle,' Beth said quickly. 'There's no romance between me and Kieran, and as for Luke…'

She explained how Luke had turned up and she'd told him the truth – that he was chasing the woman she used to be, not the one standing in front of him now.

'Good for you, hon.' The doorbell chimed. 'Hold that thought while I get the food.'

Minutes later, they were perched on opposite sofas with trays of steaming Singapore noodles, Szechuan spicy beef and fried rice between them.

'Anyway,' Beth said, chopsticks in hand, 'Luke's messaged a few times since, but I told him it's over. And I mean it. No more what-ifs.'

'Bravo,' said Diana. 'Now, on to the enigmatic Kieran. Because my love life is dead, I have to live vicariously through yours.'

Beth laughed. Diana, despite her endless admirers, was ruthless in disqualifying them. 'It's complicated.'

'It's only complicated if you make it so. Didn't you say he was single after his girlfriend dumped him?'

Beth frowned. She couldn't remember what she'd told Diana and didn't know how things stood between Kieran and Lisa. 'She's still in Cranley, I think, sort of living with him. Well, not *living* with him – I don't think he wants that – but she's persistent.'

'Reminds me of a client I once went out with,' Diana said, splashing hot sauce onto her noodles. 'Lovely muscles, terrible brain. After one date I knew it wouldn't work.'

'Because?'

'Because the size of his muscles greatly exceeded the size of his intellect. And after trying to let him down gently, Shit-for-Brains messaged me multiple times a day saying how perfect we were together.'

'Blocked?'

Diana shuddered. 'Absolutely. Once I'd steered him towards another physio practice.'

They devoured the food, then Diana rooted through her freezer for dessert. 'We need a sweet ending.'

She unearthed brownies, vanilla ice cream, and an alarming number of half-empty nut packets. 'Work your culinary magic, girlfriend.'

Beth smiled and improvised a caramel sauce. The familiar rhythm of whisking and stirring soothed her.

'So, Kieran,' Diana said, spoon in hand. 'What's the hold-up?'

Beth tried to put words to the knot of feelings inside her. The attraction was there – was obvious – but acting on it? She'd only just closed the door on Luke. And Kieran still had Lisa's shadow in his life.

'Stop overthinking,' Diana said firmly. 'Ask him out. What's the worst that could happen?'

Beth went to bed replaying those words. *Ask him out. What's the worst that could happen?*

The next morning, the journey back to Cranley was

crisp and sunlit. Diana's advice looped through her head like a mantra.

He could say no, said her inner pessimist.

Or he could say yes, another voice countered. Definitely Gigi.

Beth walked into the pub and stopped dead.

There, gleaming beside the bar, was the pinball machine.

Her pinball machine.

For a moment, she could only stare. Torn between bolting and giving Ed a piece of her mind, she watched him crouched by the power cable, screwdriver in hand. Two other newcomers had joined it: a vintage jukebox and an ancient fruit machine with a lever like a pirate's prosthetic.

'That's a one-armed bandit,' said Jimmy, appearing at her elbow in a fog of whisky fumes. 'They don't make 'em like that anymore.'

'Fascinating,' Beth managed.

Angela swooped in and steered Jimmy to safety. 'What do you think, Beth?'

What did she think? That the universe had gone utterly rogue. With Gigi loose in the main bar, anything could happen. He'd caused enough chaos in the basement.

'Beth, how did you get this thing to work before?' Ed called, tightening a screw.

'I … well … I just plugged it in.'

'Let's see. Moment of truth.' Ed plugged in all three machines. 'Bingo!'

The pub lights dimmed. The jukebox roared to life with Coldplay's 'Arabesque', while the pinball machine flared gold and hummed like an orchestra tuning up.

'That is *so* cool!' Rose bounded in, followed by a wide-eyed Mags.

'It's all very noisy,' Mags said primly. 'Can we make it quieter?'

Beth's heart thudded. Mags edged closer to the machine, eyes bright with curiosity. Jinnie, Jo and Sam hovered at the edge of the crowd, watchful.

The jukebox switched track mid-song, Phil Collins's 'In the Air Tonight' thundering through the room. The air crackled.

Oh, God, he's showing off, Beth thought.

'Can I play?' Mags asked, turning to her with childlike wonder.

'Of course you can.' Beth dug into her pocket, fingers brushing cool metal – a handful of Gigi's gold tokens. She passed them to Mags, who turned them over reverently.

'They're so beautiful. What do I do?'

Beth swallowed, aware of the silence pressing around them. She slotted a token into the machine and guided Mags's hands to the flipper buttons. 'Ready?'

'I think so.'

Lights flared, chimes cascaded, the music swelled – and the crowd gasped as Mags took off, her reflexes sharp and sure, eyes alive with focus. The ball danced; the score soared.

'You go, girl!' Ken shouted, pride and disbelief mingling in his grin.

Three hundred thousand. Four. The machine sang; the crowd clapped in rhythm. And then, finally, the last ball slipped away.

Mags stood, breathing hard, face shining. 'That was the best moment of my life!'

Beth stepped back. Across the room, Jinnie caught her eye, an unspoken understanding passing between them. Cranley wasn't normal. It had magic stitched into its seams.

'Hey,' Ken said, taking his wife's hand, eyes glassy. 'I thought our wedding day was the best!'

She laughed, leaning against him, still glowing. Ken's quick glance towards Beth said everything. *You're a star.*

Beth blinked hard, turning back to the bar as chatter resumed and the world righted itself.

I'm here to serve, murmured Gigi's voice, oddly gentle, oddly proud.

'Does this bloody jukebox play The Beatles?' Jo called.

She dropped a few coins into the slot, and 'All You Need Is Love' filled the air.

Ken and Mags swayed into a slow dance, the pub crowd smiling, glasses raised.

Beth leaned against the bar, the warmth of it all soaking into her bones. For once, she didn't overthink or analyse. She simply watched, smiled, and let herself believe – if only for tonight – that maybe Gigi was right.

Maybe love really was all you needed.

Chapter Forty-Two

In just a few days, Kieran had gathered more feedback on his app than he'd dreamed possible. Notes, ideas, wild suggestions, all bouncing round his brain like, well, a pinball machine.

He frowned. *Why did I think of a pinball machine?*

Why do you think? That voice again.

'Oh, for God's sake,' he muttered, rubbing his temples. He'd even Googled *voices in the head* and instantly regretted it. Schizophrenia, bipolar, PTSD, extreme stress – basically, a buffet of doom.

'I'm fine. A bit stressed, Prom, but that's all.'

Prom, stretched across the rug like an emperor in repose, flipped onto his back. Kieran rubbed his belly – more therapy for the cat than him.

Still, beneath the banter, a small ache lingered. He hadn't spoken to Beth since the ClosetAura event. Maybe he'd imagined the spark, the easy laughter, the current between them. Maybe she'd changed her mind.

Stop overthinking and live in the moment, the inner voice said, surprisingly gentle this time.

He tried. The moment involved clearing debris from the kitchen table before his visitors arrived.

Heather, Charlie, Jacob, and baby Ellie exploded into the cottage mid-morning, a whirlwind of chatter, buggies, and nappy bags.

'Give us a hug!' Heather cried, pulling him close. 'Good grief, you smell like my gran's sideboard.'

'Lavender air freshener,' Kieran said. 'I overdid it. Thought it would be soothing. Turns out it's more "funeral home chic".'

'Nice,' said Charlie, adjusting the sling that held Ellie. 'No hug from me, unless you fancy crushing my daughter.'

Jacob had already upended a bucket of Lego onto the floor.

'Jacob!' Heather groaned.

'It's fine,' said Kieran, crouching beside the boy. 'I used to love Lego. Fancy building something together?'

Jacob grinned. 'A rocket! With aliens!'

'Now you're talking.'

Lunch was pleasant chaos – supermarket sandwiches, hummus, pork pies, and endless toddler commentary.

'Do you have crisps?' Jacob asked solemnly.

'I do,' said Kieran. 'Badger poop, snail slime, or cowpat flavour. Chef's special.'

Jacob wrinkled his nose. 'That's *gross*! Wait … are you joking?'

'Always,' said Charlie. 'Kieran's the silliest man I've ever met – and I've met myself.'

Heather snorted. 'And he's lucky enough to be married to me, despite his silliness.'

'So far,' Charlie said.

'Fuck off,' retorted Heather, before clamping her hand over her mouth. 'Jacob, don't you dare!'

Too late. The word flew gleefully around the table.

Later, while Heather fed Ellie and Charlie made tea, Kieran helped Jacob piece together the rocket. The boy's tongue poked out in concentration, chubby fingers fitting the plastic with precision.

Kieran felt something unfurl inside him: sudden, sharp, undeniable.

I'd like children.

The thought landed like lightning. And this time the voice in his head wasn't the strange one. It was his own.

'You all right there?' Heather crouched beside him, then yelped as she knelt on a stray brick. 'Ow! These things are medieval torture devices.'

Kieran laughed, helping her up. 'So parenthood's not all soft play and cupcakes.'

'No,' she said, glancing at Jacob, who was humming happily. 'But it's worth every Lego bruise.'

He smiled. 'You've got two gorgeous kids and a husband who's definitely punching.'

Charlie lobbed a pork pie at his head. Kieran caught it and handed it to Jacob.

'Thanks!' said Jacob, taking a huge bite.

A few minutes later, Heather tilted her head towards the hallway. 'Come on, Mr App Developer. Time to talk.'

Kieran followed, braced for interrogation. Heather had perfected the *don't mess with me* stare years ago.

'Level with me,' she said. 'Lisa's history – hallelujah – but something's going on. Spill.'

Where to start? He'd moved to Cranley broken-hearted, met Beth, laughed again for the first time in months, and somehow, started to…

He realised too late that he'd said it out loud.

'You're in love with Beth?' Heather blinked. 'Oh, Kieran. You're a cliché with Wi-Fi.'

'No, I said "the best" – like, life is the best—'

'Nope. You said Beth. Don't try to fool me: I've had two pregnancies and a husband who hides biscuits in the car.'

He opened his mouth to reply, but Jacob yelled from the living room. 'Kieran! My spaceman's head's gone!'

'Go,' said Heather, smiling now. 'For the record, Lisa's fine. Saw her yesterday. She did a little fake cry about you dumping her, mascara untouched. She's already latched on to a guy who looks like Yoda.'

Kieran blinked. 'Well, that's … oddly comforting?'

'You've had a lucky escape,' Heather said. Then, more softly, 'Beth sounds like the real deal, you know. You'd be good together.'

He didn't answer, because he already knew she was right.

By late afternoon, the cottage looked like a Lego bomb site. They packed it away, and Kieran found a box to carry the rocket in.

'We'll build another when we visit next time,' Jacob declared, wrapping his small arms around Kieran's neck.

'Deal,' said Kieran, throat tight.

'You've got a friend for life,' said Charlie. 'Two, actually. Four, if you count this one.' He nodded at Ellie, now burbling in Heather's arms.

'We're always here,' said Heather. 'Through thick and thin. Though right now I'm more thick than thin.'

'You're beautiful,' chorused Kieran and Charlie.

'Fuck off,' said Heather. Then, hastily, 'Jacob, don't—'

'Fuck off, fuck off, fuck off!' sang Jacob as they waved goodbye.

Kieran leaned against the door, laughing until the sound caught in his chest. The house felt quiet again: almost too quiet.

You'd make a great daddy.

He froze. Not from fear this time, but from the truth of it.

He sat on the sofa, picking up a single red Lego brick. Fatherhood had never seemed real: not with Lisa, not even in daydreams. But with Beth…

He could imagine it. A home that smelled of soup and joy, of laughter and life.

It takes only the right coupling. Trust me.

'Not helping,' he muttered, but he smiled all the same.

He cleared the plates, stepped squarely on a Lego brick, and yelped. 'Ow! Bloody—'

Language, the voice teased.

'Fuckety fuckety fuck,' Kieran said, through gritted teeth, then laughed until his sides ached. And wished Beth was with him to share the moment.

Chapter Forty-Three

The pub was never truly silent. Even at two in the morning, when Ed and Angela had long gone upstairs and the beer taps gleamed in the half-dark, The Jekyll and Hyde retained a heartbeat. Old beams settled, pipes creaked. The ghost of a thousand conversations clung to the walls like mist.

Beth tiptoed across the wooden floor, her footsteps careful, as though she might wake the building itself. The only light came from the green glow of the emergency-exit sign, casting long shadows that made the room look bigger, or emptier. She wasn't sure which.

Her gaze drifted to the pinball machine. The Wish Master, although Beth hadn't mastered the art of making wishes. She still couldn't believe that Gigi's own wish, to be centre stage in the pub, had been granted.

Now, in the hush of near darkness, the machine looked dormant, the brass trim catching faint glimmers of light. The genie on the back glass looked half-mocking, half-inviting.

Beth swallowed. 'I must be mad,' she whispered.

'You say that as if it's a bad thing.'

Gigi's voice floated out of the shadows moments before he shimmered into existence, perched cross-legged on top of the machine like a disco Buddha. Tonight, his waistcoat was magenta sequins, his trousers a violent electric blue. He sparkled like a feverish dream.

'Sweetheart,' he said, 'you could at least knock.'

'I wasn't expecting you' – Beth gestured helplessly at him – 'to appear when it's unplugged.'

'Unplugged?' Gigi scoffed. 'Please. Don't you remember our early encounters? Anyway, technology is a suggestion, not a boundary.'

She sighed, rubbing her temples. 'I can't sleep.'

'Oh, lucky me.' Gigi fluttered his eyelashes. 'Tell Uncle Gigi everything.'

'I'm not calling you Uncle anything,' Beth muttered. 'And I'm not here for therapy.'

'Darling, I'm the only therapist you can see at two in the morning without an appointment and a three-month wait. Start talking.'

Beth took a seat at one of the empty tables. The silence pressed in around her, heavy and familiar. She steadied her breathing. 'I think I'm falling for someone,' she said. The words felt foreign and frightening in her mouth.

Gigi's eyes widened. 'Oh my. Progress. Character development!'

'Don't start.'

'I wouldn't dream of it.' He pretended to zip his lips, then immediately unzipped them. 'Actually, I absolutely would, but continue.'

Beth's heart kicked against her ribs. 'It's Kieran.'

Gigi clutched his chest. 'The techie with the soulful eyes and tragic wallpaper? Thought so. Continue.'

'No. This is serious.'

'So am I. Occasionally.' He softened. 'What's the problem, sweetheart?'

Beth stared at the floor. 'I can't let this happen.'

'Why?'

'Because I'll break him. Or he'll break me. And I can't handle any more … loss.' Her voice thinned around the last word.

Gigi nodded, his expression gentler than she'd ever seen. 'Luke.'

The name sat between them like a ghost.

Beth's throat tightened. 'We tried so hard. Everything we did – the routines, the diets, the appointments, the endless injections and scans and hopes – it all fell apart. And he walked away. He walked away because he couldn't cope and… I can't blame him. I couldn't cope, either.'

Gigi hopped down from the machine with unexpected grace. He settled beside her, sequins dimming slightly, as though he could read the room.

'You didn't fail because you didn't love enough,' he said softly. 'You didn't fail at all. Bodies are messy. Life is unfair. None of that makes you less.'

Her eyes burned. 'I can't give Kieran a family. Not the way most people mean.'

'And who told you he wants that?'

'I don't know!' Beth's voice cracked. 'But if he does … if I let him in … and then I have to explain that I'm not capable … that I'm broken…'

'Stop that.' Gigi tapped her forehead lightly. 'Not broken: bruised. There's a difference. And bruises heal faster than you think.'

Beth let out a shaky breath.

He gave her a sidelong look. 'Besides, you've got two wishes left.'

Beth snorted. 'I don't even know if the first one counted.'

'It counted, trust me. Poorly executed, very emotionally charged, zero strategic planning. A classic first wish.' He ticked imaginary boxes. 'But wishes two and three? Those could be something else entirely.'

'Like what?'

'Wish two,' he said, raising a finger theatrically, 'could be for courage. To tell someone how you feel. To believe you deserve happiness. To stop sprinting away from babies like they're wailing, pooping monstrosities. Which most of them are. And – correct me if I'm wrong, which I never am – haven't you warmed to Dahlia and Ruairi?'

Beth nodded. 'But that doesn't mean everything's OK.'

'Noted. And wish three … ahhh.' He twirled, medallion flashing. 'Wish three could be what you truly need. Not what you think you need. There's a difference.'

'And what do I truly need?'

'Healing,' he said simply. 'The messy, complicated, gut-wrenching, wonderful kind.'

The words hit her with unexpected force. She blinked rapidly, willing the sting behind her eyes to recede.

Gigi smiled gently. 'Also, a decent night's sleep. But that might be beyond my magical remit.'

Beth gave a weak laugh. 'You're insufferable.'

'I know.' He winked. 'But I'm completely fabulous.'

A soft creak sounded above them. Footsteps. Someone moving quietly across the landing.

Beth froze.

Gigi put his head on one side. 'Well, are you going to wish for courage? It's time, Beth. Carpe diem.'

The footsteps paused near the top of the stairs.

Beth's pulse surged. She rose to her feet, wiping her damp palms on her jeans.

'Go on,' Gigi murmured, fading into a shimmer of sapphire smoke. 'Say it.'

Beth drew a breath. 'Don't I have to play first?'

Above, a familiar voice called softly, hesitant in the dark. 'Beth? Is everything OK?'

And the moment was lost.

For now.

Chapter Forty-Four

Sleep wasn't happening. Not properly.

Kieran had tried herbal tea, a breathing app with a voice like warm syrup, even a podcast about the history of toilets. Nothing worked. His brain refused to power down. It kept replaying Jacob's laugh, Heather's gentle teasing … and Beth's face every time he closed his eyes.

Prom had eventually given up on him and stalked off to the spare room, tail flicking in feline disgust.

'Traitor,' Kieran muttered, staring at the ceiling.

He lay there another minute, restless, his mind stubbornly orbiting Beth – her laugh, her steadiness, the quiet strength she wore so lightly. The faint scent of good food and her distinctive perfume seemed permanently embedded in his memory.

He grabbed his phone. The screen lit the dark.

6:15 a.m.

That's when he remembered.

His laptop charger. Still plugged in behind the bar at the Jekyll and Hyde after the app meet-up.

He did have a spare.

But still.

A slow smile tugged at his mouth. The perfect excuse. Not that he needed one.

He shoved on a hoodie, grabbed his keys, and stepped out into the thinning dark.

The village was hushed, wrapped in mist. A fox slipped across the road ahead of him, fluid and silent. Somewhere, an owl called once. The world felt paused, like it was waiting for something.

As he approached the pub, he noticed a faint glow through the downstairs windows. Not the full blaze of bar lights, but a soft amber pulse.

Someone was awake.

Hopefully Beth.

His heart gave a small, traitorous leap.

He hesitated outside, debating whether to knock or turn around and pretend he'd changed his mind. Then he heard her voice.

And another.

A man's?

No, lighter than that. Musical. Oddly familiar.

Kieran frowned. *Who is she talking to at this hour?*

There was a flicker of laughter, then silence.

He pushed the door gently. It wasn't locked.

'Beth?' he called quietly.

She spun around, eyes wide. 'Kieran! You scared the life out of me.'

'Sorry.' He lifted a hand. 'Didn't mean to barge in. I left my charger behind the bar after the app night. Thought I'd grab it before I run out of juice.'

Her shoulders eased, though a faint flush lingered in her

cheeks. 'Right. Of course. It's over there.' She gestured behind the counter.

He retrieved the cable but made no move to leave.

The air between them hummed – charged in a way that had nothing to do with electronics.

'Couldn't sleep either?' he asked.

She shook her head and tapped her temple. 'Too much noise in here.'

'Yeah,' he said. 'Same.'

Their eyes held. The quiet wasn't awkward – it was full. As if something hovered between them, waiting to be acknowledged.

He nodded toward the pinball machine. 'Is The Wish Master keeping you company?'

She glanced at it. 'Something like that.'

'Looks asleep.'

'You'd be surprised,' she murmured.

He wasn't entirely sure what that meant, but before he could ask, the moment shifted. He felt it – that tipping point where you either speak or spend weeks regretting not doing so.

'Beth,' he said, heart thudding, 'can I say something without it sounding weird?'

'That depends how weird.'

He let out a breath. 'I keep thinking about you. All the time. I don't want to complicate things. I know you've had a lot to deal with. But pretending I don't care isn't working.'

She blinked, clearly not expecting that.

He forced himself not to look away. 'I just needed you to know.'

She stepped closer. Not dramatically, just enough that he felt the warmth of her.

'You don't have to apologise for caring,' she said quietly.

Then she hesitated. 'But there's something you need to know before this goes any further.'

'OK.'

She held his gaze. No flinching.

'I can't have children.'

The words landed softly but heavily.

He hadn't expected that. Not specifically. But the steadiness in her voice told him how much it had cost her to say it.

He took a second. Not because he was shocked, but because he wanted to answer properly.

'Thank you for telling me.'

Her brow furrowed. 'That's it?'

'What were you expecting?'

'I don't know. Shock. Disappointment.'

He searched himself honestly. Yes, maybe he'd imagined a house full of noise, Lego underfoot, school runs and chaos. But right now, standing here with her, that future felt theoretical. Distant. Beth did not.

'You think that changes how I feel about you?' he asked gently.

'It might,' she said. 'For a lot of people.'

'I'm not a lot of people.'

The pinball machine gave a soft ping, as if punctuating the statement.

Beth rolled her eyes, though her lashes looked suspiciously damp. 'Ignore him. He's annoying.'

'Who?'

'It's a long story.'

He wanted to ask. He didn't.

Instead, he reached for her hand. When she didn't pull away, something inside him steadied. He stepped closer.

'You don't need to be perfect, Beth,' he said. 'You just need to be you.'

She went very still.

He became acutely aware of the space – or lack of it – between them. The warmth of her. The faint scent of soap and something unmistakably Beth. Her fingers in his.

'You all right?' he asked softly.

She nodded. 'Just … remembering how to breathe.'

He smiled before he could stop himself.

Her gaze flicked briefly to his mouth, then back to his eyes. His pulse kicked up.

'Beth,' he began, and then stopped.

Because this mattered.

If he moved now, it would be easy. Too easy. And he didn't want easy. He wanted right.

She stepped back half an inch, just enough to inhale deeply. 'We should…'

'Yes,' he agreed quickly. 'We should.'

Neither of them moved.

He scrubbed a hand over the back of his neck, suddenly aware of how exposed he felt. 'I'm glad you told me,' he said. 'About everything.'

'Me too.'

The look she gave him then wasn't fearful. It wasn't defensive.

It was hopeful.

That did it.

He closed the space carefully, giving her every opportunity to step away.

She didn't.

The kiss was gentle at first – tentative, like they were tuning into the same frequency. He felt the slight catch of her breath, the softness of her mouth. It deepened slowly, warmth unfurling instead of sparking. The world narrowed to the quiet hum of the pub and the steady beat of his own heart.

When they parted, she rested her forehead against his chest.

'I should probably say this complicates everything,' she murmured.

'Probably,' he said. 'But it also feels like the start of something.'

Across the room, the pinball machine flickered once – a soft golden pulse.

'You're impossible, Gigi,' she muttered.

He huffed a quiet laugh. 'What was that?'

'Nothing.'

He should go. He knew that. Give her space. Let this be for now.

'I should probably—'

'No one else will be awake for a while,' she said carefully. 'Would you like to come upstairs?'

His entire body answered yes.

He hesitated anyway.

'We don't have to … rush,' she added quickly. 'I don't want to ruin it.'

Relief softened something in him. 'Good. Because I was trying to work out how to say exactly that without sounding like a complete coward.'

Her lips twitched. 'You? A coward?'

'Terrified,' he admitted. 'But in a good way.'

Upstairs, they sat on the edge of the bed like teenagers who'd skipped ahead in the rulebook.

Eventually they lay down side by side, a polite gap between them.

It lasted seconds.

Her fingers brushed his. Paused.

Then she laced them through his.

'Is this OK?' she whispered.

'More than OK.'

He turned his head slightly, giving her space to reconsider.

She leaned in instead.

The kiss was softer this time. Less fire, more warmth. A question rather than an answer.

When they broke apart, she rested against him, tentative at first.

'Cuddling?' she asked.

'Absolutely.'

He wrapped his arm around her. She fitted against him with surprising ease, like something aligning. No urgency. No expectation. Just breathing, warmth, the steady rhythm of two people choosing to stay.

'You're very comfortable,' she murmured.

'I'm an excellent human pillow.'

Her quiet laugh vibrated against his chest.

In the dim early light, Kieran stared at the ceiling and understood something clearly:

Whatever this was – whatever it became – it was worth going slowly.

Chapter Forty-Five

Beth woke with the vivid memory of a kiss. Of kisses. Not dream kisses, not a figment of her imagination, but real ones. Warm, tender, still tingling on her lips.

Then came the panic. She sat upright in bed, hair sticking out like a well-used toilet brush.

'Oh God. Oh … God.'

Downstairs, the faint sounds of the pub waking filtered through the floor: Ed clattering glasses, the coffee machine sputtering to life, Angela whistling as she restocked the bar. And another voice. Not one she usually heard in the morning.

Beth pressed both hands to her face. She had kissed Kieran. Properly. And he had kissed her back.

A flutter of joy skittered through her, immediately chased down by dread. *What if he regrets it? What if I misread things? What if I said something ridiculous? What if Gigi—*

'Morning, sunshine.'

She screamed. Gigi was lounging against her wardrobe

in a silver kimono and fluffy slippers, sipping from a mug labelled *Wish You Were Here*.

'You nearly gave me a heart attack!'

'You're giving me grey hairs, sweetheart. But in a sexy, distinguished way.' He ran a hand through his immaculately groomed bouffant. 'I take it last night went well?'

Beth scrambled for her dressing gown. 'I don't want to talk about it.'

'Which means you absolutely want to talk about it. Come on, Uncle Gigi needs the gossip.'

'You are *not* my uncle.'

Gigi flopped on her bed, glitter puffing off him as if he'd been rolling in craft supplies.

'Fine, we'll skip to the highlights. Number one: you kissed him. Number two: he kissed you back. Number three: nobody spontaneously combusted, which frankly is a win, given your track record.'

She glared. 'Gigi, this is serious.'

'Darling, love always is.' He softened, slipping into that rare mode where he sounded older than the universe. 'What's bothering you? Apart from the obvious: fear of happiness, emotional intimacy, and communicating your needs to an attractive man?'

Beth groaned. 'All of it.'

Footsteps sounded on the stairs – light, bouncy, familiar.

Gigi wriggled his eyebrows. 'Speak of the techie.' His form dissolved into a shimmer of turquoise smoke.

A knock. 'Beth?' Kieran's voice: nervous, hopeful. 'Are you, um, awake?'

Her stomach somersaulted. She pulled herself together and opened the door just enough to peek out.

There he stood, a vision of messy hair and kind eyes that made something in her chest melt. 'Hi,' he said.

Just a word. But it hit her like a pulse of light.

'Hi.'

He rubbed the back of his neck. 'I didn't want to assume anything after last night. So I popped home while you slept to feed Prom. And now I'm back. Ed raised his eyebrows, but in a good way.'

Beth felt herself blush. 'You're not assuming wrong.'

'That's a relief,' he said with a smile.

For a moment they simply looked at one another, a fragile new world forming in the quiet.

'Do you want to go for a walk?' he asked. 'I know Ed's gearing up for a full Scottish breakfast and I thought … maybe some fresh air? You and me?'

Beth hesitated, but only for a second. 'Yes,' she said. 'I'd like that.'

Behind her, the faintest whisper of a voice curled through the air, smug and satisfied.

A wish for courage granted, sweetheart.

Chapter Forty-Six

Kieran had told himself he'd have an early night. Be sensible. Act like a man who wasn't running on caffeine, adrenaline and the quiet terror of getting things wrong.

Instead, he was hunched over his laptop at the kitchen table, shoulders pulled tight as if bracing against a knife in the back, eyes gritty and unfocused. The screen glowed back at him, unblinking, as he tweaked layouts and menus for ClosetAura – nudging buttons, reworking colour palettes, adding filters no one had explicitly asked for but everyone might secretly need.

Make it easy to navigate.

Make it budget friendly.

Make it something we really need in our lives.

The voices from the pub replayed, looping like feedback from a badly placed microphone.

He rubbed his face with both hands and stared at the screen again, willing it to make sense.

His eyes closed for a second.

Prom brushed against his ankles, the cat circling before

settling, purrs vibrating softly through the soles of Kieran's feet. The sound folded around him, familiar and oddly comforting.

Then the cottage wasn't the cottage anymore.

The air was thick and heavy, clinging to his skin. Heat pressed in from all sides. Sand shifted beneath his bare feet, warm and grainy, each step leaving an imprint that vanished almost immediately.

Music played somewhere nearby. Not pleasant, not melodic, but discordant, insistent. It crawled under his skin.

The smell of incense hung in the air, sweet and overpowering.

Lisa flickered across his mind uninvited, but the thought of her slid away just as quickly. Whatever this was, she didn't belong here.

'I'm asleep,' Kieran said, testing the words. They didn't echo.

'Welcome, Kieran,' said a voice. It was familiar. Unsettlingly so.

Footsteps crunched behind him.

'He hears it,' another voice said. High, quick, threaded with worry. Jinnie. Definitely Jinnie.

'Of course he does,' said Jo. She was calm, measured: the voice she used at the café when stress levels were high, and she'd burned a batch of something.

'Aye, but he's no' meant to yet,' Wilma snapped. 'Not without guidance.'

'Or maybe not at all,' Sam said softly. 'This is Beth's story, not his.'

Kieran spun round.

No one was there. Just the shimmer of extreme heat and vague shadows, figures suggested rather than formed, as if his mind refused to give them bodies.

'Hello?' His voice sounded wrong here. Too solid.

The sand gave way beneath his feet. He stumbled forward – and suddenly he was inside a building.

A corridor stretched ahead, impossibly long, its walls smooth and pale, the floor polished to a blinding sheen. His reflection warped beneath his feet as he walked. Overhead, a massive fan turned lazily, stirring the thick air.

The corridor opened into a vast room. At its centre stood a pinball machine. Not *the* pinball machine. And yet it was – but larger, taller, brighter. Its lights pulsed with a slow, steady rhythm that matched the beat of Kieran's heart. The familiar music grated at his nerves, louder here, distorted.

'Don't touch it,' Jinnie said sharply.

'Touch it,' Wilma countered immediately.

'Who's the demi-Djinn around here?' Sam muttered.

'Careful, love,' Jo said, and this time there was no mistaking the warning.

Kieran didn't mean to move, but his hand pressed the launch button anyway.

The ball shot up the channel. It wasn't the usual cheap silvery metal. It was gold. Warm, almost alive.

It struck the bumpers, and with each impact the room flashed.

The night of the storm at the pub.

Candles guttering.

Prom wearing a paper crown.

Beth's laugh.

Beth's mouth on his.

The score climbed. Faster. Faster.

A burning sensation crept into his wrists and his chest ached as if something inside him was being wound too tight.

'Stop,' he said, though he wasn't sure who he was talking to.

The glass rippled.

A face pressed through from the other side, the features forming slowly, deliberately. Amber eyes. A smile that knew too much. 'You wonder why you hear me,' it said.

The voices rose again, overlapping.

'He's not ready.'

'He will be.'

'You're already involved.'

'You always were.'

The machine shuddered violently. Lights flickered.

The face leaned closer, flattening against the glass until Kieran could see every line, every glint of amusement. 'You're closer than you think,' it murmured. 'And she's closer than she knows.'

The ball dropped. The music cut out. Darkness enveloped him.

Kieran gasped awake.

His chair scraped loudly against the floor. His heart pounded so hard it made him dizzy. His mouth tasted of metal, sharp and unpleasant.

The cottage was unchanged. Lights on, laptop open, cursor still blinking at the end of a line of code.

'It was just a dream,' he whispered.

Prom lifted his head from the windowsill, blinked slowly at him, then turned round and went back to sleep.

Kieran swallowed. Deep inside him, something stirred.

Not a voice.

Not a laugh.

Just the unsettling certainty that whatever he'd seen wasn't done with him yet.

Chapter Forty-Seven

Beth had burned the onions. Again. The air smelled rancid, the extractor fan failing to eliminate the stench.

She stared at the blackened pan and sighed. For someone supposedly good at cooking, she'd had some spectacular fails in the past few days.

'You're thinking about snogging, not sautéing.'

She didn't jump this time. Gigi's presence was both infuriating and comforting. Right now, it was the former.

'Go away,' she muttered under her breath.

'I am away. Technically, spiritually and emotionally.' Gigi lounged against the industrial oven, dressed like a low-budget 1940s film star with a paisley-patterned silk scarf round his neck. 'I'm just … observing.'

'You're haunting my kitchen.'

'I prefer the term *supervising*.'

Beth scooped out the onions and started afresh. Butter, this time, with a sprinkle of sugar. Gentler. Kinder. She needed gentle and kind today.

Her phone buzzed on the side. She wiped her hands and flipped it over. Diana. She read the message.

Morning, oh enigmatic one. Did you ask him out? Slip your tongue down his throat? Blink twice if yes xx

Beth huffed and typed back: *Might have. I'm wrangling burnt onions right now. Later xx*

A second later: *The way to a man's heart is through his stomach. Not sure burnt offerings count.*

Beth smiled despite herself.

The pub kitchen warmed as the lunch crowd began to turn up. Steak and ale pies slid into the oven. Soup simmered. Pastry cases lined up like obedient little soldiers. This was her rhythm: this was safe. And yet…

Her thoughts kept drifting.

Kieran's hesitant smile in the doorway. The way his hands had hovered, as if he was afraid to touch her and afraid *not* to. The warmth of him, solid and careful.

It scared her. Not because it felt wrong. Because it felt right.

'You're doing that thing,' Gigi said, leaning over the prep table. 'The frowny thing. The "I like him, but the universe will punish me" thing.'

'He's real,' Beth said quietly. 'This is real. But you're not. That's the problem.'

'Rude.'

'You're magic, Gigi. And he isn't.' She brushed pastry edges with beaten egg. 'I don't know where you end and life begins anymore.'

He tilted his head, oddly thoughtful. 'That's because you've never allowed yourself good things without paying a price for them.'

The lunch rush hit with relentless force. Ed shouting

orders, Rose clattering plates, Jo popping her head in to ask if she could 'borrow' a batch of sausage rolls.

Beth moved on instinct. Knife flashing, pastry folding, taste, stir, season.

Life felt normal again, almost.

Until she felt that faint vibration in the air. That prickle at the back of her neck.

Gigi drifted closer.

'Oh no,' she said quietly.

'Oh yes,' he whispered back. 'He's starting to feel it.'

'Feel what?'

'The edges of me. The corners of the truth. The bit you've been standing in all this time.'

Beth's hands stilled. 'What happens when he figures it out?'

Gigi looked gentle. 'People run,' he said. 'Or they stay.'

Beth slid a tray of pies into the oven, leaned against the counter. Wondered which kind Kieran would be.

Upstairs, wood creaked. Footsteps.

Not his: not now. But she felt him anyway.

Like a loose thread pulling, slowly, at her heart.

Chapter Forty-Eight

Kieran hadn't planned on going to the pub. He'd planned on making lunch, staring at his laptop and pretending the dream hadn't unsettled him in a way that felt far too real to be shrugged off with a cup of coffee and a cheese and ham toastie.

Snippets of the dream looped through his mind like a poorly edited film. He groaned, and Prom, unhelpful as ever, gave a disgruntled miaow.

It had started innocuously enough. A faraway land, exotic and unfamiliar. Then, the voices. Not loud. Not frightening. Just … recognisable.

Jinnie's practical tone, Jo's quiet sarcasm, Wilma's murmured asides, Sam's calm, thoughtful cadence. All talking about something he couldn't see. Except … he *had* seen something. Something close. Something connected with Beth. A pinball machine, that was it.

And he had heard another voice. Achingly familiar, yet also beyond his mental reach.

By the time Kieran reached the pub, his thoughts were a jumble of contradictions.

It was just a dream.

But what about the pinball machine?

Beth's behaviour is odd at times.

Strange things have happened in the pub.

You need a holiday.

The Jekyll and Hyde smelled of coconut milk and spices. A comforting, safe smell. The specials board promised Thai Green Curry with aromatic rice. No quirky name.

Beth appeared from the kitchen carrying plates, her hair pinned back loosely. She looked tired.

She looked gorgeous.

'Hi,' she said, when she spotted him.

'Hi yourself,' Kieran replied. 'Can a starving man get a plateful of Tantalising Thai Curry with a side of torture?'

Beth laughed. 'We're over the daft descriptions, in case you hadn't noticed. Simple is best.'

'Then I'm your man. Simple runs through me like water through a pipe. Which is a completely rubbish analogy.'

Beth nodded. 'Stick to what you're good at.'

'Have you got … a minute?'

She glanced towards the kitchen. 'I can steal one.'

They moved into a small room to the side – half pantry, half breathing space for staff. Its shelves were crammed with dried ingredients and jars containing unknown substances. A smell of paprika and washing-up liquid permeated the air.

Kieran ran a hand through his hair. In a film, it would look sexy. Right now, he suspected he resembled a well-used pot scourer. 'This might sound stupid.'

Her mouth curved faintly. 'Try me.'

'I fell asleep at my laptop last night. I was working on the app, trying to make it better.' He huffed out a breath. 'Trying to make *me* better.'

She didn't interrupt, just nodded for him to carry on. He liked that.

'I dreamed,' he said. 'But not like normal dreams. It felt … completely bonkers. As if a theatre group were improvising inside my head.'

'Didn't you once tell me that Kate Bush broke your sunglasses, and something else off the wall about Black Sabbath?'

Kieran shrugged sheepishly. 'I might have made that up. But this dream… It felt so real.'

Beth's shoulders stiffened.

'I could hear people. Conversations. Voices I don't even know how I recognised. People I barely know. Jinnie. Jo. Wilma. Sam.'

Beth said nothing, but her eyes widened.

'They were talking about Cranley. About something … old, I think. Or powerful. That's all I can remember. Not details, just the *feeling* of it.'

Kieran waited. Beth stayed silent.

'It made me feel like I'd walked into a story halfway through. Like I'm a bit-part player who doesn't know their lines or what they're supposed to do.'

Beth wrapped her hands around her mug. 'Strange things do happen here,' she said quietly.

'Like what?'

She paused. Her face was inscrutable: a bit like Yoda. Hard to understand, in a deliberately annoying way.

She glanced towards the stairs, then back at him. 'Electrical quirks. Machines not behaving normally.' A beat.

'That pinball table Ed dragged upstairs … it's temperamental.'

'Temperamental how?' Kieran felt lost, as if he'd been tossed into a turbulent river and forced to swim against the tide.

Her mouth tightened. 'Old wiring. Old parts.'

Not quite an answer, but he didn't push. Something in her eyes told him *not today*.

He rocked slightly on his heels. 'I just … needed to tell someone. It felt daft keeping it in.'

Her gaze lifted to his. 'You can always tell me.'

He felt that land somewhere deep. He moved a fraction closer. 'I don't feel daft when I talk to you.'

Beth brushed his cheek with her hand. 'I'll take that as a massive compliment, but I need to crack on now. There's a table of ten arriving in half an hour.'

Kieran took her hand and kissed it lightly. 'Go forth and feed the masses,' he said. 'If you're free later, do you fancy coming to my place?'

Beth bit her lip. Kieran's heart sank. *Too much, too soon.*

'Actually,' she said, 'it's looking quieter this evening. Let me have a word with Rose and see if she'll hold the fort.'

A minute later, Beth returned. 'All good. What time, and should I bring leftovers?'

Kieran grinned. 'Believe it or not, I can cook. Is seven OK?'

Beth nodded.

And Kieran practically skipped home, all thoughts of crazy dreams banished for now.

Chapter Forty-Nine

'Beth's got a date! Beth's got a date!' Gigi chanted like a naughty schoolboy, twirling a moustache he'd never sported before.

'Oh, shut up,' she retorted. 'It's just dinner at his cottage. No big deal.'

Gigi pursed his lips. 'Hmm. Dinner with a man at his place. Isn't that the definition of a date? And weren't *you* supposed to ask *him* out?'

'I never said that! Wait— Diana told me to ask Kieran out, which means…' Beth scowled at Gigi, who adopted a butter-wouldn't-melt expression.

'Sorry, not sorry.' He giggled. 'It's just too much fun tuning into your life, even the boring bits. And there are lots of those.'

Beth huffed out an exasperated breath. 'Well, I don't think it's *boring* that Kieran had a dream where the Cranley genie posse spoke to him. What do you make of that, oh wise one?'

Gigi frowned, giving his moustache another twirl. 'This

ridiculous thing' – he whipped out the WIFI gizmo – 'has been flashing like an overexcited traffic light for days. I think it's picking up some kind of signal within the village. Or it needs new batteries.'

Beth doubted a genie's wish-giving wand required AAs but hadn't the energy to discuss it. 'Right, I'm off,' she said. 'Please behave yourself. Poor Jimmy nearly had a heart attack when he played you the other day.'

'Pah, not my fault. It was only a teeny tiny electric shock. Serves him right for spilling whisky on me.'

As Beth headed to Kieran's cottage, she remembered how Gigi had granted her the wish of courage. Without needing to play pinball, but he made the rules. 'It's like *The Wizard of Oz,*' she mused. 'The Cowardly Lion got courage, the Tin Man a heart, and the Scarecrow a brain.'

Except they already possessed those things. They just didn't know it.

'Hi, and welcome to my humble abode.' Kieran beamed, taking Beth's jacket and pecking her on the cheek.

Courage.

Beth manoeuvred until their lips met and they kissed properly.

'Wow.' Kieran stepped back, his smile even wider than before. 'I may need a cold shower now.'

'Not until you feed me,' said Beth, sniffing the air. 'Something smells good.' She bent down to stroke Prom, who'd sauntered into the hallway.

'Alas, the cottage is more eau de damp, and Prom isn't necessarily the most fragrant puss on the planet.'

As if wounded by the words, Prom strutted off.

Beth slumped on the sofa. 'What's on the menu?'

Kieran looked sheepish. 'Mince and tatties.'

'A true Scottish classic.' Beth's stomach growled. 'Sorry, forgot to have lunch. Or breakfast.'

Seated at the tiny table in Kieran's kitchen, Beth's mouth watered at the steaming pan of seasoned mince, topped with fluffy dumplings and awaiting a side of buttery mash.

'If Rose ever gets sick, you can stand in,' she said when Kieran served up the food.

Kieran topped up her glass of red. 'This is one of three recipes my mum taught me. The other two are spaghetti bolognese and beef stew. So I'm glad you're not vegetarian.'

They chatted easily. About Kieran's app, Beth's best friend Diana, Charlie's daily message updates on baby Ellie.

'He sends pictures,' said Kieran. 'Gross ones. Poop and stuff. Oh, sorry – probably not the best dinner-table conversation.'

Beth steadied her breath. Talk of babies wouldn't freak her out. She inhaled her new-found courage and embraced the here and now. With Kieran, in his cottage, which…

'Doesn't your cottage have a name?'

'Is it illegal not to?'

Beth laughed. 'No, but a place like this deserves a name. Not a number.'

'Won't that confuse the postman or woman? If I go from being number six to *The Wee Scruffy Hoose*?'

'My place was – is – called Bilberry Cottage.'

'Nice name. Although I have no idea what bilberries are. Would you like to name this place?'

Beth pretended to ponder the question. Then she leant in for a kiss. A mince-and-tatties flavoured kiss. 'Let me think about it.'

Kieran cleared up, shooing Beth into the living room

with a mug of coffee and a box of chocolates. She nudged a snoozing Prom to one side, and he crept onto her lap.

Cottage names ran through her head. She leaned back, feeling cosy and safe. Where she wanted to be, with someone who made her feel … what?

Don't over analyse, Bethikins.

'I'm not,' she murmured sleepily.

Prom purred. Beth drifted off, into that state between wakefulness and sleep. Until…

Kieran's voice. In the kitchen, talking low, as if he was on the phone and didn't want to disturb her. 'I don't want to mess it up this time.'

She leaned forward and picked up the cooling mug.

'No, not like with Lisa. I just… I know what I want more now.'

A faint murmur from the other voice, too quiet for her to make out.

'I want something steady. Not chaos, not drama. I want a proper life, mate. Like you.'

Beth sensed rather than knew he was talking to Charlie. She didn't want to eavesdrop, but she couldn't help herself.

'A home. A future. I want kids one day, a proper life … a family. But it's complicated.'

The world tilted on its axis. Beth placed the mug on the table with a shaking hand.

Kieran gave a small, breathless laugh. 'Yeah, I know. Shocks me, too.'

Beth stuck her fingers in her ears like a child. *Like a child.*

Her body made the decision before her mind. Carefully, she tiptoed into the hallway. Found her jacket, slipped out.

On the street, she fought back tears. For what she'd already lost. For what might have been.

She waited for a whispered word of comfort from Gigi.

Silence.

Courage. Well, she'd shown a distinct lack of it there. Instead of staying and confronting Kieran, she'd once again bolted like a startled horse.

Stumbling towards the pub, she remembered a ceramic heart Diana had given her one birthday. It had hung in Bilberry Cottage once: now it was probably lost.

'Courage is the small, stubborn light inside you that whispers *not yet* when the world says *enough*.'

'Not ever,' Beth muttered, and flung up her head. Much as she wanted to throw herself onto her bed and howl like a banshee, she had work to do.

She glowered at the pinball machine, ignored the customers and stomped into the kitchen.

She was reorganising the cutlery drawer for the umpteenth time when Kieran appeared. She kept her head down. Rose, who'd been making a bechamel sauce, slunk off.

'Are you OK?' Kieran asked gently.

'Fine.' She tossed a pile of forks into their compartment with a satisfying clatter.

He stepped forward, grabbed spoons and mimicked Beth's action. 'You took off without saying goodbye. And I had cherry cheesecake for dessert. Which I also made myself, with a little help from Nigella.'

'Nigella Lawson works for you, does she? Impressive.' She hated her snarky tone. Hated how her heart pounded when Kieran was inches away.

'Gordon Ramsay turned me down. Beth, look at me, please.'

Beth looked at him. Silence stretched between them. She felt sick, stomach churning, mince and tatties threatening to make a reappearance.

He shifted closer. Not touching. 'Did I … do something?'

Beth swallowed. The drawer slid shut with a soft, final click. 'No.'

A big, fat lie.

Kieran watched her for a long moment. Beth kept her gaze steady, unblinking. She wouldn't cry. *Courage.*

'Right,' he said eventually, his voice gentle but confused. 'I'll … get out of your way.'

She heard his footsteps leave the kitchen. Her breath shuddered out, leaving her feeling hollow inside.

That night, alone in her room, Beth lay staring at the ceiling.

Kids. A proper life. A family.

She curled up, fists tucked under her chin. 'But I can't give you that,' she whispered into her pillow. 'Maybe you need to find someone who can. I'm so sorry.'

Downstairs, deep inside the pinball machine, something stirred.

But Beth didn't hear it. She heard nothing but the sound of her own sobs filling the room.

Chapter Fifty

Beth hadn't looked at Kieran properly since that night.

Scrub that. She'd actively ignored him.

Kieran drifted around the cottage, dodging the pile of laundry, the dishes piled in the sink, and the unfinished app work. Even Prom, perched on the arm of the sofa with his tail flicking in disapproval, seemed fed up.

'You think I should say something?' Kieran asked.

Prom blinked at him slowly. Judgement oozed from his furry frame.

Right. He paced the living room, feeling the cottage shrink around him. He could try the pub again, but the last two attempts had gone nowhere, and she'd ignored all his texts.

Kieran thought about how she'd disappeared. Left without a goodbye or explanation. He'd been chatting to Charlie about the future – kids, maybe, a family. The sort of conversation you only have with your best mate when you think no one else is listening.

But Beth had heard him. And she'd left.

'Idiot,' he muttered.

Prom yawned in agreement.

By evening he'd worked himself into a lather of self-loathing, so he headed to the pub.

'Hi.' Angela greeted him with a tight-lipped smile. *Great.* Kieran sensed he wasn't in anyone's good books at The Jekyll and Hyde. Even Jimmy at the bar side-eyed him – although that might have more to do with the whisky tumblers lined up in front of him.

Beth emerged from the kitchen, flushed and carrying a tray of food.

'All right?' he asked.

'Yep,' she said, striding past.

He waited till she'd delivered the food before approaching her. Tentatively, in case she whacked him over the head with the tray.

'I'm busy,' she snapped.

'Beth, I know I've upset you. And I think I know what happened.'

Tension prickled the air, sticky and uncomfortable.

'I think you heard something the other night,' he said, finally. 'Something that sounded … bigger than it was.'

Beth's shoulders tensed, but she didn't move away.

'What I said to Charlie, I meant it in theory,' he went on. 'Like saying I might climb the Munros one day. All 282 of them. Obviously, not *all* in one day.'

Beth's mouth twitched a fraction. She nodded towards a quiet area of the bar and set the tray down on a nearby table, fingers lingering on the edge as if she needed something solid.

'You weren't wrong,' she said suddenly. 'About kids.'

Kieran frowned. 'Beth—'

'No. Let me.' She drew in a breath that shook on the

way out. 'It's what I've always wanted.' A brittle smile flickered and vanished. 'I just don't get to have it.'

The words landed between them, heavy and final. 'When I heard you—' She gestured vaguely, unable to finish.

Kieran stepped closer, instinctively, then stopped himself, letting her set the distance.

'I'm not broken,' she added, her voice firm now, as if she'd rehearsed the words a thousand times. 'But I am *done.* And I can't be the reason for someone to give up the life they want.'

Silence stretched. The pub rumbled on, oblivious.

Kieran swallowed. 'Beth. I haven't forgotten what you told me. Not for a second. But the life you're imagining, it's not a dealbreaker. It's not even the deal.'

Her brows knitted together, disbelief warring with hope.

'I don't want a checklist future,' he said. 'I want *you.* Exactly as you are.' He paused, then added softly, 'Anyone who makes you feel love is conditional on what your body can do is stupid. Dumb, and very, very stupid.'

Her eyes shone, furious and wet. 'You really mean that?'

'I really do. I wasn't saying that I need children to feel complete. And there are other ways, by the way. Which I know you know. I was just babbling to Charlie, that's all. And I'm so sorry that I upset you.'

Beth nodded, brimming eyes fixed on Kieran.

He took a step closer. Not too close: just enough that she'd hear him without straining. 'I don't know what my future looks like yet,' he said. 'Does anyone, really? But nothing I said meant you're in the way of it. You're … the bit that makes it make sense.'

'I didn't want to be a problem,' she said quietly.

'You're not something I have to work around, like my stupid app,' he replied. 'You're someone I want to be with.'

A faint, wobbly laugh escaped her. 'You're terrible at timing, you know.'

'Consistently.'

Another pause. Then she stepped forward a fraction, enough for her forehead to rest lightly against his. He didn't move, didn't push, just breathed with her in the low rhythm of the pub.

'By the way.' Beth's breath warmed his cheek. She stiffened slightly, as if her next words might seem flippant. 'Your cottage has a name now.'

'Really?' Kieran raised an eyebrow. 'Does it have anything to do with berries?'

She gave him a small, shy smile that punched him in the ribs. 'Now I've visited it… Whiskers Rest.'

Kieran's chest warmed in a way he hadn't expected. 'Whiskers Rest,' he repeated. 'Prom will love that.'

'It suits him. It feels right.'

It did. More than he'd admit. And for the first time since Beth had walked out on that conversation, she didn't look as if she was about to disappear.

Chapter Fifty-One

Beth had rehearsed the words half a dozen times on her walk from the kitchen to the pub garden.

No. More than half a dozen. She'd gone through versions ranging from breezy – 'Hey, funny story' – to mildly deranged – 'So, you know how life sometimes hands you a magical crisis?' – to downright cowardly – 'Have you ever considered moving to Australia?' None of them seemed remotely suitable.

You thought you'd told him the hardest thing of all, but this will send him screaming for the hills.

But if she wanted to make this work, she needed to be completely honest.

Kieran was waiting at one of the picnic benches, jacket zipped to his chin, two flasks in front of him. Steam curled into the cool afternoon air, mingling with the faint aroma of chips drifting from the kitchen.

He smiled when he saw her. A warm smile. A filled-with-love smile.

A smile that made Beth's heart expand and panic in equal measure.

'Thought you might need this,' he said, nudging a flask towards her. 'You sounded stressed when you called. I thought of lacing the coffee with rum, but as you're working…'

Beth would kill for a shot of something alcoholic, but she needed a clear head. 'Thank you. Getting blind drunk might not be a good idea.'

Kieran sipped his coffee, clearly unnerved by Beth's demeanour.

She took a deep breath. *Right.* She needed to do this. She needed to stop lying by omission. She needed to—

'Kieran,' she blurted, 'you know how weird things have been happening?'

His brow creased. 'Weird how?'

'Lights flickering. Odd noises. Music starting up on its own. The pinball machine doing things that defy every known law of physics, and possibly a few unknown ones.'

'Right,' he said slowly. 'And you think … what? That your pub is haunted?'

'No!' Beth winced. 'Well, sort of. Not haunted. More … occupied.'

'Occupied,' Kieran repeated. 'By…?'

Beth opened her mouth. And of course – of *course* – that was when the pub lights flickered, the jukebox inside the bar whirred to life and the first ominous bars of 'I Put a Spell on You' blasted through the open door.

Kieran's head jerked round. 'Did you—'

'No,' Beth said quietly. 'I didn't.'

'Then who…?'

A small puff of sapphire smoke drifted into the beer garden, curled in a perfect spiral over Kieran's flask, and shaped itself – unmistakably – into a chubby, glowing hand giving a jaunty wave.

Kieran froze.

The hand vanished.

'Right,' he said faintly. 'That wasn't steam, was it?'

Beth felt her stomach drop. This was it. No backing out now.

'Kieran, I need to tell you something. I've been dealing with it for weeks, and it'll sound mad. Completely bat-shit mad. Please don't run away, call a doctor or suggest I take up meditation.'

He stared at her, wide-eyed, waiting.

'I…' She swallowed. 'There's a genie in the pub.'

Silence. Actual, honest-to-God silence.

'A genie,' Kieran said.

'Yes.'

'As in magic lamp, wishes, Aladdin. *That* kind of genie?'

'More sequins, less Disney,' Beth muttered. 'But yes.'

Kieran blinked at her. Twice. Then he rubbed his face with both hands. 'Beth…'

'You think I'm joking,' she said miserably.

'No,' Kieran replied, surprising her. 'I think I'm having a stress-induced hallucination. But if I'm not… Could you possibly clarify what you mean by "a genie" before I lose my bloody mind?'

She took a breath. Time to rip off the plaster.

'He lives in the pinball machine. His name is Gigi. He granted me a wish. A few wishes. Sort of. It's complicated. And he might have … occasionally … interfered in your head.'

'Interfered in my—' Kieran's eyes widened still further. 'The voice!'

'Yes,' she said quietly. 'The voice.'

'The one that calls me "handsome" and tells me to lighten up?'

Beth grimaced. 'That sounds like him.'

Kieran leaned back, staring at the sky as if hoping for written instructions.

'OK,' he said eventually. 'Right. There's a genie in the pub. In a pinball machine. And he's been … chatting to me.'

'Yes.'

'Bloody hell.'

'You're taking this better than I expected,' Beth admitted.

'I'm not sure I am,' he said. 'I'm just delaying the freak-out.'

Before she could respond, a camp, disembodied voice drifted from the doorway: 'You're welcome, darling.'

Kieran yelped.

Beth groaned. 'Gigi, go away!'

'I can't help it if the man radiates confusion,' Gigi said breezily. 'Honestly, you humans take everything so literally. "Oh no, the genie is meddling again." Well, yes. That's literally my job.'

'GO,' Beth snapped.

A beat of silence, followed by a wounded sniff. 'Rude,' Gigi muttered, before vanishing with a faint crackle.

Kieran stared at the empty space where the smoke had been. Then at Beth. Then at his coffee.

'You have a genie,' he said, faintly. 'A real genie.'

She nodded.

His gaze softened, confusion giving way to something like understanding. 'And you've been dealing with that alone?'

Beth's throat tightened. 'I didn't know how to tell you.'

Kieran reached across the table, covering her hand with his. 'Beth … you could have told me anything.'

A wave of emotions rushed through her. A mixture of relief, fear and hope. 'Are you … all right?' she whispered.

'No,' he said bluntly. 'But I'm here. And I'm not going anywhere.'

She managed a shaky smile. Then, without knowing why, she sprang away. 'I have to go. Now. Immediately.'

'Go where?' Kieran tried to grab her hand, but she dodged him.

'I need answers. They're waiting for me. I'm so sorry.' And she took off, running as if the hounds of hell were snapping at her heels.

'Beth, wait!'

But Beth kept running until Kieran's shouts faded and she was alone.

Chapter Fifty-Two

How did I get here?

Beth looked down at her feet. Normal, unassuming feet, clad in comfortable, trusty trainers. She half-expected to see little wings attached, like Hermes in Greek mythology. But no. Just bog-standard footwear.

'Hi, Beth.' Jinnie stood in the doorway, her face showing zero surprise at Beth's appearance. She turned. 'Sam, Beth's here,' she called.

Sam appeared behind her, holding a wine glass like a small emotional support object. 'Come in,' he said. 'We've just opened some wine. I've a feeling we might need it.'

Beth stepped inside. She bent to remove her trainers, but Jinnie waved her on. 'No need, unless you've trodden in a cowpat. Which seems unlikely, given the complete absence of cows. Unlike genies.'

Sam cleared his throat. 'Sweetheart…'

Beth followed them into a large, warm kitchen. Gleaming appliances, a double oven, granite worktops: the sort of space that screamed *life sorted*. In normal circumstances, she'd have taken time to swoon over it. Tonight, it barely registered. 'I suppose you know why I'm here,' she said.

'We do,' said Jinnie gently.

Beth jumped as Jo and Wilma entered behind her. Wilma was holding Dahlia, who chose that moment to announce her digestive opinions loudly.

Wilma tutted. 'Timing's impeccable. Back in a minute.'

Beth sat at the table, accepted a glass of red she hadn't asked for, and stared at it as if it might explain things. 'I feel as if I've wandered into a very strange cocktail party,' she said. 'And I don't remember agreeing to come.'

Jo smiled wryly. 'That'll be the genie.'

Beth swallowed. 'Is it usually a man?'

'Yours?' Wilma asked, returning with a freshly changed Dahlia. 'Definitely. Only men announce themselves like that.'

'His name's Gigi,' Beth said weakly. 'He lives in a pinball machine.'

Wilma barked a laugh. 'That's new. Ours were lamps. Very traditional.'

Beth stared at them. 'So you all had one.'

Jinnie nodded. 'Yes.'

'And they don't hang around forever,' Jo said softly. That landed harder than anything else so far.

Beth set her glass down carefully. 'What happened to yours?'

There was a pause. A collective, unspoken agreement.

'They helped,' Jo said, finally. 'In strange ways. Then they went.' She paused. 'I got a day with my parents again,' she added. 'Just one, but it was enough.'

Beth felt something twist in her chest.

Wilma shifted Dahlia higher on her shoulder. 'Mine was

a menace,' she said briskly. 'A baby with an appetite like a horse. But in the end, I didn't want wishes. I wanted peace.'

Peace. Beth thought of Gigi's grin. His singing. The way he'd threaded himself into her thoughts and manoeuvred his way into Kieran's.

'Did anyone else know?' she asked. 'About the genies?'

They all shook their heads.

'Then why does Kieran?' The words tumbled out. 'Why him?'

No one answered straight away.

'Some people are more … receptive,' Jinnie said eventually.

'And some are gloriously oblivious,' Wilma added. 'Gus wouldn't spot a genie if it danced naked in front of him.'

Beth barely smiled.

'We thought it was over,' Sam said, twisting the stem of his glass between his fingers. 'When they left.'

'But now Gigi's here,' Beth said. 'And you think he'll leave too.'

Sam met her eyes. 'We don't know. But … there are signs.'

'Like what?' Beth demanded.

Wilma shrugged. 'My teapot vibrated.'

'I dreamt Cranley got swallowed by a glittery black hole,' said Jo.

Beth stared. 'That's it?'

Sam spread his hands helplessly. 'It's never clear-cut.'

Something inside Beth cracked. 'I don't want him to go,' she whispered. 'He's mine.' The thought surprised her with its ferocity.

A low croon brushed her mind. A familiar Sinatra song about the end being near.

'Did you make a wish?' Jo asked gently.

Beth nodded. 'I asked for a sign that life can be good.'

'And?'

'I saw the most beautiful butterfly.'

Wilma snorted. 'Gus saw one too. Thought it was a moth escaping his wallet.'

'Gran!' Jinnie hissed.

'Did you make another wish?' Jo asked.

Beth's hands began to shake. 'I think so. I asked for courage. But I don't feel very brave right now.'

Images flooded her mind. Leaving Bilberry Cottage, arriving in Cranley, panicking about the job, reacting badly to babies. Luke, the pinball machine, Gigi … and Kieran.

Wilma's eyes narrowed. 'Ah.'

'What?' Beth said sharply.

'You're in love, lass.'

'No, I'm not.'

Wilma tutted. 'Your aura's glowing golden and brighter than a bonfire on Guy Fawkes Night.'

Love burns inside you. Never extinguish the flame.

Beth tried to stand, but her legs gave way. Jo caught her as she folded, arms firm and steady.

'He knew,' Beth sobbed. 'Gigi knew all along.'

'Of course he did,' Wilma said softly, patting her back. 'Genies have a habit of seeing straight through us.'

Sam cleared his throat. 'Right, who needs another drink?'

Beth clung to Jo, grief and hope tangled together, knowing one terrifying yet wonderful thing for certain.

Whatever happened next, she wouldn't face it alone.

Chapter Fifty-Three

Kieran had created a clothing app from nothing. Built it from the ground up, often doubting himself, but stubborn enough to keep going. He trusted logic. Cause and effect. Coding, calculations and cold, hard facts. He knew the difference between a minor glitch and a system failure.

So a genie in a pinball machine should have been easy to dismiss, right? Because nothing about Gigi complied with logic. Every ounce of Kieran's being told him that genies didn't exist.

And yet…

He sat at the small table in his kitchen, Beth's words drifting through his head like snow he couldn't brush away. She hadn't been dramatic, hadn't tried to persuade him. Just told him plainly, as if she were discussing the weather.

He lives in the pinball machine. His name is Gigi. He granted me a wish. A few wishes. Sort of. It's complicated. And he might have … occasionally … interfered in your head.

She'd looked relieved when she said it. Not unhinged or

fanciful, just relieved to have shared her fantastical story. And she'd chosen to share it with him.

That was the part he couldn't shake.

He turned his mug between his hands, watching the tea ripple. If Beth had exaggerated like Lisa used to, he'd have clocked it instantly. But Beth was careful. Measured. Sometimes painfully honest.

And she was frightened. Not of the genie, exactly, but of what came after. Of what the wishes would cost. Of endings.

'Right,' he muttered. 'Magic's real.'

Prom sat on the windowsill, licking a paw, entirely unconcerned.

The signs lined up, now that he let himself see them. The hesitations, as if Beth were listening to someone else. Her odd reaction to the basement. The strangeness at the pub quiz and the open mic night. Things he'd dismissed because they didn't fit.

What unsettled him most wasn't the genie. It was the sense that Beth was standing at the edge of something, and he didn't know whether he was meant to follow or simply watch.

He cared about her. That was no longer up for debate.

Then his mind returned, unbidden, to the other truth she'd shared with him: the miscarriages, and the heartache that had followed. What that could mean to someone else. Someone like him.

Only now did he understand what she might fear people seeing. Damage, limitation, terms and conditions.

The thought tightened his chest.

Children had always been theoretical to him: a future he hadn't interrogated too closely. Beth wasn't theoretical: Beth was here. Real. The idea that her losses might make her less to him felt not just wrong, but ridiculous.

That part of her story wasn't something to weigh or negotiate. It simply was. And it changed nothing about how he felt.

What mattered was Beth, sitting at his table. Trusting him with the truth. But this wasn't something he could control.

'What happens next?' he asked the empty kitchen.

No answer came. But the question refused to settle.

If wishes were real, then endings were, too.

He went upstairs on autopilot, but sleep didn't come easily. The house creaked and settled. Prom curled against his legs, solid and warm.

Beth filled his thoughts. Her restraint, her careful distance. Not a fear of being hurt, he realised, but fear of hurting him.

The understanding arrived fully formed and undeniable.

He loved her.

Not dramatically. Not recklessly. But in a way that meant staying when things became complicated. And things *were* complicated.

Beth had trusted him. Chosen him. Out of everyone, she'd told him the truth. Not because he could fix it, but because she didn't want to carry it alone. That mattered.

He reached for his phone, then stopped. *Tomorrow*, he thought.

And then the word curdled. Tomorrow felt inadequate. Cowardly. Beth wasn't waiting for tomorrow. She was somewhere *now*, standing at the centre of whatever was happening. And if something was ending – if wishes were running out – then he was already late.

Kieran sat up sharply, heart thudding.

Sam and Jinnie's. The certainty hit him with the same instinct he trusted when a system was about to fail.

Beth was there. And something was happening to Gigi.

He didn't overthink it. He pulled on yesterday's jumper, grabbed his keys and coat.

Prom lifted his head, offended.

'Sorry,' Kieran murmured, closing the door.

The night air felt charged as he locked the door behind him. He ran, then forced himself to slow. This wasn't about rescuing anyone. It was about showing up.

Sam and Jinnie's house glowed warm against the dark. Without hesitating, he pushed at the unlocked door and stepped inside. Immediately he felt it – the sense of something wrong, something off-kilter.

Beth stood apart from the others, arms folded, eyes fixed on the corner of the room.

The genie – Gigi – shimmered there, faintly. Small. Like a star about to go out.

Kieran crossed the room and stood beside her. He didn't speak, didn't touch her. Just stood close enough to be felt.

Beth's hand slid into his, trembling.

This was the moment. Not about wishes, explanations, or even goodbyes. Just the choice to be here for whatever came next.

If some kind of magic ended tonight, then whatever followed, one thing was certain.

Kieran wasn't going anywhere.

Chapter Fifty-Four

'I don't want you to leave!'

Beth sobbed as Gigi shimmered in front of them. Like a badly pixellated film, he faded in and out of view.

'But it's time, Bethikins. Wishes almost granted, happy-ever-afters cooking like gas, and all that jazz.'

Sam stepped forward. 'Do I need to perform some ritual? Please say no.'

Jinnie tugged at Sam's arm. 'I think this time, Gigi gets to do his own thing. Right, Gigi?'

'Does this mean he'll be shacking up with Dhassim, Aaliyah and DJ?' Wilma cackled. 'Rather him than me, although I do sometimes miss the lad.'

'I do not know where I am destined to go,' said Gigi, cheeks wobbling with emotion. 'Maybe a lava lamp, Beth?'

Beth choked back a soggy giggle. Kieran squeezed her hand.

'Ach, the auras are all over the shop tonight,' Wilma said to Jo, who shrugged. 'Purple, pink, grey, a touch of orange.

That's a new one. Have you been dipping into the fake tan, Gigi?'

The madness of it all threatened to derail Beth. She'd moved to Cranley with a broken heart, met a genie, been granted three wishes and found Kieran. Sweet, lovely, honest Kieran, who'd put her back together. Like a reverse Humpty Dumpty.

'So, what happens next?' asked Kieran.

Jo finally spoke. 'Shouldn't you play one last time, Beth?'

No one replied, but the room thrummed with pulsating energy. The pinball machine appeared, as solid as the first time she'd seen it. Right there, in Sam and Jinnie's living room.

'Can I, Gigi?'

All eyes turned to Beth. She opened her hand, showing a gold coin in her palm. Their mutual gaze shifted to an ethereal butterfly, fluttering above her head.

'Of course.' Gigi settled cross-legged on top of the pinball machine. The epitome of calm, albeit calm with a sense of closure.

Beth played like she'd never played before. Fingers flying, flippers working at warp speed. Ball bouncing, ricocheting, rebounding, score mounting.

'Go, girl!'

She didn't register the final tally: she only heard a cacophony of beeps, jingles and music. Voices, whoops, everything was a blur as she fell to her knees.

'Beth.' Kieran knelt beside her. Through a mist of tears, she took in his lovely face. 'It's going to be OK,' he whispered. 'You, me, whatever the future has in store. We'll deal with it, one step at a time.'

As stifled sobs echoed around the room, Gigi gestured for quiet. 'I think we're forgetting one little thing.'

'That genies don't exist and we're in the middle of a herd hallucination?' Kieran's words were laced with residual disbelief. He helped Beth to her feet, and she blinked at Gigi.

'Your third wish, darlin'. That one nearly slipped by. Close your eyes and say it.'

Beth paused. Gigi's words from before played through her mind. *Healing. The messy, complicated, gut-wrenching, wonderful kind.*

'Is it really that simple?' she said. 'Shouldn't I wish for something more … I don't know, meaningful? That makes other people happy? Thanks to Kieran, thanks to *you*, Gigi, I'm already healing.'

Gigi smiled. 'Of course you are. And that's how it should be. But wishes can spread further. They can fly, like your gossamer-winged friend.'

'What in the name of the wee man is he talking about?' Wilma frowned at Jinnie, who shook her head.

'I think Gigi's saying that Beth's wish – wishes – go further than ours did.' Jo looked at Sam. 'Does that make sense to you?'

'Absolutely nothing in Cranley makes sense. Right?'

Heads nodded in agreement.

'But we each got a set of wishes. OK, some got more than others, some wishes were completely off the wall. And we accepted them. Why is it different now?'

Gigi did the pixellation thing again. There one minute, barely visible the next. 'I could bore you all to death with the FBI, CHUG and the silly WIFI thing, but here's the rub.'

They waited. Prom strode in, tail in the air, attitude through the roof.

'How the…' Kieran stuttered. 'I locked all the doors and windows. I know I did.'

A collective mutter of 'don't you get it yet' rumbled round the room.

'Kieran,' said Jinnie, in the manner of a mother addressing a toddler. 'We're in the presence of a genie. I don't think Prom going walkabout is relevant.'

'Ah, what an intelligent cat.' Gigi stroked Prom, who purred appreciatively.

'Yep, he's a regular Einstein,' deadpanned Kieran.

The butterfly hovered over everyone's heads, showering them with gold glitter.

'Just like the open mic night.'

'We all knew something magical was in the air.'

'We just didn't realise who or what it was.'

Gigi chuckled as they chatted among themselves, but even his voice sounded diminished. Shrunken, as if he was no longer the confident, often arrogant genie Beth had grown to love. Love? It came in all shapes and sizes. Lesson learned.

'Erm, can we wrap this up soon?' said Sam. 'I've a book signing in Edinburgh later.'

Jinnie raised her eyebrows at Sam. 'Darling, you're off the demi-Djinn hook and we're all emotional wrecks. Scrawling your name on a few paperbacks can wait.'

Sam looked put out. Perhaps the 'few' had stung.

'Beth,' said Gigi.

She reached out, grasping Gigi's hands. 'You're d-disappearing,' she stuttered. 'What happens – I mean, what do we do with the pinball machine when you're gone?'

'Keep it, store it, bin it. It doesn't matter. Once the Wish Master has gone, it is a mere relic of a bygone era.'

'Sounds like me,' said Wilma.

'Shush, Gran,' said Jinnie.

'It is almost time.' Gigi smiled, but tears glistened in his eyes. Tears matched by those in Beth's. No, now her tears cascaded down her cheeks. She felt a sharp pang of loss. Not like the loss of her precious babies: nothing would ever match that. This … this felt like losing a dear friend. A pal, and a confidante.

'But is it *really* the end?' said Jo.

As she spoke, the butterfly zapped around the room, its iridescent shimmer dimming, glitter tumbling from its wings. It landed lightly on everyone's head, finally resting on Gigi. A second later, it was gone.

'Does this mean no more genies in Cranley?' Sam gave a helpless shrug before pulling Jinnie into his arms.

'Will we ever see anyone like you again?' asked Wilma. 'Or is that top-secret, hush-hush stuff?'

Gigi puffed out a breath. It vaporised as if the air was ice cold. 'Mortals get endings: I just reset. But you, Beth – you grew.'

The words lingered, heavier than the glitter still drifting lazily to the floor. Gigi's outline softened, his edges blurring like breath on glass.

'You can't just reset,' Beth said, clinging to him. 'And I hate goodbyes.'

'So do I, although I've been practising for centuries.' He winked, though the wink juddered. 'Besides, magic never really leaves. It lingers.'

Wilma snorted. 'Like a bad smell, which reminds me of DJ.'

Gigi laughed, the sound thinning. 'Cranley's a funny little place. It has a constant electricity, like a plug socket that's never switched off. You lot did that. Community, kindness, chaos. My favourite cocktail.'

The pinball machine flickered. The lights dimmed. One final, triumphant jangle rang out, then silence.

'Beth,' Gigi said softly, 'it has been a pleasure to serve you.'

He pressed a kiss to Beth's forehead. It felt warm. Solid. Real.

Then he was mist. Then sparkle. Then nothing at all.

The pinball machine sat inert, its dull glass reflecting a group of stunned villagers and a disgruntled cat.

'Well,' Sam said eventually, 'that's another moment to add to the Cranley craziness collection.'

Kieran laughed shakily and wrapped Beth close. She rested her head against his chest, listening to his heartbeat.

Outside, a sound like a volley of fireworks disturbed the silence, then ceased.

'Did anyone else hear that?' Jo asked.

Wilma smiled. 'Aye. Cranley's got magic left in it yet.'

Beth squeezed Kieran's hand. 'I hope so,' she said, with a smile.

Chapter Fifty-Five

Two weeks later

August settled over Cranley without ceremony, warm and lingering, the days stretching lazily into evenings that lent themselves to leisurely walks and cold drinks. The air smelled of cut grass and honeysuckle, and even after sunset there was a softness to everything, as though the village itself wasn't ready to let go.

Beth didn't mind.

A welcome week of sunshine didn't fix things. It didn't smooth the edges or make grief evaporate. But it helped. It made the days feel longer, the pauses less heavy.

It gave her room to breathe.

She'd started collecting small victories the way Janette collected opinions: loudly, regularly, and without asking anyone's permission.

The new menu had landed. The punters approved. There'd been no kitchen fires, no mass food poisoning, and no rogue customers declaring that 'THE STEAK PIE RUINED MY LIFE' on TripAdvisor.

That alone felt significant.

The day had been busy – the good kind of busy, where her feet ached and her apron looked like it had lost a fight with tomato sauce, but the atmosphere had been easy. People lingered over drinks. Someone laughed too loudly. Someone else ordered pudding despite insisting they were full to bursting.

Beth turned the key in the pub door and listened to the familiar, grounding clunk of the lock. Safe. Shut. Finished.

She tucked the keys into her jeans pocket and stepped outside. The air was sultry, the sky a cloudless blue.

'You smashed it again,' Kieran said, falling into step beside her as if he was still working out where he fitted, but was content to wait. 'Wilma told me she'd have licked the plate if social convention allowed.'

Beth snorted. 'I doubt Wilma has ever been restrained by social convention.'

'True. She also asked if the cauliflower cheese was sent from heaven.'

'Did she?'

'Everything you cook is heavenly. Now I sound cheesier than the cauliflower.'

They walked down the street, the village quiet but not asleep. Just pausing between moments.

Their hands brushed. With things still new and uncharted between them, Beth half-expected the familiar flicker of retreat, the instinct to pull away before things tipped into want.

Instead, Kieran took her hand properly. No hesitation. No ceremony. She let him, feeling the warmth zing between them.

They passed the boutique with its summer display and A Bit of Crumpet, lights still on inside. Beth could picture Jo pulling a late shift, sleeves rolled up, judging a tray of baked goods with forensic seriousness.

'How are you doing?' Kieran asked.

'I'm good, I think. Steadier than I was a week ago. It still feels surreal, as if he was never here.'

But he was, and life will never be quite the same again.

'You've got a lot on in the next few months,' she said, to change the subject. To swap memories of a madcap genie for the reality of Kieran's in-the-works app launch.

Kieran grimaced, although his eyes sparkled with anticipation. 'Don't remind me. If ClosetAura tanks, I'll have to move into my parents' shed and live off tinned soup.'

'I'll make you fresh soup and batch-freeze it.'

'Thank you. Although heating it in a shed might prove tricky.'

Beth squeezed his hand. 'Trust me, it won't tank. People are raving about it already, even in the early testing stages. You're a genius.'

'You're biased.'

'I am deeply objective.' She paused. 'Also, Janette's already spread the word near and far.'

'That's either brilliant or catastrophic.'

They strolled on, spotting Wilma pushing Dahlia in her buggy. 'Evening, lovebirds,' she said, with a twinkle in her eye.

'Evening, Wilma,' Beth replied. 'So glad you enjoyed the food.'

'Always hits the spot, pet.' She peered at Kieran. 'You look a tad twitchy, lad.'

'Just getting my ducks in a row for the app launch,' he said stiffly.

'Ach, stop fretting. Keep calm and carry on. At least your aura's settled down.'

They reached the small bench near the edge of the village. Beth slowed, memories tugging at her of sitting outside the pub with Luke. Of apologies, of heartache.

All the losses were still there, just quieter.

'I still miss them,' she said.

'I know,' Kieran replied.

'I'm not fixed.'

'I know.'

'I might never be.'

'I know that, too.'

Beth looked at him properly then: not searching for reassurance, not bracing for disappointment. Just seeing him. 'And you're still here?'

'Still here,' he said. 'Still choosing this. One day at a time.'

Something eased in her chest. Not relief, exactly. As if room was being made.

They stood there for a moment, close but not pressed together, learning the shape of whatever this was becoming. When he kissed her, it was gentle. As if he was just checking in.

Beth kissed him back, slower this time. More present.

Above them, something fluttered. She pulled back slightly. 'Do you see that?'

Kieran squinted upwards. 'A butterfly?'

They followed its movements as it flitted overhead as if dancing to a silent melody.

The butterfly hovered for a moment, its wings catching the light in a way that seemed oddly deliberate. Or maybe that was just Beth's imagination, primed by everything that had come before. Then it drifted away.

Beth laughed softly, the sound threaded with something tender and unresolved.

'If a genie pops out of a bin,' Kieran said, 'I'm pretending I didn't see it.'

Beth smiled. 'If a genie pops out of a bin, I'm charging him rent. Emotional growth doesn't pay for itself.'

They started walking again, hand in hand, their pace slightly uneven but matched enough.

As they passed the pub, Beth glanced through the window. Inside, the pinball machine sat dark and ordinary.

Just a machine. And yet…

She leaned into Kieran, feeling the solid reassurance of him beside her. Not a promise of forever, not a guarantee of happiness, but a willingness to keep showing up.

The future wasn't written. But for the first time in a long while, that didn't frighten her.

It felt like possibility.

Also by Audrey Davis

vinci-books.com/CleanSweep

Love doesn't follow the rules—and it never checks your age.

Widowed Emily isn't looking for love—until a charming young chimney sweep shows up. As secrets surface and relationships are tested, five women find that it's never too late for second chances… or a little romantic chaos.

Turn the page for a free preview…

A Clean Sweep: Chapter One

Young people in England are the most illiterate in the developed world and are floundering in maths, according to a global ranking.

'It's not only the young ones,' mused Emily as she put her laptop to sleep and headed upstairs for a shower. Every day she cringed as she scrolled through her Facebook page or flicked through the comments section of the *Daily Mail*. If she had a pound for every "definately", "should of" or incorrect use of its/it's she could feast on sirloin steak instead of rummaging through the Value section of her local Tesco. She was equally appalled at people's inability to do the most basic arithmetic in their heads. Surely it wasn't rocket science to calculate that if an item cost 84p and she proffered £1 then 16p change was due?

Jim had always scoffed at her devotion to the trashy world of tabloid journalism. He was a *Telegraph* or *Times* man. 'Real news, Emily. Honestly, your brain will rot reading all that nonsense.' Then he'd settle down for his nightly dose of *Channel 4 News*, while she wondered if she could catch up with Kirsty and Phil once he'd retired for the night. She loved Kirsty. All womanly curves and clipped vowels. Which brought her back to the *Daily Mail*. It might not be highbrow – more articles on which brow shape was currently in vogue – but it did raise some interesting questions. Like how a woman could build a multi-million-dollar empire purely by virtue of having an unfeasibly enormous bottom. Emily's rear was far from superstardom status, but it did seem to grow in direct proportion to the shrinking of her grey matter. Einstein could probably have created a mathematical equation to address the conundrum.

Twenty minutes later she was sitting at her dressing table, dragging a comb through her hair. The reflection that stared back at her wasn't too bad, at least for a fifty-two-year-old. High cheekbones, thick hair and good skin, kept in check with liberal applications of whatever cream or serum promised to work miracles. Her bathroom cabinet resembled a suburban branch of Boots. Yes, she had a few fine lines but failing eyesight had its compensations. She had reading glasses stashed everywhere – bedroom, kitchen, bathroom – but she happily applied her make-up without visual enhancement. Her daughter had bought her a magnifying mirror for Christmas which still languished in its box. Some things didn't need to be brought into sharp focus. A gentle blurring of the edges was just fine.

'Mum! Are you there?'

Emily started at Tabitha's voice from downstairs, the front door slamming behind her. A minute later she bounded into the bedroom, all blonde curls and breathlessness. Sometimes her daughter made her think of the Duracell bunny on amphetamines, ricocheting from one crisis to another, bumping and crashing her way through life at full pelt.

'Washing machine's on the blink again, brought some laundry round, hope you don't mind.' Tabitha threw herself down on the bed. Today she was wearing tight red jeans and a floppy black sweatshirt emblazoned with 'Don't walk, dance'. She kicked off her ballet pumps and regarded her mother with blue eyes the shade of stone-washed denim. Emily was quite partial to skinny jeans herself, despite reading several articles declaring that certain outfits were off-limits when one reached a certain age. Bollocks to that! She still wore cut-off shorts in the summer when the sun decided to appear and had yet to witness anyone fainting in horror or disgust.

'That's fine, darling. We'll pop it on in a little while. Fancy a cuppa?' Emily got to her feet, smiling as Tabitha leapt off the bed and headed back downstairs. She'd already done a few stretches and yoga positions, part of her daily routine. Luckily her faculties were still intact. She knew of at least two friends of friends who had been diagnosed with dementia in their forties. Her morning Sudoku and crossword puzzle were her way of kick starting her brain, although there were days when her thoughts bounced around like globules in a lava lamp, connecting then dispersing in no apparent pattern.

In the kitchen Emily flicked on the kettle. She liked her kettle – bright orange to match the toaster and bread bin – bursts of colour in an otherwise bland environment. Wall-to-wall cream cupboards and grey floor tiles. They'd been Jim's choice; a man whose idea of daring was to swap his usual butter-slathered toast for a muesli mix in a concession to healthy living. She couldn't abide the stuff – like sawdust mixed with unidentified animal droppings – preferring a boiled egg or some fresh fruit. Not that his muesli had done much good. Found slumped over his desk four years ago when he should have been presenting at a strategic planning meeting.

Emily nursed her cup of instant coffee and watched as Tabitha began dragging out miscellaneous clothing from a black bin liner and stuffing them haphazardly into the washing machine. The cycle started, she pulled up a chair and launched into a rapid-fire summary of her escapades that week. She often thought of Tabitha – thirty next birthday – as a human whirlwind, constantly teetering on a precipice of euphoria or despair. Today was a good one, her smile like sunlight breaking through the clouds, words tumbling from her mouth and tripping over each other in the way of toddlers with only a basic grasp of walking.

'How's Tom?' she asked. Tabitha's boyfriend of more than a year seemed a decent enough sort. Easy on the eye, unfailingly polite and hugely appreciative of her Sunday roasts. Particularly since her daughter's recent evangelical conversion to all things organic and wholesome. And gas-producing. A good fifteen to twenty-minute gap was necessary before entering the bathroom after Tabitha. She could rival napalm in the toxicity stakes. *Apocalypse Now*, or certainly a short while after a nut roast had been consumed. Emily sometimes found herself humming "The Ride of the Valkyries" as Emily emerged from the loo. She hoped it was a passing phase. Her daughter had been through more phases than the moon. With a few total eclipses along the way.

'He's good. Busy at work.' Tom worked for a small but niche travel agency on the High Street in Little Hambledon, a picture-postcard village a few miles away from Emily. She and Jim had bought their seventies-built detached property just over twenty years ago. It wasn't exactly a candidate for a *Country Living* double-page spread

– too boxy and functional – but its location in Tattler Green was considered highly desirable. Easy access to the motorway and Heathrow airport, the village itself boasting a pretty common with duck pond and various pubs and small shops. They'd done a lot of work to it over the years; new bathrooms to replace the hideous sludge-brown suites and even darker tiles, the bland but eminently practical kitchen, polished oak floorboards throughout instead of swirly shag pile in shades of mud brown and fluorescent blue. Emily had wondered if there had ever been a study into why so many people in the 1970s had been so utterly devoid of taste. Or simply had severe eyesight problems. 'Ooh, this is a tiny little bathroom with barely any natural light so let's give it an avocado green loo and matching basin shaped like a shell. And tile it wall to ceiling in khaki with a hint of pink. Lovely!'

'So, what's new with you, mummy dearest? Any deep, dark secrets I should know of? Like a hot man, perhaps? You really need to get back in the saddle, so to speak. Can't spend all your days cloistered away turning verbal diarrhoea into something readable!'

Tabitha was always teasing Emily, both about her part-time work proofreading and editing short stories for women's magazines and her lack of a love life. She didn't mind. The former brought in a bit of extra cash, the latter she tried to ignore. In the years since Jim died, she'd had a handful of dates – chiefly with men around his age and widowed – but had failed to click with any of them. She had a nice circle of friends but was happy being on her own a lot of the time. She certainly wasn't prepared to hook up with any old codger just for the sake of it.

'For your information, I've been having *amazing* sex with

my car mechanic for weeks now. And no cracks about my big end, thank you!'

Tabitha snorted in laughter. She knew very well that Ken Crompton was nearing retirement age and had all the wit and warmth of a dead haddock. The only reason they both used him was because he was cheap and reliable, unlike many of the other garages in the area.

'Ha ha, very funny. Seriously though, you should think about on-line dating. There are tons of websites out there and they can't *all* be mad stalkers or porn-obsessed saddos. I can check some of them out for you if you like?' Tabitha looked imploringly at Emily, who scowled back in exasperation.

'Tabitha, I am perfectly capable of sorting out my own love life. If I choose to. And right now, I choose *not* to. I am quite happy with my life as it is, even if it seems deadly dull to you.' Cue massive eye roll from Tabitha, before she began rummaging in the fridge in search of a snack. 'If I happen to meet someone and it feels right then I'll take it from there. Until then – don't you *dare* scoff my last piece of Cheddar – I'll continue with my vows of celibacy and get my thrills from my work. You have no idea the shenanigans some of these characters get up to. Gets me hot under the collar sometimes!'

Almost an hour later and Tabitha had departed, washing duly going through its cycle and barely enough Cheddar to satisfy a mouse left in the fridge. Luckily all the really good stuff was hidden away in the overflow fridge in the utility room. Tonight, it was Emily's turn to host book club, and she'd shopped earlier for the requisite canapés – devils on horseback, mini spring rolls, a platter of French cheeses – as well as an assortment of sweet nibbles. Under pressure from her older sister Celeste she'd agreed to join the merry-go-round of monthly meetings where novels were analysed, dissected and discussed in depth, the focus being on literary content, intellectual stimulation and relevance in today's multi-cultural society, Or, as Celeste's husband Michael put it, 'Ten minutes on the book, the rest shoving nibbles and booze down their necks and bitching about some poor soul or other.'

As she skimmed a duster over the coffee table and gave the bookcase a quick once-over, she smiled at her large collection of paperbacks. Most people she knew, herself included, downloaded everything on to their Kindles or similar devices. Certainly, a lot less baggage weight when going on holiday, but there was something special about turning the pages of a much-loved book. Her fingers came to rest on one. A present from Jim. *Blood Angel – A Tale of Gory Revenge.* About as far removed from Emily's tastes as possible. Pushing it back into position she realised with a jolt that today would have been their thirtieth wedding anniversary. Thirty years since Emily had turned to Jim and said, 'I do'. When a little voice in her head had been whispering, 'Are you sure? Really, really sure?'

She'd only been twenty-two when they'd got married, Jim five years older. Far too young to be trussed up in white taffeta that stretched uncomfortably against her slightly protruding stomach. Yes, caught in the age-old trap of finding herself pregnant just a year after finishing university. They'd met there, at the students' union, a rather tipsy Emily flattered by the attention from this rather earnest postgraduate with his unruly brown hair and tattered Jimi Hendrix T-shirt. He drank wine rather than beer – which she thought the height of sophistication – and had a vinyl collection that filled his parents' spare bedroom.

In the early days of their burgeoning romance, Emily felt safe and a little smug as her singleton friends bed-hopped around the campus. Moaning continuously about their scruffy student boyfriends with their bacteria-gathering bathrooms and mountainous heaps of dirty washing that festered in corners of their cupboard-sized rooms. Jim was different, a grown man with a future in marketing already mapped out. He owned his own place, thanks to a legacy from a dotty old aunt who'd secretly stashed away a fortune betting on greyhounds and took her to nice restaurants. Dependable, devoted, financially secure, what was not to love? Except Emily couldn't help wondering sometimes if something was missing. Passion, perhaps? That feeling of a delicious fizz of anticipation when you were waiting to see the supposed love of your life. The sex was fine – well, *OK* – not that she had much to compare it to. Apart from the odd steamy novel or TV show that had her dad coughing furiously and her mum rocketing out her chair to deal with some suddenly urgent matter in the kitchen. Not so much a fizz, perhaps, more like a glass of two-day old Lilt. Still drinkable but lacking sparkle.

For their silver wedding anniversary, Jim had bought her a pretty pair of earrings. Shame he hadn't noticed in all these years that she'd never had her ears pierced. Her mum deemed it akin to self-mutilation – 'You might as well get your neck stretched like those African women!' – so she'd never got around to it. She, in turn, had searched the internet for the perfect decanter with a delicate silver base in a pattern of intertwined grapes and leaves, Jim's love for wine and all things tastefully alcoholic having blossomed over the years. He would sniff, swill and pontificate on its provenance, whereas Emily just liked the way it made her feel mellow and couldn't care less if it came as part of a 'dine in for a tenner' deal.

What was the symbol for thirty years? Pearl? Couldn't imagine Jim fishing a tantalising little faux-suede box out of his pocket, nestled inside a single lustrous drop on a fine gold chain. Not one for romantic gestures, his gifts had been of a more practical nature. Like the Christmas before he died. She'd bought him a bottle of vintage Armagnac produced in the year of his birth. He'd given her an electric foot file designed to slough away dead skin and callouses. 'Look, Em!' he'd exclaimed as she attempted to generate some kind of enthusiasm. 'It's got real diamond crystals!' Try as she might, Emily couldn't imagine Eartha Kitt purring with pleasure over finding *that* in her stocking. Poor old Santa Baby would most likely have been shoved unceremoniously back up the chimney.

Speaking of chimneys, it had been more than four years since her own one had been lit. Metaphorically speaking, more like ten years since any kind of flame had smouldered in Emily's life. After Tabitha was born – and both she and Jim had been smitten by their daughter from day one – she had hoped to expand their little family. However, it was not meant to be. No clear-cut medical reason, the doctors said. And as the months and years passed and Jim retreated to his own study/guest room at night – 'hate to keep you awake with my snoring, my dear' – her dreams of a brother or sister for Tabitha faded along with her libido. A perfunctory peck on the cheek or the lips, the occasional pat on the bottom, the very occasional coupling which lasted as long as a TV ad break. And usually followed a fine bottle of St Emilion Grand Cru if Jim had been celebrating a particularly successful campaign.

There was still a basket of logs next to the fireplace. And, if her memory served her correctly, a box of firelighters on a shelf in the garage. Jim had disapproved of firelighters.

'That's the cheat's way, Em. It's all about arranging the kindling correctly, a few scrunched-up pages of *The Telegraph*, and Bob's your uncle!' Then he'd huff and puff and almost blow the house down as the flames failed to take hold. On the odd occasion when Jim was travelling, Emily took gleeful delight in lighting the fire herself. With the aid of the illicit firelighters, it took her approximately five to ten minutes to produce a roaring hearth. Curled up with her Kindle and a glass of passable plonk she'd congratulated herself on a job well done, and with the minimum of fuss. Then made sure to clear away the evidence before Jim's return, lest his masculinity be reduced to a pile of cold ashes.

It was just after seven and Emily had set the stage; the fire ready for the touch of a match, the food artfully arranged on plates adorned with seedless green and red grapes. Candles burned on every surface, suffusing the air with a hint of wild berries and cinnamon. The lamps were turned down low, both for atmosphere and because women in their fifties and sixties preferred the subtler approach of ambient lighting. Going into a brightly lit changing room these days was akin to torture; every lump, bump and line thrown into sharp relief by the brutal glare and wall-to-wall mirrors.

First through the door was Celeste. At almost sixty she was remarkably well preserved, like a plump Christmas ham glistening under the hallway light. She'd recently taken to having hair extensions after complaining that her once-crowning glory was thinning at an alarming rate. 'I'll be damned if I end up with a bloody comb-over like that Bobby Charleston!' she'd decreed, before emerging from the salon more footballer's wife than footballing legend.

One of her sister's more endearing traits, in Emily's view, was her proneness to malapropisms. Hence the Charlton/Charleston mix up.

'Hello, darling! You look fabulous! Haven't seen that top before, is it new?' Celeste clamped her sister to her bosom, nearly asphyxiating her in a cloud of La Vie est Belle. Emily smoothed down the simple but fitted teal blue number with its daring – for her – halter neck. At a time in life when women were forming campaigns like twenty-first century suffragettes to bring back sleeves, she was inordinately pleased that she had succumbed to neither bingo hall nor bingo wings. And, with hopefully a real fire to keep them warm this evening, she felt a little flesh-baring wasn't too over the top.

Celeste followed her sister into the kitchen, opening the fridge and retrieving a bottle of Pinot Grigio. Pouring herself a generous measure, she sank down on a counter stool and scooped up a handful of Bombay mix. Duly chewed and swallowed, she surveyed Emily with an appraising eye. 'A bit outré for book club, ma petite?' Celeste had briefly taken a French course at night school and liked to toss in a few Gallic phrases in a bid to impress. 'Shame we don't have any male members; I'm sure dear Arnold Pettifer would be quite smitten with your defoliage.' As Arnold Pettifer was nudging seventy and had a smile reminiscent of yellowing tombstones – with an odd familial gap or two – Emily didn't feel it too much of a loss.

'Did you enjoy the book? Found it a bit boring myself. All that weeping and wailing and endless doom and death! Give me a good Sheila O'Flanagan any day of the week.'

On this, Emily had to reluctantly agree, even though it had been her selection. Over 700 pages of painstakingly researched historical fact/fiction did not make for a light bedtime read. It might have won several major prizes but to her it served only as a more effective sleeping pill than those prescribed by her GP. She'd managed a quarter before giving up and downloading something frivolous but eminently more entertaining.

'Last month was really interesting, shame you couldn't make it,' continued Celeste, as her sister looked at her watch and wondered if anyone else was going to show up. 'Not my usual cup of tea, but I'm now an Ernest Hemingsworth devotee.' Oh help, thought Emily, wondering where this train of thought would crash spectacularly. 'Alice chose it, she's always been a bit pretentious, but I found it quite fascinating. All about bullfighting in Spain. You know, the tradition behind it, the way those men saw themselves as warriors fighting a noble cause. You really should read it, Em. Here, I've written down the name for you.' Celeste scrabbled in her bag, produced a tiny notepad with a flourish worthy of Paul Daniels at his peak. '*Murder in the Morning!*' she pronounced. Emily simply prayed for the doorbell to ring. Which it did.

Half an hour in and book club was in full flow. Emily's living room was filled with the thrum of ceaseless chatter. Glasses chinked and plates clattered as oozing wedges of Brie were spread on crackers, spring rolls dipped in sweet chilli sauce, horseback thingies taken apart to cries of 'Ooh, it's a date, thought it'd be an oyster! Or is that the angel version?' Michael – damn him – had been proven right as this month's weighty tome had barely warranted more than five minutes of their time.

'Watching paint dry would have been more fun,' said Esther Thompson, licking a particularly gooey St. Augur from her fingers.

'Too true,' chipped in Susan Wainwright. She had sped her way through the savouries like an Olympic athlete with an eye on the gold, which in her case was Emily's fabled mini cheesecakes. With a crumbly butter biscuit base and meltingly creamy in the middle, they were topped with a layer of sweet but tangy blackberry compote. Emily felt slightly miffed that her book choice had failed to captivate her fellow members. Still, at least she'd got beyond the first chapter.

'Oh, I really shouldn't, but …' Susan bore the expression of a woman who'd just spent the past hour in the throes of ecstasy with George Clooney/Brad Pitt/take your pick of desirable males as she grabbed another cheesecake. Her third, Emily noted, relieved that she'd made a double batch. Susan then launched into a blow-by-blow account of what some random woman she knew was up to these days. Which involved latex, whips and something about the headmaster of the local secondary, who'd always seemed a perfectly nice man to Emily, if you discounted his fur-lined anorak and encyclopaedic knowledge of feathered creatures.

Nancy Edwards, a mousy little soul who had barely contributed a word to the proceedings, was currently fanning herself with a copy of *Good Housekeeping* purloined from Emily's magazine rack. Gosh, it was a little hot in here, thought Emily. Even with her wispy Arnold-attracting top. Taking a large gulp of water, she glanced at the fireplace and realised her fire was more than blazing. It was now raging like a mini-Hades and belching out eye-watering plumes of smoke. Esther was in the midst of a spectacular coughing fit, Alice's face was turning a vivid shade of scarlet, and Susan had put down her dessert plate and looked vaguely distressed. And not just because the cheesecakes were finished.

'Emily!' squeaked Celeste, having just returned from a nose-powdering session in the cloakroom. 'I think we have a problem!' No kidding Miss Marple, thought Emily, as smoke continued to billow around the room. All the women were now convulsed in a cacophony of honking and spluttering like consumption sufferers in a modern-day sanitarium. What to do? Call the fire brigade? Much as the thought of hunky hose-wielding men storming her semi gave her a little frisson of excitement, it seemed to her that the problem was more to do with a blockage in the chimney than an out-of-control inferno.

'What the hell's going on in here?' Through the pall of smoke emerged the robust figure of Celeste's husband, Michael. Often on taxi duty – Celeste never knowingly under drank – he forged a path towards the fireplace, pausing only to grab a vase of fast-wilting tulips. Tossing aside the blooms, he chucked the water on to the smouldering embers. Which hissed, spat and emanated an astonishing amount of steam. *From hellfire to hammam*, thought Emily. All we need now are fluffy white bathrobes and a reflexology session.

A short time later, the book club ladies said their goodbyes.

'Most excitement I've had in a long time!' Nancy gave Emily an uncharacteristic hug, her usual lavender and old lace fragrance tinged with a hint of charcoal.

'Wait until I tell the women at yoga about tonight!'

chirped Susan, although Emily suspected they already knew, had seen the high-definition footage and were on to the next domestic drama-to-be.

Michael, a pink-faced and slightly droopy Celeste clinging to his arm, paused at the front door. 'Have you ever had your chimney swept, Emily?' For some reason – maybe one too many glasses of Pinot consumed or just the sheer exhaustion of it all – Emily couldn't help but giggle. Not recently, she wanted to retort but thought better of it. Michael was solid, reliable and adored her older sister, but he was not over-endowed in the sense of humour department. Particularly the section marked 'slightly smutty'. 'Well, I think you should call someone in. Have a look on Google. Could well be something dead up there. Goodnight then.'

Emily, having cleaned up the kitchen, sprayed liberal doses of air freshener around the living room and taken a shower to wash away the stench of smoke, sank down on her bed. A chimney sweep. Did they even exist anymore? Suddenly her head was filled with pictures of Dick Van Dyke dancing with penguins, alongside Julia Andrews being practically perfect in every way. 'A spoonful of sugar makes the medicine go down …' She shook her head forcefully. The last thing she needed right now was a night's sleep plagued by Mary flipping Poppins. She'd investigate the existence of men with long brushes and soot-smeared faces tomorrow.

A Clean Sweep: Chapter Two

Back home after several cups of coffee with her mum, Tabitha sank down on the loo seat. What a relief! It was all very well drinking the recommended eight glasses of water a day (plus tea, coffee, wine etc) but not if your bladder was the size of a peanut. OK, it was probably perfectly normal sized for a twenty-something female, but it always seemed to scream 'time for a pee!' at the most inopportune moments. Like ten minutes into a movie when she was squashed into the middle row of the cinema between a man the size of Magic Johnson and a woman the width of a small bungalow. Both nursing buckets of popcorn that could have fed a small African nation for a week. And as reluctant to budge as a soon-to-be neutered spaniel on its way to the vet. Or – even worse – on a rickety old bus in the middle of nowhere in Indonesia where the choices were behind a bush where goodness knows what creatures lay in wait or a delightful hole in the ground with strategically placed foot markings on either side. That was a memorable trip, thought Tabitha. She'd been proud of her pelvic floor, lasting two excruciating hours until the relative luxury of the backpackers hostel.

She'd read somewhere, the *National Geographic* perhaps, that an elephant could urinate around 160 litres in one go. Or was it David Attenborough? Not who could pee so copiously, of course, just where that little gem of knowledge had come from. Apparently, the average human managed a mere 600 to 1000 ml. Which was only a bottle of Sauvignon Blanc, give or take. What was *really* fascinating, however, was that both elephant and human took about the same time to empty their bladders. She found that hard to believe. Ah well, the miracles of nature. A quick dry off, up with the pants and jeans, hands washed, time to make something to eat. Quinoa with feta and lentils, part of her new health kick. Although egg, chips and beans might be quicker. And tastier. She grabbed the door handle, turned it and … shit, no. Oh, damn and bugger! Tabitha gazed in horror at the handle, now detached and in her squirty soap-scented hand. She rammed it back on the sticky-out spindle thing and tried again. Nothing. It wouldn't budge. Not an inch. She was locked in the lavatory, just like the old ladies in the song.

Right. Tabitha took a long, deep breath. Don't panic. Stay calm. She checked her watch. 5.30pm. Barring hold ups, Tom should be home in half an hour. She can't call him as her mobile is in the kitchen on charge. I mean, who takes their phone to the loo? She remembered giggling when her former boss Denis related the tale of his tumbling into the bowl mid-stream. No amount of drenching it in rice grains saved that poor Nokia. An ignominious end.

But wait a minute. Didn't Tom mumble something this morning over his Shreddies that he might go for a pint – or two – with Clive and Keith from work? Maybe even a curry if they hadn't put the Premier League to rights in the pub? Tabitha, sitting at the kitchen counter with her tongue sticking out as she applied her mascara, had barely been listening. She'd had a long day ahead – sorting out new stock, packing up internet orders, listening to the latest tales of dating disasters from her boss – so Tom's after-work movements hardly warranted more than a cursory 'whatever'. He could be at least an hour, probably more like two – or three – or …

Feeling her heart racing faster than Usain Bolt, Tabitha attempted to clear her mind, particularly of the image of two lightly fried eggs, crispy golden chips and a side of Heinz's finest. She could survive without food for a few hours. Might even help lose some of that excess flab she packed on over the Christmas holidays. But water? Wasn't the maximum survival time something like a week, less if you were in the baking heat of the Australian outback? Which, of course, she wasn't but the bathroom was pretty warm. What if Tom, strolling back from a tasty chicken tikka Balti and garlic naan, got hit by a bus? Or an asteroid? Or collapsed with an undiagnosed brain haemorrhage? And, having left his wallet in the Delhi Delight, was now lying in intensive care while staff desperately tried to trace his next of kin.

Tears began to well in Tabitha's eyes, then spill down her cheeks. Which made this morning's mascara – a departure from her usual brand – join the cascade. Blinking hard, for there was now a nasty stinging sensation, she squinted painfully at the mirror. Great, just great. Now she resembled a blinking giant panda. As she turned on the tap and grabbed a wodge of toilet paper to wipe away the smudges, she ever so slowly registered the trickle of water that gradually became a steady flow. OK, so she might not die a horrible death by dehydration just yet. Or be accepted as a member of Mensa anytime soon.

The morning after the night before and Tabitha unlocked the door of The Little Shop of Treasures, plonked her handbag on the counter and wandered through the back, the beaded curtain jangling behind her. Her boss was already there, opening boxes of greeting cards and sorting them into neat piles. ABBA's 'Take A Chance on Me' played in the background and the air positively reeked of a consignment of scented candles meant to enhance a romantic evening but more likely to bring on a migraine.

'Darling, you're late!' Meryl tapped her watch pointedly but with a smile. Clearly last night's blind date had gone well. A blow-by-blow account would follow, but for now it was time to get the shop ready to open in thirty minutes.

Tabitha had worked there for almost eighteen months now. It wasn't quite what she'd had in mind when she'd graduated with a degree in events management. She'd stood there proudly on the stage, clutching her empty cardboard tube (for photo purposes only), and beamed at her mum. And begged her silently not to leap to her feet and scream 'Love you!' hysterically like a pubescent One Direction fan. Sadly, her fantasies of micro-managing high-end parties, teetering around in Jimmy Choos and barking orders at minions laden with hideously pretentious canapés – sautéed snails a la croûte, anyone? – and balancing trays of Pol Roger had not been realised. She'd managed a couple of corporate events, but these were more vol au vents, paint-stripping wine and a couple of unfortunate incidents involving ageing executives with bad breath and wandering hands. The closest she'd got to celebrities was assisting at the end-of-season wrap party for reality TV show, *Scots Wa Hae.* This featured a delightfully colourful cast of Glaswegians being filmed going about their day to day lives. There was Wee Jock, a six-foot three bundle of tattooed joy, who claimed to be in the *Guinness Book of Records* for most pints of Tennents Lager consumed in one minute, Senga, boasting of bedding half a Scottish third division football team (presumably not all on the same night), and Big Tam, her personal favourite. A die-hard *Braveheart* fan, he had watched the film a mind-boggling 250 times and still blubbed like a baby whenever Mel made his 'freedom' speech. A surprise nationwide hit – with subtitles, of course – the show was scheduled for a second series. So a rather inebriated Tam informed her, his blue-striped face coming perilously close to her crisp white blouse. 'Aye, hen, we've had better ratings than *Emmerdale* and *Corrie* put together.' Swaying slightly, he proffered a congealing plate of deep-fried Mars bars. Tabitha politely declined.

So here she was, hardly in the job of her dreams but it paid the rent, and she was very fond of Meryl. Somewhere in her mid to late forties, she'd never been married but still believed the perfect man was out there somewhere. Her real name was Beryl, but she'd changed it in homage to her favourite actress who also happened to star in her number one movie, *Mamma Mia*. Such was her devotion she frequently sported dungarees and would burst into ABBA songs at the drop of a hat. Unfortunately, Beryl/Meryl made Pierce Brosnan sound like Alfie Boe.

'If you change your mind, I'm the first in line,' warbled Meryl. Tabitha looked at a display of hand-painted wine glasses and wondered why they didn't shatter as her boss did a passable impression of a cat being administered an enema. Grabbing a Stanley knife, she began attacking a box of cutesy fridge magnets bearing such slogans as "Cleaning the house while the kids are still growing is like shovelling snow while it's still snowing". As she began to arrange them on their special board, Meryl – thank you, God – switched off the CD player.

'Time for a brew, methinks, before the hordes descend.' Tabitha nodded in agreement. She'd overslept this morning, still traumatised by her near-death experience in the loo. Luckily, Tom was home sharpish as Clive had been off sick and Keith under threat of castration from his missus if he wasn't back in time for the kids' bath and bedtime story. Once he'd released her from captivity – and stopped laughing long enough to put the oven on – she'd felt vaguely sick and more than a little miffed at his lack of sympathy. Then her sleep had been peppered with vivid nightmares involving killer toilet brushes and lakes of elephant wee.

'So, how was last night?' she asked, sipping her builder's brew. Meryl had recently joined an online dating service. She'd only been on four dates so far – including this one – but the first three had been unmitigated disasters. The first, with recently divorced car salesman Dave, mainly involved him weeping openly about how his wife had run off with his best friend. The second – Nathaniel (call me Nate) – started more promisingly until she discovered his passion for taxidermy. 'Just finished the most amazing ferret. It's getting the eyes right, that's the tough bit,' he'd enthused, eyes glittering with all the fervour of a mass murderer. Slapping down a fiver for her drink, she'd fixed him with her own beady stare and the parting words, 'Get stuffed.' Which she was really rather proud of. Date number three – accountant Alan – might have had potential if he hadn't so blatantly lied in his profile about his height. His alleged five foot eleven could only be achieved if he carried around a large crate to stand on. More like five foot two, and she suspected even then that he had lifts in his highly polished brogues. Which meant, standing up, his nose came perilously close to nesting in her not-inconsiderable cleavage. Admiring her décolletage was one thing but using it as a set of well-padded earmuffs was quite another.

'It went really well!' exclaimed Meryl, more than a hint of joyous disbelief in her voice. 'We hit it off straight away. So many things in common. He loves going to the movies and cooking and he was really interested when I told him about the shop. His name's Miroslaw, from Poland originally, but lived here for yonks. Still got a hint of an accent – quite sexy, actually – and he looks a little bit like a younger Al Pacino. Honestly, Tabbie, I think I might have hit the jackpot this time! He runs his own building business, mainly fitting conservatories, new windows, that kind of thing, *and* he drives a Range Rover!'

Tabitha smiled, genuinely delighted for her boss, who she also considered a friend despite the age gap. She was one of the few people Tabitha tolerated calling her Tabbie, an abbreviation she hated as it made her feel she should be coughing up fur balls and depositing dead birds on her neighbours' doorsteps. Her mum had chosen the name because of her love for the old US TV show *Bewitched*, in which the main character Samantha's daughter was similarly monikered. She generally insisted that it never be shortened – Tom once called her Tab and was lucky he'd ducked in time – but for some reason Meryl was incapable of getting it right. Shame she hadn't also inherited the character's ability to perform magic by twitching her nose. That would have come in useful last night. Both to escape the lavatory and to have zapped a zipper across Tom's guffawing gob.

'Sounds too good to be true! Are you sure he's not married, or gay, or just has appallingly bad eyesight?'

Meryl swatted at her young assistant with a copy of the local free newspaper. 'Less of your cheek, young lady! He was the perfect gentleman. All holding doors open and pushing in chairs. He said he'd nearly been married once, about twenty years ago, but it didn't work out. And he can't possibly be gay, I'd have spotted the signs right away!'

This from the woman who for years had been adamant that Graham Norton was straight and only holding out for the right woman to cherish his impish Irish charms.

'So, when are you seeing the incredibly manly Miroslaw again?' asked Tabitha. She was now ripping open cardboard boxes of newly delivered merchandise, cursing as yet another fingernail snapped in the process.

'Tomorrow evening. We're going to see the new Meryl Streep movie then have a bite to eat at that nice tapas place. What do you think I should wear? I've got a lovely new little floral dress I picked up at Bab's Boutique the other week. Or should I play it down? Maybe jeans and a fitted top?'

Tabitha eyed her boss carefully. Anything but bloody dungarees, she thought. Also, considering Meryl's sizeable bosom, she'd err on the side of caution when it came to anything too fitted. Lest a button popped and took out poor Miroslaw's eye.

'The dress sounds good. Maybe play it down with your nice denim jacket and those cute suede boots? So, when will I get to give him the once-over? If he doesn't pass the Tabitha Five Point Test, then I'm afraid it's *'do widzenia'*.'

'Do what? And what is the Tabitha Five Point Test when it's at home?'

Tabitha prided herself on knowing how to say a handful of key phrases in around ten different languages. Not that *'donde esta el bano'* (where is the bathroom in Spanish) had served her particularly well since she'd never been to Spain. Still, one never knew when these little nuggets of knowledge might come in handy.

'It means 'goodbye' in Polish. The Tabitha Five Point Test is just something I came up with after dating a couple of real duds a few years ago. It's pretty simple. If they can meet the following criteria then they're worth considering.'

- *Must have good teeth. Preferably their own. Dental hygiene majorly important.*
- *Absolutely no nail biting. Chewed nails and gnawed cuticles are a no-no.*
- A *nice head of hair is good but will accept partial or full baldness if done with taste. Grey is fine, dodgy dye jobs not.*
- *Should be polite, attentive and have a good sense of humour. An ability to cook would be a bonus but not essential.*
- *Doesn't have to be a genius in bed (although that would be lovely) as long as he knows which bits go where and considers his partner's satisfaction equal to his own.*

She ticked off each item on her fingers, Meryl gaping either in awe at her wisdom or disbelief at her *actually* having a list compiled. Tabitha was pleased to note that Tom generally complied with all the above, although cooking wasn't his strong suit and sometimes his humour was gained at her own expense.

'Gosh, Tabbie. You've got it all worked out, haven't you? Mind you, having met Tom I can see he fits the bill. How is he, anyway? He hasn't dropped in here for a few weeks now.'

Meryl was minutes away from turning the shop sign to 'open'. Tabitha deposited the contents of her final box on the counter, a selection of magnifying reading glasses in funky patterns and prints.

'He's good. Business has been a bit ropey lately but hopefully things will pick up soon. Listen, I was going to invite a couple of people over for dinner next Friday. How about you come too and bring lover boy? I'd love to meet him. Promise I won't give him the Spanish Inquisition. Just want to make sure his intentions are honourable!'

Meryl beamed a smile at the first customer of the day. A young woman clutching the hand of a toddler and attempting to push a pram at the same time.

'I'll run it by Miroslaw but I'm sure it'll be fine. Just let me know what time and if I can bring anything. And promise me you won't put him on the rack. Even the dish-drying one!'

Tabitha cackled in her best Monty Python impression. 'Nobody expects the Spanish Inquisition! Now let's get this show on the road. Good morning, how can we help you today?'

About the Author

Audrey Davis is the bestselling author of sparkling romantic comedies that blend warmth, wit and just a touch of mischief. She burst onto the scene with *A Clean Sweep* and its prequel *A Clean Break*, before bewitching readers with her ghostly romcom *The Haunting of Hattie Hastings*, first published as a trilogy and later as a standalone novel.

Her feel-good Cranley Wishes series began with *A Wish for Jinnie* and went on to delight fans with *A Wish for Jo* and *A Wish for Wilma*. Along the way, she also delivered the laugh-out-loud *Lost in Translation* (2021). Her latest standalone, *The Lexicon of Love*, charmed readers in September 2025.

Originally from the UK but now settled in Switzerland with her husband, Audrey divides her time between writing, shopping, cooking, and indulging her love of red wine. She's a voracious reader, a keen storyteller, and never fails to get a little giddy when readers reach out.

About the Author

www.ingramcontent.com/pod-product-compliance
Lightning Source LLC
La Vergne TN
LVHW030917080826
845145LV00013B/2932

* 9 7 8 1 0 3 6 7 3 3 9 5 7 *